INDIAN SCHOOL DAYS

A CHARLES BLOOM MURDER MYSTERY

To Jeff, one of my favorite people in the world whose immense talent always amazes me.
Best, Mark Sublette

MARK SUBLETTE

JUST ME PUBLISHING

Copyright © 2018 by Mark Sublette
Author's Note by Mark Sublette Copyright © 2018

All Rights Reserved. This book may not be reproduced, in whole or in part, in any form, without written permission. For inquiries, contact: Just Me Publishing, LLC., Tucson, AZ, 1-800-422-9382

Published by Just Me Publishing, LLC.

Library of Congress Control Number: 2018938516
Indian School Days / Mark Sublette
ISBN 978-0-9998176-1-2
1. Fiction I. Title

Quantity Purchases
Companies, professional groups, clubs, and other organizations may qualify for special terms when ordering quantities of this title. For more information, contact us through www.marksublette.com.

Jacket and book design: Jaime Gould
Author photo: Dan Budnik

Printed in the USA by Bookmasters
Ashland, OH · www.bookmasters.com

AUTHOR'S NOTE

The books in the Charles Bloom murder mystery series are all works of fiction. Two Trees Indian School, all the teachers and principal are fictitious. In the real world, Toadlena Trading Post had a nearby Indian school for local children to attend. Any resemblance to any boarding school, teachers or students, is strictly coincidental.

Indian boarding schools varied greatly for many Native Americans: some found it to be a great experience; others felt it devastated their culture and individuality. In many cases, the memories continue to be a source of angst. To my knowledge, no boarding schools stole cultural patrimony from any students, but there is no doubt that many focused on obliterating the link between the children and their tribal heritage—often through removal of cultural, religious, and language traditions.

All characters in *Indian School Days*—including police officers, trading post pawn people, artists, the art dealers and their galleries exist only in my mind. Both the Native Americans and references to any of their religious practices or beliefs are fictional; any relationship to real life—by name, clan, or description—is purely coincidental.

The Toadlena Trading Post, a central component of all the Bloom murder mystery books, is a real working trading post that exists as described on the Navajo Nation. This historic post specializes in Toadlena/Two Grey Hills weavings, and is well worth the effort to visit. I would like to thank its proprietor, author Mark Winter, and his wife Linda for their invaluable insights as well as for Mark's editing prowess, and thanks to the Brown family for critical insight and helping my book ring true.

No book is complete without a great cover, and I'm most appreciative to Jaime Gould for her graphic design skills. I'm also grateful for Patricia West-Barker's careful manuscript editing and thoughtful suggestions.

I have added a glossary of geographical, Navajo, medical and art terms that will hopefully make any unusual words more accessible to readers.

All the photographs of Santa Fe and the Navajo reservation were taken by me to serve as points of reference correlating to each chapter. Other images are courtesy Medicine Man Gallery. I hope the images will help the reader experience the same sense of place and moment in time I experienced when I took them.

"In Indian civilization, I am a Baptist, because I believe in immersing the Indian in our civilization and when we get them under, holding them there until they are thoroughly soaked."

—Richard Henry Pratt, founder of the Carlisle Indian Industrial School, *Battlefield and Classroom: Four Decades with the American Indian, 1867-1904*, edited by Robert M. Utley, Yale University Press, 1964

"Assimilation made us feel ashamed of what we were, where we came from, how we spoke, our stories, our families, how we dressed, and for speaking our language."

—Laura Tohe, *No Parole Today*, West End Press, 1999

CHAPTER 1

NOTHINGNESS

For the first time, the black silhouettes looming on the skyline of the remote homestead on the Navajo Nation made Marvin Manycoats' favorite climbing tree something to fear. The tangle of ancient juniper branches adjacent to the Manycoats' family hogan was no longer an inviting shelter from the hot afternoon sun. Now it was a dangerous place, something to avoid. Under night's spell, the tree had taken on the form of a witching figure, a dark sign that the coyote spirit is near, Marvin reasoned, as his father's telling of the Navajo creation story—when coyote steals fire for Etsa-Assun (first woman) and Etsay-Hasteen (first man)—played in his head.

The boy wondered how he could escape his current predicament. Could he fly deep into the northern vista like the bats that buzzed the weak kerosene lantern swaying above his family's parched wooden porch? Marvin's eyes focused on the heavens as he prayed to the celestial bodies to fly him wherever the bats might call home and keep him safe from tomorrow's impending ordeal.

Marvin was wise for an eleven-year-old. He wasn't necessarily book smart, but he had a good grasp of what it meant to be Navajo. His father, a respected man among his people, had prepared the boy well. Before long, the frightened child would be forced to navigate perilous adult situations, but on that lonely late summer night in 1961 he was desperately looking for a way out of a difficult situation. He didn't know it yet, but Marvin would soon become the chronicler of his people's struggles.

Tomorrow morning many children's lives would change dramatically—and not for the better. Tomorrow, Marvin would be entering the bilagáana world, and there didn't seem to be any viable options to avoid this head-on collision with the white man's orders. The pale-skinned enforcers had a new home, called Indian boarding school, waiting for the children.

Marvin was required to attend middle school regardless of his clan's wishes. "White man's law," his father had repeatedly told the family. "All Navajo must attend Indian boarding school or face the government's hard hand."

The Navajo people had been imprisoned in 1864 for four miserable years at Bosque Redondo in eastern New Mexico, well beyond the embrace of the Navajolands and the power of their four sacred mountains. The story of the trauma had been devastating for generations, the tragic event remaining fresh in the memory of many elders. No sane parent would dare disobey the bilagáana's wishes—not even Ned Manycoats Sr., himself a product of the cruel Indian school system—no matter how destructive it would be to the Manycoats family's home life.

Marvin was considering every possible option that night, even if it meant defying his stern father's insistence he leave tomorrow morning for the white man's world. Ignoring Ned Manycoats' wishes would be a first for the wiry kid with shoulder-length black hair and an oversized smile.

His childish fantasy was to head west with a few days' provisions as the midnight moon rose, hiking the backcountry at night. He could then seek refuge on top of Fortress Rock in Canyon de Chelly, just as his ancestors had when Kit Carson was chasing them. He didn't know how he would be able to scale a mesa top that even Carson's soldiers couldn't conquer, but details like that seemed small in comparison to what was awaiting him at the Toadlena Trading Post the next morning.

A distant relative lived in Canyon de Chelly and Marvin was sure he could navigate the moonlit route. He thought he could do it in two days—and maybe someone would give him a ride—but the daunting tree face was looming large in the darkness. Standing paralyzed in the doorway of his boyhood home, Marvin was unable to act, and could summon no courage to go against the Holy People that seemed to be at hand. A backpack filled with dry venison and hard crackers was now the only remaining sign of Marvin's deflating plan.

Like a clap of thunder, the boy's inner thoughts broke free when a whiff of hot mutton stew filtered into his consciousness, and his trademark grin returned to the boy's face as his nose and mouth instinctively turned toward the recognizable aroma. The delicious smell mixed seamlessly with the thick, warm night air. Last year's hardened deer jerky was no match for a home-cooked meal made with plenty of his mother's love. Dinner was at hand and lamb was Marvin's favorite meal.

The food was a going-away present from his parents to their youngest child. Marvin's mother had slaughtered a potentionally valuable wool sheep for the occasion, a rare gift indeed. It was a night for presents, and the boy's father had earlier bestowed on Marvin an old squash blossom necklace.

When Ned returned from World War II, he traded two of his silver bracelets and $25 for the magnificent turn-of-the-century squash blossom necklace by Slender Maker of Silver, one of the best silversmiths to ever construct jewelry. Born between 1850 and 1860, not far from Toadlena near Whiskey Creek, New Mexico, Slender Maker—or Slim as he was called—was taught his craft by his brother

Atsidi Sani, also a celebrated silversmith who had learned the art of working with the metal from the Mexicans. Slender Maker was a man Ned revered not only for his abilities as a silversmith but also as a community leader for his people.

Ned decided to make the necklace his own by adding almond-shaped aquamarine turquoise. Each stone tab was bow drilled then interspaced between the heavy coin silver squash beads, creating a uniquely distinctive necklace. A string of round, polished Number 8 turquoise beads formed a double row of heishi along the wearer's neck. Each fine bead had been meticulously graded for color, size, and thin black matrix. The necklace represented a sizable source of wealth to its owner. Number 8 was some of the most valuable turquoise ever mined.

Ned wore the piece with pride at social gatherings, and often told of its creation by Slender Maker, who had also made necklaces for Henry Chee Dodge (Hastiin Adiits'a'ii) the chairman of the Navajo Tribal Council in the 1940s. Like his father before him, Ned's silversmith skills were legendary among his people; bilagáana and Navajo alike coveted a Manycoats necklace or silver bracelet—especially a piece that was a marriage of two of the tribe's great silversmiths. Ned secretly hoped Marvin might follow in the family business and become a silversmith.

A Navajo craftsman rarely keeps what he or she produces. Jewelry is a commodity made for commerce, not an heirloom or a religious item, its sale providing for the necessities of everyday life. Occasionally a unique piece was passed down. The Slender Maker squash blossom necklace was one of those, and it now belonged to Marvin—a significant gift for one so young.

Ned realized it was risky to give a necklace of great value to someone of Marvin's age, but he recognized his son's maturity and hoped the constant reminder around his neck of his family's love might help him cope in the difficult months to come. He had lectured the boy on the importance of not flaunting the piece, especially to the whites, as they would only see it as another form of money. "Keep it under your shirt, next to your skin for protection," he advised.

But for now the necklace was proudly draped around Marvin's brown neck for all to see, its manly size incongruent with the boy's small body. The weight of the turquoise and silver beads already symbolized the burden of being a foreigner in the white man's domain and reminded him not to forget his Navajo roots.

Stroking the necklace, Marvin felt a sharp twinge of guilt for thinking of disobeying his father's wishes after receiving such a wonderful—and unexpected—present, especially since his older brother had not received the necklace when he went to Indian boarding school.

The Manycoats party had included nine other little boys from the vicinity, all at the terrible age of eleven when they would be taken away to learn to read and write the bilagáana language. Most of the boys, like Marvin, were scared but too naïve to realize what was waiting for them in the shadows at boarding school. Marvin understood all too well what was coming: Ned Jr., his older brother by three years, had warned him of the dangerous possibilities that lay ahead for those sent to the school with the wrong headmaster.

Numerous Indian boarding schools dotted the Southwest, each with its own particular curriculum and tone set by the school's headmaster—usually a stern white man with a bilagáana name. Marvin's only hope was that he and his fellows would be lucky enough to end up with a headmaster who liked or at least tolerated the Navajo. If that happened, the school year would be livable, with moments of happiness sprinkled in; even real learning would be possible. But there were a few notorious schools with weed-strewn cemeteries filled with the decaying bodies of young Navajo children on their grounds. Illness seemed to strike suddenly and often at these schools. Ned Jr. had attended such a school for one year and told Marvin what he must do to survive, if he were unlucky and drew a coyote headmaster.

Tomorrow, Marvin would find out what the Holy People had in store for him. Had he been able to see the future at that moment, he would have skipped the tasty mutton meal and headed to the hills with the bats, dining on venison jerky instead. Serious danger was coming, and there was no way to escape.

CHAPTER 2

MATCHSTICK WOMAN

Sunlight streamed under the front door of the Manycoats' one-room hogan. His day of reckoning had arrived. The hogan was traditional in construction, with an east-facing entrance to greet the sun's warmth and bless the house's occupants at the beginning of each day.

Marvin prayed for Changing Woman's metaphorical gift of a rebirth for himself as he pondered his fate. Sitting upright on his rusty metal cot, he could feel his heart pounding in his ears—a fight or flight response in full tilt. A dry mouth complemented his tight throat as the early light of the sunrise glistened off his wet cheeks. The boy asked Mother Earth for protection as he stroked the slick beads of turquoise that had graced his father's neck for decades. His repetitive, quiet chant calmed his anxiety and his breathing returned to normal.

Today would be Marvin's first test of courage. His family's embrace had always been a given; five months in a foreign land would surely test his mettle. Two lost sheep and a nearly two-day trip with his father to find the animals was the only meaningful time he had spent away from his hogan's immediate vicinity. Today there would be no father or sheep, only scared children to accompany him; no loving mother's face or delicious food for months on end—and eating was an important part of Marvin's world.

No roadmap to Marvin's final destination was forthcoming; the sole information given to family members waiting at the Toadlena Trading Post at 8:30 a.m. was to board the yellow bus.

Being late would not be tolerated. The Toadlena Trading Post was the central pickup location, the only place a large vehicle could easily navigate.

The locals referred to the bus as the "yellow summer squash on four wheels." Marvin's father tried to reassure him so the boy would not worry about riding the bus to school, but the eleven-year-old's vivid imagination pictured an ominous, gigantic hollow gourd resting on wooden wheels in which he and his friends were expendable seeds, just waiting for the raven's mouth.

Few Navajo owned clocks. The sun was a reliable compass of approximate time; no man-made device was needed in the Navajo world. Today the parents would all be early, not knowing exactly when 8:30 a.m. would arrive.

Ned's favorite stallion was tied to Marvin's climbing tree, ready to go. Seeing the animal, Marvin's throat swelled again.

There was no small talk during family breakfast. Marvin's time was short, and introspective thought ruled the day; homemade salted frybread and a thick slice of last night's mutton graced the hand-hewn table. The food was delicious and Marvin savored the juices of his final home-cooked meal.

His brother had warned him that white man's food was strange, and told him that they were never served lamb or corn during his entire school year. The bilagáanas' favorite dish, Ned Jr. said, was hot dogs. Marvin could imagine eating a young tender dog if hungry enough, but hoped he would not know the animals he consumed, as he loved all creatures, especially dogs.

Marvin understood that in periods of great need animals had to sacrifice their lives for the greater good of his people. He had grown up hearing the stories of the Navajo using dog as a food source during these times of hardship, and assumed his fate was to eat dogs. His brother assured him that he would like the hot dog meat, saying it was quite tasty. His brother recommended eating the dog meat hot. Otherwise, he said, it tasted slimy. Marvin assumed this was why the bilagáana referred to their food as "hot dogs." Thoughts of strange meals to come were streaming through his consciousness as he sopped up the last drops of bacon grease and strengthened his resolve to leave.

Marvin's mother engulfed her son in a bear hug as he reached the front door, refusing to release her grip. Chants and soft sounds of crying filled the small room as Ned Sr. finally pried loose the protective mother's embrace.

Marvin tried not to cry. He was a man, after all, going to elementary school. His father's gift draped around his neck said as much, but he could not help himself. His mother's emotions were infectious and tears rolled freely over both their cheeks, splattering on the hard dirt floor of his hogan. He wondered, as he saw the small drops, bouncing then disappearing into Mother Earth's bosom, whether any more of *his* tears would fall on the floor—or whether they would only be tears from a mother's grief.

A bad schoolmaster could mean Marvin might never see his family again, and that only a pine cross in a white man's cemetery somewhere near the unknown bilagáana school would testify that he had ever existed.

The whites claimed the few children who died while at boarding school were unavoidable losses from diseases that no man could stop, like polio or a virulent flu. The whites said these were rare events, and told the parents not to worry as they, too, had great medicine men in hospitals who would take care of their children as if they were their own.

The Navajo had voiced requests in the past that when their children were sick, they should be returned home for traditional treatments. They complained that the white medicine never worked and the faraway, unknown graveyards kept adding to their untold secrets. Many families had lost children to these graves. Bodies had to be buried within twenty-four hours according to the white man's law. Having a child die at a boarding school far from home was the greatest fear of all Navajo parents. Not only did they lose a beloved child, they were not allowed the proper Diné burial. There were no goodbyes or proper send-offs to the next part of one's journey—just a white cross far away from home.

Ned Manycoats Sr.'s intervention with his wife's grief triggered memories of leaving his family as a child. Boarding school was part of the Manycoats legacy; Marvin's grandfather had been sent to the Carlisle Indian School in Pennsylvania in 1902 when he was Marvin's age. The trauma affected Ned Sr.'s father when he, too, was sent to boarding school. These events played vividly in his mind moments before he pulled Marvin from his mother's loving arms. He hated seeing his youngest child leave for an unknown school and a potentially hostile world—a world that didn't understand or care about the Navajo way of life—but he had little choice.

The white man had spoken, and, just as Ned Sr. had gone to boarding school and then to war, he would now give up his youngest son to the arms of another. All he could do was pray that he had taught Marvin enough of the Navajo ways to keep pure of heart and strong of mind. He hoped the precious squash blossom necklace would somehow help him stay on that path.

Indian school had perfectly prepared Ned Sr. for the military's special Code Talker team. Many Navajo Code Talkers had boarding school in their background and could speak and communicate in more or less proper English. These select individuals were used to wearing a uniform, keeping their hair short and following orders. All were native speakers; their Navajo was flawless. The Japanese army was never able to break the code they created, rooted in the Athabascan language of clicks and guttural utterances. Without the Navajo Code Talkers, the war effort would have taken much longer and many more lives would have been lost.

No one knew of the Code Talkers or their heroics as their war service efforts were classified. Although their service was declassified in 1968, the Code Talkers weren't officially recognized by the U.S. government until 1982. At the time Marvin was leaving for boarding school, these forgotten Navajo men, who had risked their lives for the United States, were a footnote in U.S. government files.

This was fine with Ned Sr. He had returned to his Diné roots and tried to forget about the war, using English only as needed. He had taught both sons to speak Navajo and English, but to be Navajo at heart. Ned Sr. was more of a disciplinarian then the boys would have liked, but his father's and his own early boarding school indoctrination followed by military service had damaged that part of his personality.

The sun's shadows said it was time to go; the earth's circadian alarm was ringing. Marvin must leave now; it was his turn to attend Indian boarding school, a Manycoats tradition. Ned Sr. grabbed his son's shirt for stability and mounted his favorite horse's back in one fluid movement, beginning the five-mile journey to meet the yellow squash bus at the Toadlena Trading Post.

Marvin rode to Toadlena in a slow-motion time warp, recognizing every ant mound and deer scraping along the way to the old stone trading post. There was no talking, only the sound of hooves beating and the thumping of his heart. A faint smell of burning juniper and horse sweat permeated the warm air of the Toadlena basin. Marvin wondered, as did his father, if this would be the last time he would see the land they both loved so much, and he took in the sights and smells to help him remember his home.

The Indian school system had changed some since Ned Sr. was a student. Children were no longer taken halfway across the country. A more humane understanding of the family unit had taken hold; Navajo children were now mostly boarded in Arizona, New Mexico, Oklahoma, or Utah though California was also a possibility. The children were allowed to come home for Christmas and the summer, but that seemed far away and Marvin couldn't let his mind go to that place.

The Toadlena Trading Post's natural stone façade loomed on the distant ridge, and Marvin prayed that somehow he would never arrive. He begged the Holy People to stop his father's horse and make him run in the opposite direction so he would never reach the stone outcropping that was gaining prominence in the open landscape at the base of the Chuska Mountains—but the building kept getting larger.

The faded yellow bus parked below the post's entrance was surrounded by small groups of people clumped in bunches in no apparent order, all saying their goodbyes to departing sons and daughters. The scene was awash in grief. There was no "farewell, see you at Christmas." The community was gripped by the somber moment as they waited for their children to be taken away by the white man's machine.

Peter Booten, the bus driver, had grown up near Toadlena but now lived in Gallup and worked for the Indian schools. Having found Jesus Christ, he preferred to answer to his Christian instead of his Navajo name. On Sundays, Booten liked to visit Toadlena and preach the Christian way of life to those he felt were lost to God—an activity not appreciated by his traditional Navajo neighbors. Ned Sr. did understand Booten's need to work, but taking Diné children from their families did not fit his idea of a job. He equated the driver's religious predilections with his career choice, and cared little for either.

A white woman with fire-orange hair wearing black-rimmed spectacles sat rigidly upright in the front row of seats. The glasses forced onlookers to focus on their rhinestone edges and distracted them from the fact the woman had no visible eyebrows. She sported a pink sweater that had "Mrs. Pingry" handwritten on a brown paper tag, the bright colored fabric popping against her unhealthy pale skin. She was everything a Navajo woman wasn't, and Marvin couldn't take his eyes off her. She was mesmerizing in her oddness.

Mrs. Pingry's arms were the size of small broomsticks and looked as if the slightest pressure would snap them in half. This woman had apparently never wrangled a sheep or dragged a baby lamb out of a deep crevice. Ned Sr. wondered how a woman with no physical strength could be in charge of a group of active, athletic, Navajo children—and he was not the only one wondering about her fitness as a leader; she was the subject of much of the current conversation in the huddled masses. Peering in at the scarecrow woman through the bug-splattered front windshield, Ned Sr. observed in Navajo to no one in particular, "If they had respect, the whites would know that this person is not a leader and should not be in charge of any Navajo—not even children." Many nodded their heads in agreement.

When the white woman spoke it was as if a small bird were chirping in a deep canyon. Her voice was immediately lost in the cavernous bus, so she rose from her seat and exited the vehicle, positioning herself on the highest point in the parking lot. This time, Mrs. Pingry yelled to capture the crowd's attention.

"Excuse me. Excuse me, people. It's time to go. Please have your children line up in a single file line and give me their ENGLISH name so we can mark them off. Please don't use any Navajo or War names until the children return for Christmas break. If you're able to write letters to your children, do so in English and make sure you use their Christian name if you want the letters delivered."

Ned Sr., who spoke and understood English very well, cringed when he heard the reference to Christian names. He had experienced the same attitudes thirty years earlier at his boarding school, and recognized that his son was heading into trouble. Nothing had changed for Navajo children at Indian boarding schools, except that now the whites were so entrenched in their power that they sent a matchstick woman as their leader to further humiliate his people—and did so right under their noses.

As requested, the children lined up and responded to their names one by one. Small cries from distraught mothers would sound when their child's bilagánna name was read aloud. Mrs. Pingry never lifted her head from her clipboard as she systematically checked off the name of each individual, grunting an acknowledgment as each parent and child called out. She finally looked up after no affirmative voice spoke for Ricky Begay.

"Ricky Begay. Where is Ricky Begay?" she demanded. No one answered, although all knew his father had taken him to their high country camp and refused to be part of the boarding school process.

"Does ANYONE know where Mr. Ricky Begay is and why he is not in attendance? The time and place were very clear in the letter you all received." Everyone knew, but no one would say. An elderly Navajo woman at the back of the crowd said in a hushed voice, "He is safe from you, fire devil; I wish they all were."

A few giggled at her Navajo words. The small, frail white woman frowned at the laughter. She did not understand the words, but the tone of the crowd was evident.

"You'd better let Mr. Begay's family know that if he does not appear in Gallup by the end of this week he will be treated as truant and breaking the law," she sternly cautioned, "and a subpoena will be issued for his arrest. Our headmaster Stanton Soliday will not brook this kind of behavior. Attending school is serious business, and the law is clear that when it comes to Indian boarding school all must participate—no exceptions."

Many in the audience did not understand the white words, but the tone of her voice was stern enough to hush the crowd.

Mrs. Pingry started moving back toward the bus, her tiny arms mechanically pumping back and forth to emphasize that she was the leader of the pack. "Time to go, my little warriors," she shouted. The children instinctively filed into the bus and took any vacant seat, their heads peering out of the windows like prairie dogs looking out of their burrows for danger.

Parents scattered to whichever side of the bus their child's head popped up in, many chanting and all upset at seeing their children leave for unknown parts. Mrs. Pingry told the parents their children would be processed in Gallup and no visitors were allowed. She left a handful of flyers detailing where they could send letters—but with few able to write in English, their children wouldn't be hearing from parents anytime soon.

The old bus's engine sputtered to a start and headed down the deeply rutted dirt road toward the blacktop over ten miles away. Ned Sr. stood alone thinking about his decision to let his son leave and wondered if Ricky Begay's family might have made the better choice. Seeing the bus turn the corner out of his sight, he impulsively jumped on his horse and spiked its side as never before. The horse reared up in surprise and bolted forward in a flash of red dirt, Ned Sr.'s body as close to the animal's mane as possible to reduce all possible drag. He caught the bus in a full gallop and saw his son's face looking out of the window in amazement at the way his father was riding, wondering why he was acting this way.

What Marvin couldn't understand was that his father was well aware that his son's fate was now sealed and that the boy was caught in the Matchstick Woman's divisive grip—a hold not even he could break. All Ned Sr. could hope was that he had given Marvin the tools to survive the white man's schools. Ned kept his horse parallel to the bus, held his body erect and spoke directly to Marvin: "Be strong my son," he said. "Remember you are a Navajo brave, stand tall and with honor. I will think of you every day from when the sun comes up until the stars appear." The little stallion couldn't keep up with the bus's mechanical power, and fell back as Ned Sr. reluctantly gave up his futile chase. His son was gone—possibly forever.

CHAPTER 3

WELCOME ABOARD

The bumpy, seventy-four-mile ride from Toadlena to Gallup took two hours, and the late August heat was oppressive. There was no water or food, and the only breeze was the hot wind that blew through the open windows. Mrs. Pingry's red bun was slightly ajar, and a line of tiny perspiration beads had formed on her unusually high forehead. A large lemonade jug was at her ready. She drank from it heartily, never thinking to share its contents with anyone, including Pete Booten.

Finally the old bus pulled up to another stone building with a semicircle sign perched over a rock entrance that read "Indian School—Gallup District," its impressive red sandstone exterior no doubt built by the sweat and muscle of Navajo workers.

The boarding school on the far outskirts of Gallup turned out to be the group's final destination, and Marvin was delighted that he was not too far from his hogan. If he had to run away, he thought he could borrow a horse and be home in a day-and-a-half if he rode hard. His family's ancestral lands were within a raven's daily home range; this gave Marvin hope that evaporated when he spotted a cemetery adjacent to a blue water tower marked "Two Trees Indian School." The overgrown plot filled with neat rows of white crosses inside a freshly painted picket fence welcoming new arrivals.

"Navajo chindi," he thought.

The graves were a sign to beware, and Marvin instinctively took his father's gift from around his neck and stuck it inside his underwear, giving him the appearance of man rather than a prepubescent boy. He loved that necklace, and he would guard the piece even if it required an uncomfortable hiding place for the moment. The little crosses had struck a cord; Coyote was nearby, the proof lined up in front of him. He would have to be cautious.

Mrs. Pingry stood up as the bus came to a rolling stop. Pete Booten looked back at the children for the first time and smiled as if to say, "You're in their world now. Good luck…." The door made a sucking sound as the ratty rubber edge opened, letting a new blast of hot air pulse through the bus's interior.

Mrs. Pingry's voice was no longer that of a small bird, but an angry raven screaming at them.

"No talking, children. You are now at school and expected to follow all the teachers' commands. Never speak unless spoken to. You are here to learn a civilized way of acting; you are no longer to be savages. When you talk, do so in English. Anyone speaking Navajo will be punished, with no exceptions and no second chances. This is your only warning, and I advise you to heed my words.

"Mr. Soliday, our headmaster, can be very strict and will not tolerate any insubordination. He is not a man you want to trifle with. That means don't talk back or think you have the right to speak to him. He is the big chief here and a man of God, one who expects you to learn what it means to be a good Christian. Now out you go. Follow the white lines to your first stop—and remember, English only!"

Most of the children comprehended only bits of what Mrs. Pingry had said, so they followed those few individuals who spoke fluent English. Marvin, who understood nearly everything, including "insubordination," a word his father had used in the past, was terrified. "NO NAVAJO, NO NAVAJO, they will hurt you," he said under his breath in English. "ONLY ENGLISH." Still, Marvin felt the need to help his Navajo brethren. He must stand up and be brave; his father would expect this of him. It was why he had given him the Slender Maker necklace. He was a man now.

Mr. Soliday came out of his office and looked up at the bus as the children slowly filtered down the worn steps. He looked odd to Marvin, but, unlike Mrs. Pingry, who seemed to have a soul, Soliday's eyes were black and hard. Marvin could tell this was a man who meant business and that he would have to be very careful in his presence. There was no smile of welcome as he examined each child as if he or she were his new horse.

"He's making up his mind about who we are as people," Marvin thought. He felt as if he were one of many sheep penned in a corral corner, waiting for one of the flock to be picked out for slaughter. Marvin prayed he wasn't the tasty one in Soliday's eyes.

All of the children looked like typical Navajo in 1961. Except for a few, the boys had shoulder-length hair, and many had turquoise jewelry on their arms, necks, and ears. One child, Ernie Yazzie, was wrapped in an old Navajo blanket that his grandmother had given him. A family treasure, its red diamonds and blue and brown stripes more than covered Ernie; he looked like a dignitary awaiting court. The blanket was all wool and the heat was stifling—yet Ernie proudly wore the weaving as close to his body as if it were mid-January.

Mr. Soliday walked up and down the line inspecting the troops. When he had completed two laps looking intently at the children, he spoke. He had an odd-sounding accent, one no Navajo child had ever heard before. Soliday was from back East, and had a pitch and rhythm similar to that of a rabbit being killed by a pack of coyotes—both startling and irregular.

"Children," he said, "I am your headmaster at the Two Trees Indian School. This is your final stop, and it's where we will teach you how to become good human beings and not savage Indians. You may think I am harsh at times, but I assure you that I am a fair man of God who will treat you well if you learn to respect yourselves and the white men and women that teach you.

"I'm sure Mrs. Pingry has told you that absolutely no Navajo shall be spoken while you are at this school—not during school hours or after school hours. You are here to learn English and become a good citizen of the United States of America, not the Navajo Nation. Any deviation from these rules will be punished. The first time you break this rule, your mouth will be washed out with the big yellow soap; the second time you will be whipped with a switch from the two trees for which this school is named. The third time you will be whipped and placed in the corrective box. So far, no one has broken that rule a fourth time." As he spoke, he turned his head and scanned the little white crosses, as if to say, 'Don't let this be you.'

"Please take two minutes to discuss this with your neighbors so there is no misunderstanding of how serious I am about speaking English. This is the last time you will be given the opportunity to speak your native tongue while on school grounds."

The dumbfounded children looked at each other, and all at once started talking to each other in Navajo, their predicament with the requirements at Two Trees Indian School soaking into their consciousness.

Marvin, who was fluent in English, shuddered at the thought of all those whose ability to speak English was limited at best. They would mostly become mutes. He tried to take charge and use this one opportunity to speak in swift, full sentences in the Navajo language.

"No Navajo! Don't speak unless you use English. This man is very serious and will hurt you if you do not obey. No exceptions. If you don't understand something, do not talk. No Navajo!"

Mr. Soliday looked at the children's heads twisting back and forth, their fear palatable. As the sound of an ancient language filled the dry, dusty New Mexico air, a slight grin came over Soliday's face. It was barely noticeable, except to Marvin, who realized that the sight of children in distress gave this bilagáana some twisted pleasure. It was something Marvin could not understand, other than to be very afraid.

"Enough! You have spoken your last words of Navajo; it's time to become good citizens. The boys and girls need to separate. Gentlemen, you will follow me. Ladies, you will go with Mrs. Pingry to get checked in for the year. You have some kerosene baths, inoculations, and haircuts to attend to, and will receive some new clothing. We will not tolerate lice at this school, which is more than I can say about your own homes."

The children, many with tears running down their faces, diligently followed the two biláaganas and headed to their new homes—or prisons—depending on your point of view.

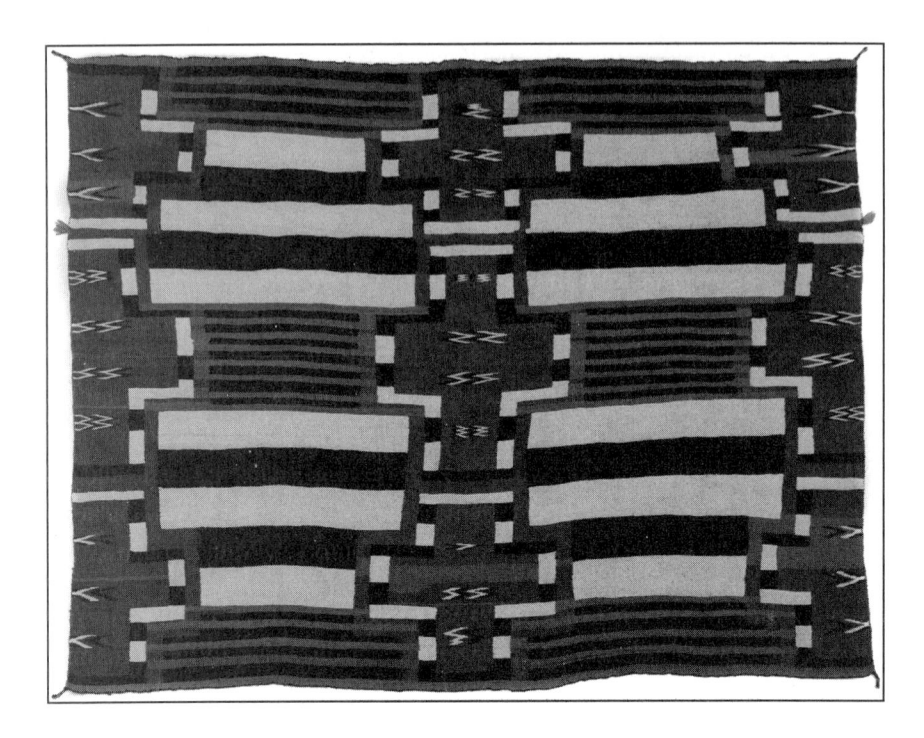

CHAPTER 4

AN UNWELCOME ALLIANCE

Marvin's first week was uneventful until he received a note from Mrs. Pingry, whom the children called Matchstick Woman, to go directly to Mr. Soliday's office. Marvin stood quietly next to an impressive hand-carved desk waiting for Soliday to finish writing a letter, while his mind was racing, wondering why he was there.

He tried to focus his eyes somewhere other than on the man's stern face. An Albuquerque newspaper splayed on the end of the table had a bold headline reading "Six Flag's New Park—Record Crowds." The newspaper showed a photo of a weird mountain with the largest log Marvin had ever seen, hollowed out and filled with young white smiling faces plunging into a watery pool. The image captured Marvin's imagination; he wondered what it must feel like to be freefalling without worrying about the consequences, knowing someone was always there to catch you. The contrast with his own situation hurt him to the core. Another article, set in much smaller type, was something Marvin understood well. It was about the Freedom Riders being arrested and beaten in Alabama. The civil rights battle was in full tilt in the South, but no one in New Mexico knew or cared about the Indian condition.

Soliday's voice snapped Marvin back to reality.

"Well, Marvin, I must say I'm impressed with you. You've been here only a week, but it's obvious the other boys look up to you. Your spoken and written English is quite good. And I like the fact you don't wear any of that Native jewelry. It's refreshing to see."

Marvin had decided to hide his precious necklace and found a safe place under the floorboards of the boy's dormitory. He would keep his piece out of sight for the duration, then smuggle the necklace out over Christmas break and leave it at home with his father. Two Trees Indian School was too dangerous a place for the Slender Maker necklace. On the second day of school, all the boys had had their "Native" items confiscated, to be held until they were going back home—or so they were told.

Ernie Yazzie's grandmother's beautiful chief's blanket was now folded into a square that sat on top of a bureau in the corner of Soliday's office. A small paper attached to the top of the weaving read, "Springer's Trading Post inventory." The barely visible scribbled note was a wake-up call to Marvin. The blanket was not being stored until winter break, but appeared to be heading off to a trading post for sale.

"Mr. Manycoats, how is it that your English is so good? This is your first year at a white school, correct?"

"Yes, sir. This is my first year at boarding school. My father was very strict about us knowing both English and Navajo. He told us we had to understand the outside world if we wanted to do well in life."

"Sounds like your father is a very wise man. Did he go to boarding school?"

"Yes, sir, he did, and his father, too. My grandfather went to the Carlisle Indian School in Pennsylvania."

Soliday smiled. He knew that school, in particular, was demanding and made good Christians out of those who attended it—a godly thread that undoubtedly had been ingrained into the Manycoats men. The young boy's family's boarding school history and Marvin excelling above his peers confirmed Soliday's beliefs that the Indian school system worked. "Take the savage out of them," he would tell his friends about his long-term goals.

"Excellent. Did your father get any other education?"

"Well, he was in the military in World War II, but I don't think he ever went to college or nothing."

"What did he do during the war?"

Soliday guessed his father may have been a Code Talker, which was classified information. Soliday had been briefed about the details of the program because many of the boarding school graduates were Code Talkers. Soliday also knew that if Marvin's father had done his duty, he would not have discussed his role with his son, as any aspect of his work was still a secret to the general public.

"I don't know, Mr. Soliday; he never would say anything about the war or what he did other than he helped this country and was glad he was able to make a difference."

Another grin came over Soliday's face. Marvin's father was clearly a disciplined man, which meant his son could follow directions and keep his mouth shut if ordered to do so.

"I see. Well, I'm glad to hear your father served our country. You know this boarding school is also serving our country. Our job is to make sure Indians become good Christian citizens and help improve the lives of their own people and the country as a whole, just like your dad did. Do you want to help me with this task Marvin?"

Marvin knew he was in a no-win situation; there was no real freedom of choice here if he hoped to survive what was going to be a demanding and potentially dangerous year.

"Yes, sir. I will help if I can."

"Excellent, Marvin. You can be of great help to my staff and me. We need someone who has an ear for Navajo and the respect of his peers. We also need someone we can count on, someone who is loyal to the ideals of the school and to me. Are you a person I can count on for help?"

Marvin hesitated just for a second to avoid what he knew he had to say. Soliday didn't notice the brief delay.

"Yes, sir."

"Great. I'm sure you and I will be good friends. I love your slick new haircut and crisp uniform. Don't you?"

"Yes, sir."

"I'm afraid that kerosene is smelly, but at least you don't have any of those pesky lice."

Marvin wanted to scream, "Screw you!" in Navajo, but knew he could never speak Navajo to the headmaster if he expected to keep his freedom. The kerosene for the nonexistent lice had burned his scalp, and he hated the haircut that exposed the pale skin of his neck. The first layer of burnt skin was peeling off and itching, and his right arm throbbed unmercifully from the white man's shots.

"Yes, sir. I like your clothes and short hair."

Marvin could not help but refer to his new dress as "your," as it was a foreign look, and he decided to avoid the lice comment altogether. He had not seen himself in a mirror—there were none on the campus—but his classmates all looked odd in their new hairstyles, and he figured he must look as un-Navajo as the others.

"So, Marvin, I need an ally in the boy's dormitory to help me keep things under control. I know many of the boys are speaking Navajo during their downtime, and I have looked the other way—but this has to stop. I also need to know if there are any troublemakers who might try to stir up problems. Do you understand?"

"Kind of, sir, though I'm not sure what you mean by 'Al Eye.'"

"Well, Marvin, it's like two clans that work together, each respecting and helping the other. You and I would be our own clan."

Marvin shook his head yes, but thought he knew of no clan heads who would beat someone with a stick for speaking Navajo.

"I will try to help, Mr. Soliday, and I will make sure the other boys don't speak Navajo."

"That's a good start Marvin, but I want you to take notes that we can go over each week to ferret out any troublemakers before they become a problem. I particularly want you to watch Ernie Yazzie. He seems to have a tendency for trouble and is very attached to Navajo traditions."

As Soliday talked, Marvin looked at his feet. He liked Ernie Yazzie and didn't want to hurt him. Thinking of himself as a ferret—a vicious predator—didn't fit Marvin's self-image, but that was what Soliday wanted.

The headmaster handed Marvin two small black notebooks and said, "Take these notebooks and keep detailed notes, meaning anything that anyone says that's bad about the school or any individuals speaking Navajo. No one will know you are my ally. It will be our little secret. Just keep the notebooks hidden so your bunkmates won't be the wiser.

"By working with me, I can help your friends become better citizens just like your dad, a man who has shown great honor and fought for his country."

Even at eleven-years-old Marvin knew this was a ploy to win him over and that his dad would never rat-out his friends. His father did not particularly care for white people, especially those like Soliday who were prejudiced against Indians. He never spoke of the military and didn't like anyone to bring up his past.

Marvin felt like he was far from home, watching a sheep caught in a crevice with the sun going down. He had to decide whether to spend the night and maybe have to fight off a coyote, or even a cougar, or leave and hope the lamb somehow survived the night on its own. It was decision time and he had to act quickly. Neither option was good, but Soliday was waiting.

"OK, Mr. Soliday. I will try to help you. I will write down anything I see that seems important, and I won't tell anyone or let others see me writing. Can I go now? I still have homework, and I need to do something on my woodworking project before supper."

"Fine, fine. It's nice to have an ally in the camp. We will meet next week to discuss what you have found out. Remember to watch Mr. Yazzie closely and keep notes on him for any suspicious behavior. He's a bad seed, Marvin, not good for our school. He may be a coyote in sheep's clothing."

Marvin's skin got clammy and his heart raced as he listened to Soliday's last statement. All he could do was shake his head in agreement as he peered over the headmaster's shoulder at the old Navajo blanket folded on his bookshelf. He hoped Soliday wouldn't realize that he had seen the note, or he could be the next Ernie Yazzie on the wrong side of the true coyote: Soliday.

CHAPTER 5

A NEW BEGINNING

The smell of green chile was hanging in the late September air, shifting Charles Bloom's attention from mounting his October gallery show to his gurgling stomach. Roasting chile in Santa Fe is a fall ritual that locals anticipate as much, if not more, than the leaves turning yellow. No grocery store visitor can enter the premises without being bombarded by the sweet aroma of cooked chile.

"I'd say it's time to make a trip to the farmers market." Bloom was talking to himself—something he often did.

"Rachael would love a fresh batch of chile for my famous green-chile cheeseburgers."

Bloom, a fan of the Blake's Lotaburger fast-food chain, had been working on replicating the delicious Santa Fe tradition and had decided chile was the critical ingredient. He liked an Anaheim variety of green chile grown north of Albuquerque with a particularly sweet taste that didn't kill you on the Scoville heat scale.

Charles had been especially attentive to his wife, who had not recovered from a recent trauma, and in his mind nothing showed love more than fresh green chile on a steaming-hot burger.

The Bloom family was trying to return to a normal life rhythm. Rachael had experienced a near-death scenario at the hands of Felix Zachow, a deranged Canyon Road art dealer, who was currently in the Santa Fe jail system awaiting trial. Zachow, who was planning to kill Rachael, had strung her up by her shoulders and wrists in a sick ritual. Bloom and Detective Billy Poh of the Santa Fe Police Department had rescued her at the last moment; it had been big news in the state of New Mexico.

Rachael tried not to think of the man who almost took her life, but each time she went by Zachow's gallery, which was located next to Bloom's on Canyon Road, she felt nauseated. So Rachael had been keeping a low profile, spending most of her time at their rented house in La Cienega in Santa Fe County, and avoiding going into town to see Bloom at work.

Her doctor had recommended that she do no weaving for at least three to four months, possibly six, to allow her joints to heal fully. Both wrists were wrapped in ugly neoprene sleeves during her waking hours. Rachael had been told not to carry their young daughter Sam in her arms for more than a few minutes a day, which of course was not happening. The black sleeves reminded her of the events of that horrible day. She was ready to be well, physically and mentally, so most days the slings stayed on the bathroom counter.

Not being able to weave was compounding her distress. She loved to create beauty on her grandmother's loom, and the money she earned was essential to the family finances. Spider Woman kept calling Rachael in her dreams and she had no way to answer. Taking an unwanted break from her life had confused Rachael. She was grappling with what was truly important.

Bloom understood why his wife wanted to avoid the gallery. Rachael was a terrific salesperson and a big asset to his business, but she was not ready for tourists and their blunt questions. "What happened to your wrist?" would not be good for her mental health, even though it made a fantastic story. Bloom couldn't help but think about how the tourist would be amazed to hear the details of the art world gone mad.

Without an active loom to occupy her time, Rachael's world had slowed to a crawl, even with children to help fill the gaps. Little Willard—Willy as they called him—had started preschool and didn't seem to need his mom as much. And Samantha, whom they called Sam, was almost three and a challenge to a mom with sore arms who was used to being physically active. Rachael knew she was not her usual happy self. She had lost her inner balance and no resolution to her problems seemed to be at hand; staying at home seemed to be her only option.

A dose of Toadlena's healing landscape and a curing ceremony were needed if she hoped to return to walking in beauty. A long trip back to the rez to visit Hastiin Johnson, a medicine man, was in order, and she hoped Bloom would be receptive to the idea. Johnson was a longtime friend of her late grandfather Hastiin Sherman, who had also been a powerful medicine man. Johnson was in his early nineties but still a vibrant and respected healer and community leader. Getting a sing from the influential Johnson would be an honor, and Rachael knew he would be willing.

All these thoughts were swirling in Rachael's mind as Bloom unexpectedly burst through the door at two p.m.; he rarely left his gallery before four. The big smile on his face said there was something special going on and the aroma of green chile that followed his entrance was the tip-off.

"Guess who's got fresh Anaheim chile from the farmer's market?" he crowed. "I'm going to put Lotaburger to shame!"

Rachael, who was sitting at the dining room table working on a crossword puzzle, looked up and smiled, thinking how lucky she was to have found this man.

"What wrong? Do you need help with your puzzle? I know English is a second language for you," Bloom teased, "so don't take it so hard that you can't figure out who was one of the first American abstract expressionists. I'll give you a hint: the name has seven letters." Bloom was poking fun at his wife, who, with a fine art degree from Santa Fe's Institute of American Indian Arts, knew more about art history then he did.

"Who is Jackson Pollock for $200?" Rachael retorted.

"Correct!" Now, how about some fresh green chile straight from the Río Grande basin—and can you believe you don't have to peel them?"

Peeling freshly roasted chile was the worst part of the job as the Capsicum, the active heat-producing ingredient, penetrates all parts of your body. The fact that this batch of chile was pre-peeled was an exciting proposition for Bloom, who refused to wear plastic gloves when cleaning chile.

"OK, I'll cook the meat, if you set the table. I want to talk to you about something, Charles." When Rachael called him Charles instead of Bloom, he knew it was serious.

"What's up? You don't like me coming home early?"

Bloom was hoping a little levity might break the sudden chill in the room, but Rachael was not biting.

"You know that's not it; I'm just not happy like I should be. I'm sure you've noticed that." An almond-shaped tear rolled down Rachael's right cheek; she flicked it away reflexively.

"Honey, you've been through an ordeal, and it's going to take a while to get back on track. Maybe you need to go talk to someone, get some professional help?"

"I agree, but it's not a psychiatrist I need—it's a healing sing. I need to get my hózhó back. I want to go back to Toadlena for few months to find my footing in life. I can do my arm and wrist exercises just as easily sitting in my own house, looking at the tip of Shiprock, as I can here. Santa Fe is not really my home, and I have relatives and friends on the rez who can help me with the kids if I need it."

Bloom considered his options before he spoke; he realized he might have to stay in Santa Fe by himself and that Rachael might take the children with her to Toadlena.

"What would we do with our kids? Willy just started school, and I'm not sure it's a good idea to pull him out. Maybe he should stay here with me?"

Rachael smiled, realizing that Bloom would be good with whatever path she chose.

"I know it's a tough decision, and that I've sprung this on you. It's Willy's first year socializing with other children, but I think it would be best for you to stay here to focus on the gallery while I take the kids back home. You know the teachers are pretty good at Tohaali Community School. Remember when I worked at the high school? That's where we had our first kiss so many years ago." Rachael smiled, feeling a sudden rush of blood through her body.

"Yes, I remember that huge pothole that got me into so much trouble—and cost me two kids, in fact."

Bloom moved close to his wife and pulled her to his chest, giving her a long hug and a gentle kiss on her forehead. He knew she was right. Rachael needed Toadlena. The rez would be good for her soul, but Charles wondered if a sing would be enough to get their lives back to normal.

CHAPTER 6

PACKING UP

The Bloom family had been living in its small, rented adobe house nestled in the cottonwoods of La Cienega for only five months, but for Bloom the place was already home. Rachael's sheep had fattened up on the high grass of northern New Mexico, and it wouldn't be long until shearing time would be upon them—even if the wool wouldn't be used for a rug anytime in the near future.

Bloom's gallery was getting lots of press since Spanish conquistador Juan de Oñate's sixteenth-century treasure chest—now housed in the Museum of Indian Arts and Culture for safe keeping and research—was discovered on the premises last summer. Owning what might be one of the oldest homes in America had been great for business, and everyone wanted to hear the story of the chest's discovery. Bloom was tired of repeating the details, but sales were sales, and Bloom was happy with the upswing. Rachael had made up her mind, though, and there was no changing the outcome; she was going back to the reservation for the foreseeable future.

Ten days had passed since Rachael decided to go back home for her Toadlena therapy. A friend had gone to Hastiin Johnson's hogan and asked, on Rachael's behalf, if the medicine man would perform a sing. Hastiin Johnson agreed to take her as a patient, even though he was now doing only the occasional ceremony; a new young recruit named Preston Yellowhorse would assist him.

Having raised him from a baby, Rachael considered Preston her son. She had no idea he was being mentored by Johnson and was proud of him. The young man had recently finished his degree at the New Mexico Institute of Mining and Technology in Socorro and had landed a good paying job at Intel Corporation in Rio Rancho, just north of Albuquerque. Every other weekend Preston returned to the reservation for training by Johnson. He was six months into the apprenticeship and apparently showed great promise.

Rachael was proud that her boy was staying in touch with the traditional world. Even if he never became a full-fledged medicine man, she felt the Diné teachings would keep him grounded, something she wasn't so sure of during his teenage screamo-band days. Rachael and Preston were on the right path. She was pleased that Hastiin Johnson would include him in her ceremony.

The sing was set up for November when the first significant snow arrived in the Chuska Mountains. Bloom would take off from work, which slowed dramatically after all the leaves had fallen in Santa Fe and come to Toadlena to be a part of the ceremony. This would give Rachael more than a month to get physically and mentally prepared for the task at hand, something that she looked forward to, as the structure would focus her attention on getting well.

Moving the sheep back to Toadlena was a challenge, but Rachael preferred to have the flock close so that her precious animals would get the attention they needed, even if she couldn't weave. The sheep were her children too. Rachael had known of weavers who treated their sheep better than their own kids. She hoped to never be one of those people, but it was somehow understandable in the alternative universe of the rez.

In addition to caring for the sheep, Rachael needed skilled help shearing their precious wool; fortunately, such workers were plentiful around Toadlena. The heavy monsoon rains and no sheep feeding for the better part of half a year had turned her ancestral pasture into a sea of tall yellow grass, so moving the sheep back to Toadlena made sense, even though Bloom hated the idea. The roundup, loading, and transportation of the flock had been a royal pain the first go around, and the departing sheep made Rachael's move all that more permanent in his mind.

The question was whether her loom should stay in Santa Fe or go back to Toadlena. Bloom lobbied to keep it with him, knowing that if it were in Santa Fe Rachael would have to come back in the near future—but Rachael decided to take the cumbersome loom with her on the off-chance she felt like she could begin to work again. Bloom didn't want her to start weaving before her strained shoulders were healed, but realized it wasn't his decision, and that all the westward winds were in favor of the Navajo Nation.

September was colder than usual, and the aspen were particularly colorful. Tourists were abundant and spending, even in an uncertain political climate; Santa Fe was just too beautiful to be ignored. Bloom tried to focus on sales and not on who was running the government, knowing politicians would come and go. Santa Fe had been a center for commerce for four hundred-plus years, regardless of which country or politician was in power. Walking by the continuously occupied Palace of the Governors, built in 1610, assured Bloom that Santa Fe was never going to fade away—no matter which way the political winds were blowing.

Bloom had just opened an impromptu show of Billy Poh's jewelry. The Santa Fe detective and talented silversmith had brought Bloom an unexpected collection of ten bracelets that he had made using old techniques and large cabs of Cerrillos turquoise. The pieces, fashioned with heavy-gauge silver, simple green stone embellishment and heavy sawtooth bezel, looked like they could have been made in the nineteenth century. Bloom did an email blast to his client list and sold half the pieces before the official opening, which was good news since he had decided that he just wasn't going to let Rachael go back to Toadlena without him.

Walking the floor of the gallery, impressed with the line of red dots next to the bracelets, it dawned on Bloom that his was now as much a traditional Native art gallery as it was a showcase for contemporary art. He realized that his business model had started to change when he married a Native American weaver. He was selling Indian jewelry and enjoying the process as much as he did the abstract artworks that had been his love and mainstay for so many years.

Dr. J., Bloom's manager, an archeologist by training, had been helping run Bloom's for nearly six years and had developed his own loyal client base. Dr. J. was in his late seventies and customers usually assumed he was Bloom, which was fine with Charles. It made sales easier if the clients felt comfortable that the man helping them was competent.

The Bloom gallery casita was now designated a historical treasure, and the prestige only added to Dr. J.'s sales pitch as he could work in the critical history of the Canyon Road gallery, which helped him close deals. Supervision was no longer an issue for Bloom; the store ran itself, and he was there only because he loved the action. At that moment of clarity, Bloom realized his place for now was with Rachael and his children on the Navajo Nation. The few sales he would lose because he wasn't on the gallery floor to close a deal were minuscule compared to the cost of the time away from his wife and family. Children grow up fast and he was an older father. These were necessary times for him to be a part of the family unit.

Spending an extended period on the reservation also might give him the opportunity to develop relationships with additional Native artisans. Finding new silversmiths, who were abundant on the rez, would help pay his mortgage, and he would become a better Native art dealer by increasing his understanding of the people who had helped him build a thriving gallery. Bloom assumed Rachael might put up a fight and that her concern for the family's financial welfare could cloud her emotional intelligence, so he decided he wouldn't give her the opportunity to say no; he would simply make it happen.

Rachael's old Ford truck looked like a space-age vehicle. A handmade loom of piñon pines standing six feet tall sat squarely in the middle of the pickup's bed, with kids' toys tied down at all the anchor points. The front of the cab was stuffed to the top with luggage. The deer horn she had taken from her house in Toadlena and stuck under the floorboard to await its safe return was also along for the ride. Bloom would follow behind in his own truck, loaded to the gills with clothing, sheep-related gear, most of the kitchenware and two beds for the kids. The pair looked like a caravan of hippies heading up to Taos in the 1960s.

Bloom had arranged a second mortgage on the gallery, and discussed the plan for the next six months with his gallery manager. They agreed that Bloom would handle the internet sales, accounting, and social media, while Dr. J. would run the store as if he owned the place. Dr. J. was getting up there in age so this would be his last opportunity to be the boss—something he would relish. Bloom figured if he merely broke even for the next six months and did not have to dip into the bank for the mortgage money he would be fine.

The time away from the gallery would give Bloom an excellent opportunity to get in shape and learn more about the place Rachael called home. He had spent time in her world before, but never for half a year. This was a major commitment. He would work on his language skills so he could say more than *yá át ééh* (usual greeting) and *hágoonee'* (goodbye).

"You about ready to go?" Bloom called out to his tribe as Rachael made her last check for telephone chargers, pillows, and favorite toys.

"Yes, sir!" Willy shouted, looking like he was going off to summer camp.

"Looks like someone is excited." Rachael smiled as she cradled a sleeping Sam and headed out the front door. As she secured Sam and Willy in their car seats, her inner voice told her to make one final check of the house. She headed back to the bedroom and discovered all of Bloom's clothes were missing.

"What's up with the clothes, Bloom? You moving out once I'm out of here?" Rachael said half-jokingly, while trying to figure out what Bloom was planning.

"Well, I was going to tell you when you got back home, but as it turns out I've decided to join you on your vacation of sorts." Bloom's grin showed all his teeth—a dead giveaway that he was pleased with himself in a boyish way.

"Really? What about money to pay for this house that we still owe rent on and making sales at your gallery? You know that if you're not there it won't do as well."

"Our landlord has someone in the wings for our La Cienega place, and Dr. J. has agreed to work full time for the next six months. All the bills are covered and, if things get tight, I have a second mortgage secured that I can dip into to cover any shortfall. Honestly, I couldn't bear the thought of letting you go for such a long time—so guess what? I'm coming too."

"Second mortgage, huh? When were you going to tell me about that one? You know I get all the bills and would see the statement." Rachael's look at Bloom was somewhere between amused and peeved.

Bloom sheepishly replied, "You know it's high time I start learning Navajo with my kids. Half a year on the rez should give me a great start on becoming bilingual."

Rachael's annoyed look morphed into a full smile. "Let's start with the phrase, 'Rachael's the head boss,'" she said in Navajo.

"What does that mean?" Bloom asked—but before Rachael could answer, Willy, who had undone his seatbelt and come back into the house to find out what they were doing, piped up: "Mommy is the teacher and you're the kid."

Willy started an infectious round of laughter. Rachael smiled and hugged her husband. No words were necessary.

The family piled into their respective vehicles and headed out of town. The aspen leaves were starting to change in the Sangre de Cristo Mountains and plumes of piñon smoke floated through the cool fall air. Going over the rise at La Bajada ridge, Bloom saw Santa Fe through his rear window. The place he had called home for most of his adult life was slowly vanishing into the distance, and he wondered how long it would before he returned—or if this was the start of some new life he had never expected or planned on. He was going to some strange new school and he hoped he was up for the challenge. Willy was right; Rachael was the teacher and he was the kid.

CHAPTER 7

HIGHWAY 491

Gallup's Highway 491, the old Route 666 turnoff toward Toadlena, ran directly past Blake's Lotaburger, Bloom's favorite restaurant. Today Bloom could barely see his old friend's sign peeking between the new McDonald's and a Panda Express restaurant. Modern motels were popping up on every corner. Gallup was starting to look a lot like any other American town, not Drunk City USA, its unofficial moniker.

Gallup's history of alcohol abuse and drunken Navajos freezing to death was legendary. Exposure took the lives of many poor souls each year, as did crossing roads while intoxicated. There had been many attempts to decrease the number of alcohol licenses in the town, which stood at thirty-nine in 2015—a number you would expect see in a larger city, not a town of twenty-two thousand. Bloom hoped the increased commerce might somehow help Gallup develop into a place that more people wanted to make their home.

The family stopped at the new McDonald's, much to Bloom's chagrin. After a potty break, two Happy Meals, an oriental salad, and a less than satisfying cheeseburger (in Bloom's opinion), the family was back in the saddle for the last seventy-four-mile hike into Toadlena. The excitement on Rachael's face was palpable and she switched back to Navajo time and speech immediately.

The girl working the front register was from Toadlena and was in full "Glad you came back home" mode by the time the Big Mac reached the floor. Santa Fe was small and Bloom was a known entity there—when your name is on a prominent Canyon Road sign people can't help but have some subconscious name recognition.

The rez was different; information and gossip traveled at the speed of light, and everyone knew of Rachael, the famous weaver and sister of Willard Yellowhorse, the great Navajo painter murdered in New York City over twenty years ago. Bloom was a nonstarter; no one had ever heard of his gallery. Here, he was Rachael Yellowhorse's husband, the bilagánna art dealer.

Rachael's truck led the way home, with Bloom following close behind. As usual, Highway 491 was a cluster of one-way traffic lanes as the state performed its perennial roadwork. The land surrounding the road was as fertile as Bloom could remember, with dried yellow flowers and green snakeweed filling the usually barren spots. The rains had come this year, which meant the snow would probably follow in spades.

Bloom didn't mind snow, but it wasn't like Santa Fe, where the roads were plowed within a day. Out on the reservation, if you didn't have your own grader you might not get out for a week. This was a new paradigm for Bloom; he knew to expect isolation because he had lived here before—but always with the understanding that it was nothing permanent, just a short stay. This time it felt different.

Turning west at the Shell station meant Rachael's hogan was around the bend. Tsénaajin and Tsénaajin Yázhí, the Two Grey Hills, welcomed the family home, the glistening afternoon light making the two pinnacles stand out even more prominently than Bloom remembered. He loved those two obelisks. They were not as large as Tsé Bit'a'í, their nearby brother Rock with Wings, but were no less impressive in his mind.

Rachael's sheep had been delivered the day before and were waiting near the house, recognizing the sound of her truck as she pulled into the long driveway. She stopped and told Bloom to put out her truck tire, a signal that let everyone in the community know that she was back home and to come say "Hi." The house key was just where she had left it six months earlier under a pile of broken bricks. No longer was her hogan just another abandoned home on the rez; she was back to regain her hózhó and raise a family, even if it were only a temporary stay.

The first thing Rachael did was to return the three mementos she had taken to Santa Fe—a moss-green rock she had played with as a child, a set of bleached deer antlers her late brother Willard had found in the Chuska Mountains when he was fifteen, and a broken gourd her father had used for healing ceremonies—to their proper places. The stone and antlers she gently placed under the front door stoop. The gourd she brought into the house; she would give this to Hastiin Johnson to help with her curing ceremony in November. She was back where she belonged and felt at peace for the first time in almost two months.

Bloom wrestled the kids' beds into the hogan. Willy claimed his by throwing his backpack on the unmade cot and yelling, "Dibs!"—then running back outside in one quick motion. Sam, who wanted to join her brother in the fun, was reluctantly put down for her nap. Charles moved back into their old room, with a too-small queen bed and a water heater that was only good for a five-minute shower. No use complaining, he thought. This was for Rachael. Maybe he could buy a new water heater even if a larger bed wouldn't fit in the tiny space. The hogan was home now, and he would need to get used to the surroundings if he hoped to make a go of it—which he would do for his wife's sake.

The first night in Rachael's hogan was a chilly reminder of the winter to come and what it would take to heat the place. One didn't simply turn the thermostat up to 75 degrees before going to bed, but instead must stoke an antique wood stove located in the kitchen with enough piñon and juniper logs to last through the long winter night.

Rachael reminded Bloom that the fuel wouldn't gather itself and jump miraculously into the stove, but would require the actual physical labor by going up into the Chuskas and collecting the wood. With her two bad wings, Rachael could legitimately avoid this task, but was free with suggestions for how Bloom should fulfill his fast-approaching winter duties.

"Go up to the trading post and borrow Sal's chainsaw," she said. "He will loan it to you. If you ask nicely, he might even let you borrow his mule to go way up the back side of the mountain to get some real quality firewood."

"I don't know anything about mules, Rachael! I'm a city-boy art dealer from Portales, New Mexico—not a backcountry bumpkin."

"First off, Portales is no city, and you're right about the bumpkin part. A 'mule' is a four-wheel-drive vehicle and ATV, and you, my love, are what we refer to as a Rexall ranger, a drugstore cowboy."

"Drugstore cowboy?"

"Yeah. You buy the boots and the hat from the drugstore, but don't know the first thing about being a cowboy or, in this case, a wood gatherer. Clearly, we are going to have to toughen you up. You do know how to use a chainsaw, don't you?"

Bloom made a face that implied that of course he knew how to use a chainsaw—even though he had never handled one before. How terrible could it be? He could borrow Sal's computer and watch a YouTube video to see how it was done.

"Of course! I'm not that much of a city slicker," he said.

Rachael knew he was covering up, but she let him slide; there was no reason to completely emasculate him on their first day back.

Rachael had already abandoned any vestiges of Santa Fe life and had a large cup of her favorite cowboy coffee brewing on the stove, ready for the morning's work. They had brought some eggs with them from

Santa Fe, which were cooking, along with a slab of bacon. This part of the rez Bloom could get used to quickly.

After an excellent breakfast, Bloom headed up the five-mile road to the Toadlena Trading Post. Bloom hoped Sal was in a good mood as he could use some extra work to fill in the gaps in income he figured might be coming when winter hit the Santa Fe art market. Sal and his wife Linda rarely left their beloved post, but one never knew. The trader was getting up there in age and had grandchildren in Las Cruces, so he might want a day or two off this year.

The Toadlena Trading Post never seemed to change; its old stone façade, constructed in 1909, the same year as Geronimo's death, had only become more enchanting with time. There was always human activity around the post and the large bulletin board near the front door broadcast the comings and goings in the valley.

Bloom scanned the faded tan plywood board looking for news of interest; it all seemed to be of the local variety. A veteran's meeting would be held at the Tooh Haltsooi Chapterhouse in Sheep Springs next week. There was hay for sale at $8 a bale. And there were two help-wanted ads. One was for a volunteer firefighter; the other was for the Moss Pawn and Trading Post in Farmington, which was looking for an experienced silversmith to work the bench.

The ad for the silversmith seemed like a throwback to the 1940s, but apparently being a bench silversmith was still a real job around the rez. Trading posts would employee Navajo silversmiths at low wages to make custom jewelry at a fraction of the cost to sell to tourists under the store's own brand. In the early days, great jewelry was created by posts like the Thunderbird Shop and White Hogan, which employed the best silversmiths. But, in today's world, the job might not pay much more than minimum wage, and jewelers were more likely to work for themselves. The internet had become the great equalizer.

Bloom pushed open the heavy wood door to see Sal leaning on the counter with his morning pickle half-devoured.

"Charles Bloom, I heard through the grapevine you were moving back here," Sal said in a booming voice, his hearing aids obviously not turned on.

"The Big Mac communications line?"

"Yep. Gloria stopped by yesterday after her shift and told me that Rachael was coming home—something about needing a sing to help cure her from all that trouble in Santa Fe."

"Gloria is correct on all fronts. Sorry it took so long for the word to get around," Bloom joked.

"You know, Bloom, that damn city you call home is filled with more lowlife dealers than you can shake a stick at. You're better off here. At least you know who your enemies are—and if they knife you, they do it from the front."

Bloom wondered if Sal was referring to that Farmington dealer who had the nerve to put a help-wanted sign for a silversmith on a competing post's bulletin board.

"Well, I'll miss Santa Fe, but you're right—it's nice to be in the fresh air, and knowing your neighbors is a big plus."

"Oh, you will know them all right," Sal chuckled. He knew all too well how nosey many of the so-called neighbors could be.

"Rachael sent me up here to gather some firewood; she said you might loan me your chainsaw and the mule to go up the mountain."

"Rachael's right to get you collecting wood now, before the snows come and the downed trees get picked over. Old Hastiin Manycoats has been collecting wood for half a month now. He only uses a wheelbarrow, so he doesn't go up too far. That man's on Medicare and still walks at least ten miles a day. The government is going to lose a lot of money 'cause he's never going to die."

"Sounds like he's in better shape than me," Bloom said. "I'm not sure I remember Manycoats. Is he from this area?"

"Yeah, born and raised. He's a bit of a recluse, lives in a small hogan down by the Two Grey Hills. He was a Marine in Vietnam and received two Purple Hearts. But you wouldn't know he was a war hero. I've never heard him talk about it, not even once. He prefers speaking Navajo to English and is usually pretty quiet, unless he wants your attention—then you can't shut him up. He's fluent in both languages."

"I remember him now. He likes to sit in your barber chair and listen for hours on end, has a great smile."

"Yep, that's Marvin. By the way, are you looking for any work while you're here?"

"Funny you should ask, Sal. I'm expecting to be here for a good bit, maybe six months or possibly longer, so I could use some extra work if you have some. When I worked with you a few years back, I thought it went well, and now I even know how to sell Navajo rugs and jewelry, something I didn't know before."

"Well," Sal grinned, "my wife and I want to do an around-the-world trip before we are too old, which as you can see is pretty damn close." Remembering he was mortal reminded Sal to turn on his hearing aids.

"So are you asking me to take over for a month or so?" Bloom asked.

"More like four months. It turns out it takes about as long to go around the world as it does to hike from here to Monument Valley in the winter."

Bloom got the humor of going over the Chuska Mountains in high winter snows on foot—a Donner Party-type experience.

"You know, Sal, if we can work out something fair for both of us, I might just take you up on that offer. Moving from gallery owner to trading post manager sounds like a step up to me."

Both men laughed and sat down with their pencils sharpened to flesh out the details. Bloom completely forgot about Rachael's wood. He now had a new money stream flowing his way; Sal planned to book his tickets tomorrow.

CHAPTER 8

NIGHTMARES

Marvin began having a recurrent nightmare. In the dream, the headmaster would demand to read Marvin's notes and, after handing them over to him, the notes would magically transform from English to Navajo and Soliday would start screaming and hitting Marvin with huge branches from the school's namesake cottonwoods. "English only!" Soliday shouted. "What about Yazzie? I don't see anything about Yazzie. He's a bad seed!"

Each time the nightmare was the same: Marvin would wake up in a cold, drenching sweat and then lie in bed, wide-awake. The boy began using his 4 a.m. wake-ups to record his emotions and the events of the previous day in the hidden notebooks. A blow-by-blow accounting of his school life, with no detail too insignificant, became Marvin's new routine.

White men were big on schedules and, while there were no mirrors to be found on the school property, there were plenty of clocks to remind the children of the importance of time in the modern world—a white man's way to exercise control. Marvin vowed to document time on his own terms by using the notebooks as a vehicle to vent his frustrations and record the injustices he saw on a daily basis.

Monday, Sept. 25

7 a.m. I ate cold cereal and found a mealworm. I ate the worm. It tasted better than the spoiled cereal. I hope to find more worms and have asked the others to save the worms for me if they aren't hungry.

8 a.m. Started class, woodworking, carving pencil designs, furniture for the school, best part of my day.

10 a.m. Math class, addition, and subtraction. Easy work. Very tired. Fell asleep for most of the class. Was not caught. Lucky!

11 a.m. English class, ABCs, nouns and verbs. Only a few understand what a verb or noun is. Sad class.

12 p.m. Lunch. Roll and butter. Bread old, no worms, too bad. Butter was tasty and fresh, reminded me of home, more sad thoughts. Sky is blue and wind still hot and dry. It's hunting season back home.

1 p.m. Irrigation class. Wish it was Friday when we have no irrigation class and get a second hour of English. Today we worked in the cotton field for two hours. Back hurts. Saw a hawk with a mouse in its claws flying toward Black Mesa. I thought of home. Dug up three beetle grubs and stuck them in my backpack, snack for later. Nick Tsosie was swatted twice with cottonwood twigs for asking for water in Navajo. Mr. Wellman warned him that he would tell Mr. Soliday next time. Nick received no water as punishment. I secretly gave him some of mine.

4 p.m. Religious class. Told us we would go to hell if we talk Navajo. We prayed for our salvation. I prayed to Talking God for help. No answer yet but I'm hoping for one soon.

5 p.m. Clean up around school grounds. I saw a horned lizard at an ant pile. It made me laugh. He was eating better than me. Maybe I need to try ants.

6 p.m. Dinner. Ate outside. The day's heat broke. A coyote yelped in the background, he's hungry like us. Beans and bread for dinner. Found two rocks in the beans, was lucky not to hurt my teeth. No one talks, just eat.

7 p.m. Study time. Homework easy. Helped others and tried to keep everyone's spirits up and work on their English. Most speak in Navajo during study time as no one watches us. I even talked once in Navajo. Ernie Yazzie is sad. I think he knows he has been singled out. He's afraid to speak, especially to me. He must somehow know I've lost my hózhó by being Mr. Soliday's ally.

8 p.m. Lights out. No shower today, maybe we will get showers tomorrow. I miss feeling the water on my face and hair. My hair is filled with sweat and dirt from the irrigation class. I broke a nail today on my left hand. It hurts and looks bad. Hope no evil chindi haunts me. I chanted softly to pray for good health.

As the days passed, Marvin became even more compulsive about his note-taking. He knew Soliday would expect results from their alliance and, to keep him happy, Marvin would write about some minor infraction on a piece of paper torn from his notebook, but always in general terms. His two personal logs he wedged into a crack in the back dormitory wall where they would be hidden by his clothes. He often wrote in those books after awakening from nightmares in the early morning while the rest of the dormitory slept.

Marvin knew it was odd to wake up and write down each thought and detail, no matter how insignificant the activity might seem. But writing worked for him somehow, and made him feel better about his precarious situation. If Soliday discovered the notebooks, they would be thrown out and he would be in huge trouble, so he began the laborious task of memorizing every word he wrote.

He would start from the first day he got the notebooks and follow through to the last day's entry. Once his sharp mind had memorized all the information and could repeat it twice without a mistake, he felt his task was complete. Then he would put away the notebooks and try to go back to sleep—something that rarely happened. He put the most personal material in one notebook and used the other to record more mundane daily activities. He kept the books separate so, if he was ever asked to show his notebooks to Soliday, he could give him the lesser of the two evils and claim the other had been stolen.

The days became weeks. Every Monday, Marvin had to meet with Mr. Soliday at noon. To keep Soliday from exploding, he had to report some small piece of poor behavior. Ernie Yazzie was brought up at each meeting, and each time Marvin would play down any problems. Soliday was getting impatient.

It all came to a head the day before Marvin turned twelve.

On that day, Marvin did not get to make his usual entries in his notebooks. If he had been able to write about it, he would have said, "Mr. Soliday was in a very poor mood and attacked me in a rant about baseball and Ernie; I like this word 'rant.' It's a new word for me."

"Marvin," Soliday shouted, "did you know that Babe Ruth's home run record was broken today—and by a cheating Yankee! What is the world coming to when subpar people are given such totally undeserved accolades? And Marvin, you owe me some good intelligence today. I've only been getting half-truths about Ernie Yazzie, and I want to know what's really happening!"

Babe Ruth had been Soliday's father's favorite player and Roger Maris had beaten the Babe's record on the last day of the season. The headmaster was angry and wanted blood—if he couldn't have Ernie's, maybe Marvin's would do.

Marvin didn't know much about baseball other than white people liked the game—and he would never understand their obsession.

"No, Mr. Soliday. I would tell you if Ernie's been bad. He's working on his English and is getting pretty good."

"Bullshit, Marvin! Do you know what bullshit means? It means you're lying, and if you don't come clean, I'm going to punish you instead of Ernie. Do you understand me, my little Navajo spy?"

A cold sweat broke out on Marvin's face; he didn't know what to say or do. If he didn't give Mr. Soliday what he wanted, he would definitely be punished. If he lied about Ernie, the other boy would pay dearly for something he had not done.

Ernie's grandmother's blanket was no longer around—and maybe that was the crux of the problem for both boys. Like the proverbial sheep stuck deep in the crevice, Marvin was at a crossroads. He had to make a decision, and he chose to save Ernie.

"I can't help you any more than I have, Mr. Soliday. Ernie Yazzie has done nothing wrong so far... I'm sorry. I wish I could be more helpful but I promise I'm watching him closely."

"Oh yes, you will definitely be sorry, Marvin. Just because I can't do anything about a guy named Roger Maris doesn't mean I can't do something about Marvin Manycoats, an eleven-year-old who lies. Head over to the box! I will be there shortly. You will have four days to think about your actions, young man!"

The box was a ten-foot by ten-foot wooden cell with no windows and a hard-packed dirt floor. The box's outside covering was black, which caused the interior to heat up from solar absorption. A Donald Judd-esque torture chamber, it contained no bathroom, no bed or anything other than a dark, musty environment that reeked of urine. The only light came through a hole in the ceiling, probably an old chimney exhaust. But this box had no stove, just a fifteen-inch slot for the passage of food, water, and waste at the bottom of the door. The slot was an open invitation to any snake, insect or rat that could slither or crawl through the sizeable opening.

Only one child had entered the box in the two months the kids had been at Two Trees Indian School, and he was only imprisoned for two days.

The boy had looked horrible when he came out, and Marvin thought the child might die. He was semi-delirious the first day out and was beaten on the feet with a cane for mumbling Navajo chants. The boy didn't remember much about the experience—he was just glad to be alive, and swore he would kill himself before going back into the cell.

Marvin remembered all this as he walked over to the isolation chamber.

Mr. Soliday asked him one more time for a confession.

"Are you sure there isn't something, even a small infraction, you can tell me about Ernie? Remember the box is meant to punish—and you will be punished. You know this, don't you, Marvin?"

"Yes, I know, I saw Ricky Begay come out. He was very sick and scared, and I'm very scared now. But if I tell you anything bad about Ernie it will be a lie. He has not done anything I can report. Believe me, Mr. Soliday, I don't want to go into the box. I know I might not come out."

"You're right about that, Marvin. Some don't come out of the box. Their bodies give out, and it is unusually hot right now so you should rethink what you haven't told me about Mr. Yazzie and write something on this piece of paper that tells me the truth."

Soliday was holding a sheet of his stationary and a number two pencil and waiting for Marvin to take the paper and write. Marvin knew he should give the man anything he could—but he also knew that if Ernie went into the box he would never come out. Ernie's body and mind were weaker than his, and Soliday had it out for the other boy. Marvin wasn't raised to leave the sheep in the crevice and would need luck and prayer to survive.

Avoiding looking at the paper and pencil, Marvin pleaded: "Please Mr. Soliday. I will watch harder. I will find something. Just don't throw me into the box, pleeaassee...."

Soliday grabbed Marvin by his gray school shirt collar and tossed him against the entrance to the box, which was directly in front of the headmaster's office window.

"Sorry, Marvin," Soliday sneered. "I'm not putting you in the box; you are putting yourself in there by not being honest with me. I will check on you tomorrow and see if things appear different with regards to Mr. Yazzie. I hope you can still write by then."

With that, Soliday took out his key, unlocked the heavy plank door and pushed Marvin roughly into the foreboding box. The young boy fell back hard onto the rock-solid dirt floor as something scurried out through the small slit at the bottom of the door. A loud slam put an exclamation point on the conversation, and then the lock turned.

Marvin—and all the Indian kids Soliday despised—was Roger Maris in the headmaster's eyes, and he would punish the insubordinate child for the next four days. There was always someone else who would talk if Marvin chose not to play ball with him.

CHAPTER 9

SURVIVING (DAY 1)

Sprawled on the ground, Marvin's first impulse was to scream for Mr. Soliday to come back, save himself, write whatever the white man wanted and throw Ernie Yazzie to the wolves. It was instinctual. Marvin bit his lip hard and tried not to cry. Today was the day he turned twelve, and it wouldn't be a happy birthday unless Soliday changed his mind. Marvin understood what it meant to be hot, hungry and scared. This box was not the first time in his life he battled the elements to survive, but it would be his most significant challenge.

He realized thirst could kill him—not starvation, as very little food was required to survive—but if he got too dehydrated death was certain. Marvin had seen first-hand sheep that wandered away and died in a single day of a lack of water. He decided at that moment to live and, once out of the box, to help Ernie escape, or the boy would perish for sure. They were clan brothers and Marvin must help Ernie or die trying.

Marvin picked himself up off the hard floor and began to move slowly around the box to see if any creatures were hiding in his new prison. There was just enough light filtering in from the slit in the roof to see once his eyes adjusted to the dimness. Above the box's roof loomed one of the giant Two Tree cottonwoods, out of reach and of no help other than providing some shade.

There was surprisingly little debris on the floor: a few plum-sized quartz rocks that the boys had thrown through the roof hole in a game of dexterity, and a cottonwood branch the size of his arm that must have fallen in during the last storm. In the corner, he found a small juniper twig and a dried prickly pear cactus pad, which a pack rat probably brought in to start making a home before realizing even a pack rat wouldn't want to live there. The only man-made item was a single rusty can that read Campbell Soup, its paper label partially eaten off, no doubt by the same hungry pack rat.

The bottom of the heavy plank door had a metal-hinged flap that closed, except for the last inch, which allowed a small, thin rectangle of light to shine on the red dirt floor. When fully open, the slit was large enough to slip in food and a small bedpan for bodily waste— although the box smelled like the last guest didn't get the bedpan. Marvin decided that one far quarter of the room would be for human waste if no bedpan were forthcoming. A little breeze came through if the door slit were propped open and he could relieve himself where the breeze would help keep the smell to a minimum.

Marvin took the metal can and worked the jagged top back and forth until it broke free. He then placed the empty soup can where it could hold the swinging door open for airflow and additional light. Once satisfied with his interior improvements, Marvin settled into the far corner of the room and concentrated on breathing slowly and trying to make sense of his predicament. His father had taught him that if he were ever in a life or death situation, he should think before acting and stick to a plan. No matter how poor that plan might be, any course of action was better than none.

The can's lid scraping against his upper arm as he methodically moved it up and down was reassuring. He knew the first and last days of his confinement would be the hardest. On day one he would have to conquer his fears. Day four, when the last of his body fluids were exhausted, would be when he would need all his strength. Maybe he would get lucky and Soliday would regain his composure and reconsider his harsh punishment. After all, Marvin wasn't a Yankee—he was just a little kid, but he could not count on charity from that Christian man.

As he squatted contemplating his predicament, a song came floating under the door jam; it was a sad, twangy woman's voice he had never heard before, and it was coming from the radio in Soliday's office.

"I fall to pieces

Each time I see you again

I fall to pieces

How can I be just your friend?"

The words stuck in Marvin's head and he tried to remember them verbatim so he could add them to his notebook if he got out alive. The announcer said it was a new hit song by someone named Patsy Cline. Somehow the song helped calm his pounding heart; the singer felt the same pain he was feeling, and knowing others also suffered from unfair relationships allowed Marvin to realize it was not his dilemma that was unique—just the setting.

Marvin's mind shifted back to the present, trying to determine his strategy. The door was locked and made of solid recycled barn wood covered with small splinters that he did not dare run his hand across. The dirt floor was stone-hard and stained in a butterfly wing pattern. Looking at it, Marvin couldn't help but think of home, where Shiprock was always visible in his backyard, its wings embracing his world.

He slipped his arm through the food slit and considered the possibility of digging out earth to make a big enough space to escape, or at least get more air—but the effort would use up too much energy and he had no tools. Escape was impossible except with help from the outside, which was unlikely as Soliday seemed to have the only key. It would be nightfall before his classmates would figure out he was in the box and they would be too afraid to help.

"Save my energy, that is how to live," Marvin chanted to himself, knowing that this was a good strategy. The only strategy.

Marvin had not planned to celebrate his twelfth birthday inside the box. He rolled back through the images of birthdays past in his memory, reliving his mother's special meals. Then he thought about the temperature. Some days were hot, others quite cold. Early fall was an unpredictable time of the year. As warm as it was in the box now, it could be cold in short order. The nights were already feeling more like winter, and he had to prepare for all the possibilities over the next four days. Marvin smiled, realizing how lucky he was to have been born on October 2nd, and to have a mind that could remember those past birthdays as if they were yesterday.

As Marvin sang the words of the new Patsy Cline song, he took off his outer shirt to cool down—and realized he had also worn a tee shirt that day, a lucky break. He removed the tee shirt as well and used it to wipe the sweat off his head. He checked his pockets and found a square of hard bread from breakfast and a beetle larva from irrigation class. He popped the squirming bug into his mouth; the juices tasted so good. The hard bread he would save for later.

Marvin heard his father's voice telling him to make a weapon and looked around at the few materials available to him. The branch was big and strong enough to be fashioned into a defensive tool. Ironically, the woodworking class had helped Marvin develop good shaping skills. He started cutting and chipping the end of the stick with the jagged edge of the can top until he fashioned a thin groove, in which he could slip the piece of metal, creating a homemade hatchet. Finally, half the can top slipped into the end of the stick. The boy ripped small bits of his tee shirt into long, thin pieces and secured the soup can's lid to his makeshift handle. A few prickly pear needles inserted at angles doubly secured the fabric to the porous cottonwood limb.

The work took hours, but cottonwood is soft for a desert tree, one of the reasons the Hopi use it carve their kachinas. A juniper branch would have been too difficult to manipulate. It was a birthday present from the Holy People, and he thanked the cottonwood for its welcome gift.

Marvin's stomach ached. The box's daytime heat would soon switch to night's cold. He pulled the can from under the door hinge to help keep in the warmth. He had no blankets, and the ground would sap his body heat. He felt an urgency to have the hatchet ready before the sun went down, as night also brought out the chindi and shapeshifters.

Marvin took the hatchet and hit it hard against the wall, where it stuck. It was strong and could be deadly with some additional sharpening of the quartz rocks. He had no food or water but the night would be easier to bear now that he had a weapon to defend himself or use as a tool. If it wasn't too cold, he could prop open the door slit with the juniper twig once it was entirely dark and hope that some form of food would wander in. Maybe the pack rat would be back.

Marvin relieved himself in the corner, drawing little circles in the sand with the potent, dark yellow urine. If no more water appeared it would be his last creative work for many days.

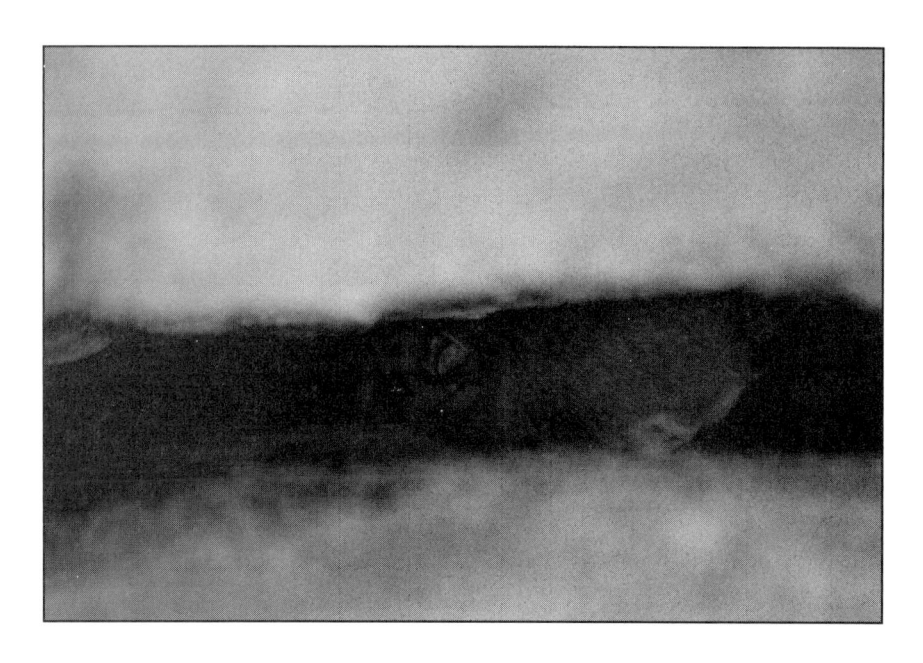

CHAPTER 10

DAY 2

Marvin was startled awake by a small animal scampering over his face—not a first for a boy who lived in the desert—but it still scared him, and he jumped up swinging his hatchet before he realized what had happened. Marvin had spent as much time sleeping outdoors as indoors in the summer months, and little varmints occasionally scurrying over you was not unusual, but the extreme stress of his situation had put him on edge. He searched in vain for the rodent, but it was gone—a lost opportunity, one he couldn't afford to miss again.

It was day two and he had received no food or water since being interned in the box. The sun had been up for three hours; Marvin could hear the school coming to life, with familiar voices filtering through the slit. It wouldn't be long before music would be coming out of Soliday's window.

Marvin decided he would try to sleep in the warmest part of the day and save his energy for the night, when he could look for a rat or snake to eat; even a juicy fall grasshopper was starting to sound good. Being awake after dark would give him a better chance of finding food.

Amazingly, he was able to sleep until he was awakened at 2 p.m. by the sound of the slot opening and something sliding in. Not a word was spoken. The metal plate was cool to the touch and contained a soggy piece of bread that fell apart when Marvin tried to lift it off the plate. There was nothing else on the tray.

Marvin devoured his meal in three greedy gulps, then licked the plate repeatedly until only a metallic taste was left in his mouth. The stale, wet bread did more for his thirst than for his empty, aching stomach. He didn't know whether to keep the plate in the box or slide it out through the slot. He decided it would be better to put it out so they would know he was alive and hopefully bring him some additional food. The plate disappeared minutes after he pushed it through—that apparently was his meal for the day.

He could now use the bits of bread he had discovered in his pocket on day one as bait. He had almost succumbed to his childish impulses and eaten the found food, but realized it could be used to bring more food to the table. He stuck the bread onto the prickly pear pad's needles, and sharpened the juniper stick so he could use it as a nail to secure the pad to ground. Marvin hoped his tasty bait would get the attention of some fat mouse that he could eat—or catch and use as bait for something more substantial. The boy was fishing—even though he had never eaten a fish in his life.

Marvin felt rested. What he needed now was the patience it would take to trap food. He removed all his clothes and waited. Finally, around two in the morning, with the moon shining through his small roof hole, his victim—a hungry deer mouse—came calling. As soon as the mouse had made its way over to the bait, Marvin stuffed his clothes under the slit in the door so nothing else could come in or, more importantly, get out.

Marvin slowly stalked the unsuspecting mouse, pouncing on his prey with the soup can. It was a perfect strike, except for the small cactus spine that punctured his palm; his meal was alive and kicking. Hunger aside, the boy now had to decide what to do next. A mouse would only be a small snack. If he were smart, Marvin might be able to catch something much more significant. Even if he didn't get what he hoped for, he would still have a nice little bite of mouse.

So he wrapped the trapped mouse in his tee shirt and rapidly spun the rodent in circles until the mouse was so dizzy he could remove it from the soup can. Then he took a strip of the tee shirt, which he had pulled into a tiny thread, and tied it to the base of the rodent's tail. He secured the other end of the cloth to the ground with the juniper nail. The mouse jumped wildly until it had wasted all its energy and—much like Marvin—was ready to accept its fate.

It wasn't long before Marvin's late birthday gift arrived: a four-foot-long Western Diamondback rattlesnake slid through the slit, honing in on the rodent's body with his heat-seeking sensors. The mouse, sensing his impending doom, started to pull at the thread that held it to the ground, frantically hoping to free itself in a last burst of energy. As the snake struck at the mouse's warm body, Marvin swung his hatchet, decapitating the snake at the base of its skull with the sharpened soup can lid. The box had two victims that night: Marvin was determined not to be the third.

The snake's headless body rolled over and over, like a balloon escaping from a circus clown's grip. The mouse had miraculously survived the deadly attack, but was in obvious distress. It had given up trying to escape and was quietly awaiting its demise. But Marvin, who felt the small creature's pain, started to hum Patsy Cline's tune. He untied his captive's tail and gently placed him outside the slit, saying to the little mouse, "You are free. Tell your brethren that Marvin Manycoats is a good human and, if you can, help me when I truly need it."

The thought of eating snake meat bothered Marvin's Navajo belief system immensely, something a good human would not do, snakes and lizards are sacred. Marvin thought of his father's reaction and then heard his voice, "You must survive and help Ernie," Marvin prayed to the snakes for forgiveness and to borrow the rattle for protection.

Marvin used the homemade hatchet to remove snake's skin, which he slipped off like a banana peel. He positioned the multipurpose juniper stick in the box's roof opening, letting the silky strip hang over the twig to dry for the moment. Then he returned his attention to the food—snake meat. As if it were corn on the cob, Marvin meticulously picked off the still-warm flesh, which occasionally twitched in his mouth as the rattler's synaptic juices fired their last cylinders. In twenty minutes nothing was left but a fine line of bones. For the first time in two days, Marvin felt content and knew he had made the right decision; dying in the box was less likely now.

After easing most of his hunger, Marvin turned his attention back to the snakeskin, cleaning the last small bits of meat clinging to the snake's smooth, shiny pelt with the little juniper stick. He used the hatchet as a hoe to pry up a chunk of the floor, then crushed the silicon block into fine sand that he could use to cover the wet inner surface of the skin. Plucking another string from his tee shirt, he rolled the snakeskin into a tight ball—a powerful reminder he made it out of the box alive, which now looked possible. For the first time since he had been locked up, no nightmares disturbed Marvin's sleep.

CHAPTER 11

DAY 3

The music that woke up Marvin next morning was sweet:

Where the boys are

someone waits for me,
A smiling face, a warm embrace,

two arms to hold me tenderly
Where the boys are...

The song was sung by someone named Connie Francis, and the melody made Marvin smile for the first time in three days. He was sure that if Mr. Soliday knew it made him smile the music would stop.

Marvin was now twelve and he had grown up a lot in his three days of confinement. He felt like a man for the first time in his life. Soon he would need to turn his attention to dealing with Mr. Soliday and Ernie.

The wet bread came the same way it did yesterday. This time, a small card with the food read:

"One more day to go. Don't ever make me mad again. Mr. S."

Marvin hated the man in the office on the other side of the box even more.

"If I had a bow, I would shoot an arrow into your heart, pull it out and eat it as it was beating in my hand," Marvin said loudly in Navajo, hoping Soliday could hear his defiance through the wooden prison walls.

Marvin squeezed the water from the bread into the soup can and saved the crust for later. He was still full from the snake and felt he should squirrel away both food and water in case Soliday added more time to his sentence.

Marvin unrolled the snakeskin and cut off the rattle, a possible witching tool for revenge in the future. The head's sharp fangs might come in handy, too, for their potent venom—though he didn't know how long the toxic poison might last. He put the snake's bones into the empty pan, slipped it under the hatch, and waited for a response.

A woman squealed. He hoped it was Mrs. Pingry; he didn't like the Matchstick Woman. "It's a bad memory for both of us," Marvin shouted. He had no other contact with anyone on day three.

The weather changed from hot to cold as a front rolled in and Soliday's radio confirmed what Marvin's body could already feel; it would be cold tonight. New Mexico can reach 100 degrees one day and snow the next. It was early October and the Yei winds could change in a moment—which they did.

Marvin realized he might get very cold. Though the box would break the wind and probably keep him from freezing to death, it could get uncomfortable. Using the hatchet, he chipped some wood from the paneling inside the box. These slivers of kindling could help start the fire he hoped to make. Cutting off a small section of the snakeskin Marvin fashioned a sling and, using the juniper stick, he began rubbing vigorously, producing a hole in the soft cottonwood handle of the hatchet. Soon the handle was smoking.

Using the slivers of wood and bits of his tee shirt, Marvin started a small fire. He was able to break a few sizable pieces of wood off the inside of the box and soon a beautiful orange flame was warming the room. Marvin took the few rocks he had found in the box and placed them in the fire, vowing that if he got out alive he would be sure to join in the game of throwing stones down the roof hole. They might come in handy for the next occupant.

The fire slowly died out, but the rocks were hot. Marvin curled up near the embers and covered his head with the remnants of his tee shirt. The rocks provided a slow, radiant heat and the shirt retained his head's warmth. For the second night in a row, he slept well.

CHAPTER 12

DAY 4

Marvin awoke with the sun and prepared for what he hoped would be his last day in the box. He cleaned off his clothes, ate yesterday's bread and drank the last gulp of water. He chipped out a large section of the floor to form a small cavity, the way the Nasazi did when leaving a cache in a cave for a later date. He placed the tomato can, prickly pear pad, snakeskin minus the rattle and head, and the hatchet in the hole in case he was ever tossed back into the box, and carefully covered them with the rectangular dirt top that now had a small X incised on it as a marker. Using yet another piece of tee shirt, he pulled a thread that he attached to the rattlesnake's long rattle and tucked the ornament next to his skin, under his shirt, a powerful charm not to be taken lightly.

He combed his hair with the juniper stick as best he could, then wedged the remaining bit of the tee shirt and twig between two of the boards on the wall. Using a piece of charcoal from the previous night's fire, he inscribed on the darkest wall farthest from the door, in Navajo: "I live. You can, too. Black Mesa will call us back soon. Under Mother Earth are gifts if you need them. Find the X." Marvin wanted to help the next child forced into the prison, and only a Navajo would understand his cryptic note.

Then Marvin sat and waited. No food came, but by noon the door opened. Mr. Soliday was waiting on the other side.

"Marvin," Soliday asked, "Are you still with us?"

His question appeared heartfelt; Soliday apparently knew there was a chance the boy had died during the ordeal. Marvin was sure the headmaster thought he would have to drag an unconscious body out of this man-made hellhole.

Marvin ducked his head under the door jam and stretched as he breathed in the cool, refreshing October air, his clothes neat and hair combed. Covering his light-sensitive eyes with one hand, he squinted up at Soliday—and then saw what was hanging from the man's neck: his father's squash blossom necklace!

The large blue turquoise nuggets looked out of place on the starched white shirt. Marvin wanted to scream, "Take off MY necklace," but he knew that the evil Soliday was looking for that very reaction. Instead, he said in his most forceful voice, "Thanks for asking, Mr. Soliday. I'm fine. I'm sorry you had to put me in the box. I believe it's time for math class now; if I can, I would like to return to my usual schedule."

Soliday looked at Marvin in complete disbelief. The boy appeared to have just awakened from an afternoon nap, ready for the rest of the day. He was apparently no worse for his ordeal in the box.

"How do you like my INJUN necklace? Nice turquoise? One of the boys turned the junky old piece in this week; some kid in the past must have hidden it under the floorboards of the boy's dormitory and forgotten it. Good heavy silver, though the craftsmanship seems to be a little poor, probably made by a beginning silversmith. I thought I would take it to old man Springer and see if he would give me anything for it—or maybe just melt it down for the silver...."

Marvin knew he was being baited. In his most confident voice he said, "I've got a necklace, too. It's pretty cool," and pulled out the snake's rattle in defiance of the man who had stolen his heritage. "If it's OK, Mr. Soliday, I'll be going to class now."

A frown slid over Soliday's face. He was expecting anger, despair, or crying. He was not expecting to be outwitted by a Navajo child. He wondered if maybe the necklace wasn't Marvin's after all—perhaps a kid really had left it under the floor and died and never got it back. But wherever it came from, it was Soliday's necklace now.

"OK, then. Go on, no dawdling. Go directly to class, don't stop for anything. We will have our usual Monday noon meeting—and I hope you will have something for me by then."

"Yes, sir. Straight to class and meet with you on Monday. I'll go now."

Soliday, who had a glass of ice water sitting on the outer corner of the box, picked it up and gulped some down, still hoping for some reaction from the boy. But Marvin just walked past him and headed to class as if he had never seen the water or the necklace. Soliday was impressed by the young man's toughness. He knew the Navajo were strong people, but he had never seen anything like Marvin Manycoats. He was a worthy adversary and one he should not underestimate. The diamondback's rattle proved that.

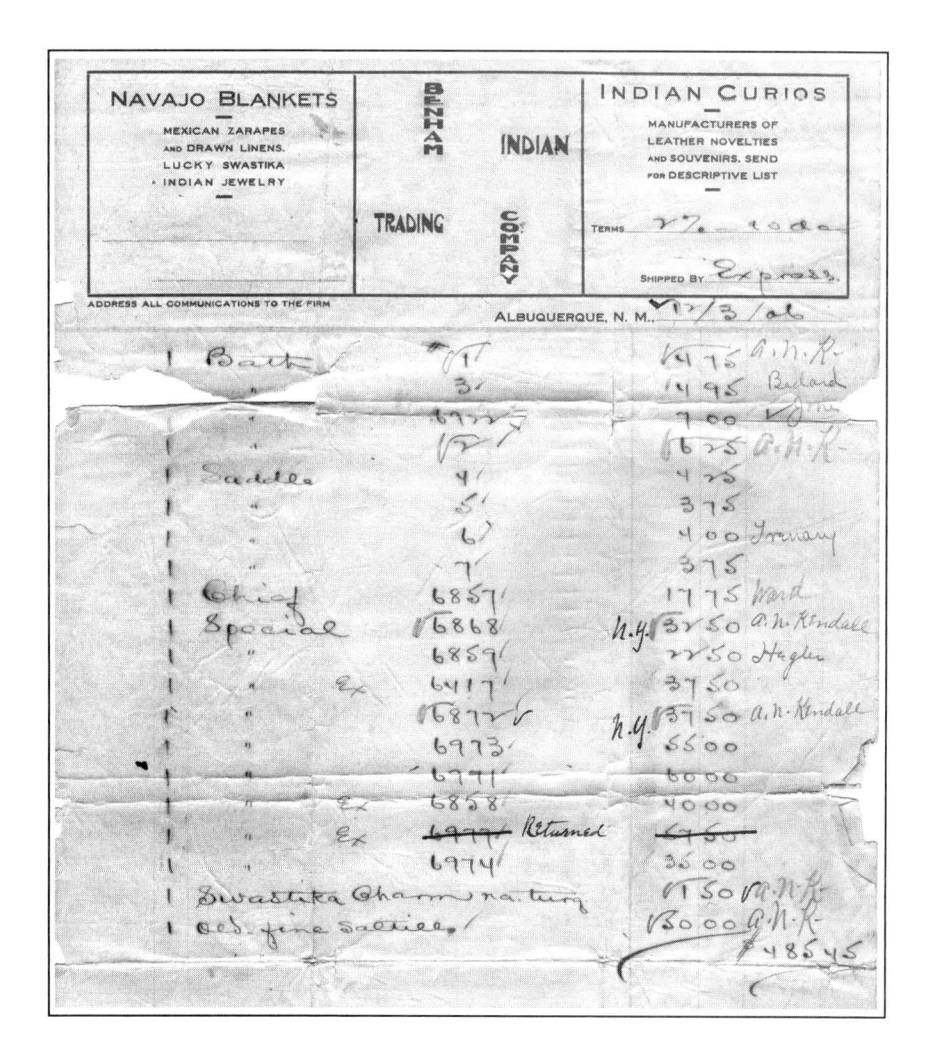

CHAPTER 13

SAVING ERNIE

Marvin headed to class, stopping first in the restroom to relieve himself; the rattlesnake meat had finally worked its way down through his empty bowels. Next, he drank heartily from the sink until his mouth no longer felt parched. Marvin's mind cleared, and he felt less lightheaded after drinking his fill. He washed his face and hair and continued on to class.

When he arrived in math, the kids were shocked. They had assumed that Marvin had given up and that his chindi had now joined their ancestors. To see him come in looking normal amazed the other students, who all smiled in unison. Mrs. Pingry looked a little afraid. She had indeed been the one who removed the metal plate containing the snake's carcass. Seeing Marvin unscathed and ready to learn, the rattlesnake necklace prominently dangling on his chest, took her by complete surprise.

"OK, Marvin. Take a seat. You are four days behind, and I expect you to make up all your work. No excuses."

"Yes, Mrs. Pingry. I'm sorry no one brought my homework to me in the box. I'll take care of the missed work."

Marvin was surprised by his own cockiness, especially the way he was flaunting the rattle. But Mrs. Pingry, the snake's skeleton flashing through her mind, was nervous enough to let the bold remark and unapproved ornament slide. Her apparent retreat gave Marvin more clout with his classmates.

After class the kids encircled Marvin, peppering him with questions and wanting to know why Marvin would have a sacred snake rattle around his neck.

"What was it like? How much food and water did you get? How did you get that rattlesnake tail? Were you scared? Why were you in the box?"

Marvin dodged the questions by saying, "Not now. We'll talk later or we all might all end up in the box—and believe me, you don't want ever to go there."

All the children became as silent as if Mr. Soliday himself had spoken, and they paid attention; there were no more questions.

The group headed from math to English class, where an elderly, nearly deaf white woman taught the kids about the importance of diction and punctuation. Marvin's mind wandered back to his father's gift, now hanging around the neck of a man who could easily have let him die for not lying. Marvin had to come to grips with the idea that he had lost the necklace and that there was nothing he could do about it unless he could kill Stanton Soliday and take it back.

"Could I kill that man?" he asked himself. Marvin was pretty sure he could if the opportunity presented itself, and the rattlesnake charm around his neck confirmed his dark side.

The box had provided him with a weapon of sorts. If he could somehow inject the venom from the severed rattlesnake head into Soliday's bloodstream, he might retrieve his heirloom. The venom would only remain potent in the dead snake's shriveling skull for a short period of time, so if he were to act, it would need to be soon, otherwise he would need to depend on the rattlesnake rattle, his witching charm.

Maybe Ernie would help him. After all, both boys were marked men, their doom only as far off as the next Monday afternoon meeting with Soliday. Marvin had no intention of going back into the box, not with the school's cemetery looming nearby. His squash blossom necklace was probably heading over to Springer's trading post to be sold, a package deal with Ernie's old chief's blanket.

The bilagáana's emphasis on time was now washing over Marvin in baptismal fashion. He was having a newfound awaking to the almighty clock and its significance—none of which was good news for Ernie Yazzie. His clan brother's time was running out, and Marvin knew he was the only one who could save his friend.

The rest of the school day dragged on. Marvin's energy was low, the lack of food, water, sleep, and high level of stress taking a more significant toll on him than he expected. He wanted to talk to his friends—especially Ernie—but after dinner he collapsed on the bed's top sheet, never removing his clothes or shoes, and none of his bunkmates dared wake him.

There were no dreams that night, just deep sleep. Marvin did not stir until the morning sun warmed his face. Awakening, he first thought he was still in the box and a chill of fear ran through his body. Then he realized he was in his army cot, not on the cold, hard ground. Looking around, he saw that everyone else was still asleep and would probably stay that way for another hour.

Marvin took out his two notebooks and started writing, making sure to accurately capture his four days in prison before the memories became blurred—or worse, repressed in some inaccessible part of his brain. He wrote feverishly—including Soliday's remarks about his father's squash blossom necklace—and didn't stop until the sun had fully risen and his bunkmates were starting to stir. By then, everything that happened had been recorded in vivid detail: the snake, his birthday, even the words to the Patsy Cline song.

Snapping out of his writing-induced trance, Marvin noticed that the boards under his bed were still ajar from when Soliday stole his family's heirloom. That invasion of what little privacy he had irritated the usually well-balanced boy, and he decided to leave a small gift for Soliday if he came looking for more things to pilfer. Marvin unwrapped the snakehead from its protective tee shirt covering and placed it upside down in the niche with the mouth open, exposing the two long fangs; he hoped Soliday would come on another fishing expedition, stick his hand into the hole and stab himself on the snake's extended fang. Marvin shuddered as he realized he was now no better than Soliday—someone who could take another's life without thinking twice about it.

"The whites are teaching me well," he thought.

Marvin had lost the inner beauty the Navajo believe not only keeps one balanced, but also helps one cope. The brutal treatment at Two Trees had extinguished his self-worth; now his soul was considering murder as a viable option.

The bilagáanas believed the Navajo ideology was savage, and their stated intention was to take the savage out of the Indian. Marvin was sick of being in the white man's world of greed, religion, and military order. He didn't understand how his father could have let him go to such a wicked place. He hoped this school was an exception and that not all Navajo children had to go through such a painful process of indoctrination.

Looking over at Ernie, who was still peacefully sleeping, Marvin wondered if it would be possible to save the friend who was unlucky enough to get on the wrong side of the sadistic Stanton Soliday. Slipping quietly over to Ernie, Marvin gently touched his shoulder.

"Ernie, wake up. It's Marvin."

Ernie's eyes opened; he smiled at Marvin and said, "Yá át ééh, Marvin. I'm glad the box didn't take you away from me. I would miss your funny face."

"That makes two of us, Ernie. Are you awake? I need to talk to you about something serious."

"Sure. What's up?" Ernie asked as he sat up on his cot.

"Ernie, Mr. Soliday has it out for you, and I'm worried about your safety. He wants me to say you are doing bad things, breaking the school's rules. He put me in the box, because I refused to do that. Why does he dislike you so much?"

"I have no idea Marvin, I really don't. I have never said anything to him except when he made me give him my blanket. I was very upset when he took my grandmother's blanket. I told him it was very special to me, and that I wanted to keep it close. He didn't like that, and said it was against school rules, and he would keep it for me until winter break. Maybe he doesn't like me for that, but why would he want you to make up things about me being a bad person? I'm sorry you had to go to the box, Marvin."

"It's OK, Ernie. Believe it or not, as horrible as the box was, I learned a lot. But you don't want to go in there—ever!

"I think Mr. Soliday is angry about your blanket. I think he wants the blanket for himself; maybe he's going to sell it and needs you out of the way. My dad told me once that some old Navajo blankets can bring big money. I'll bet yours is one of those. If there is no more Ernie Yazzie, who is to say you didn't just give him the blanket? Or maybe he could say it was stolen. That's why I think he threw me in the box, Ernie."

"I never thought of that, Marvin—but how can he sell something that's not his? That's my blanket. Won't people ask where it came from?"

"Ernie, he just has to say, 'I got it from an old Navajo family. It was a gift for helping their kids....'"

"That's not right. He's supposed to be helping us, not stealing from us!"

"Or killing us, Ernie. I think he might want to see you dead. Soliday could have killed me just because I wouldn't help him. Who's going to care if Ernie Yazzie or Marvin Manycoats dies in the box? 'He was a bad Navajo—good riddance.' There's nothing our families can do, and it won't matter if we're dead."

"Could he really want me dead for my grandmother's blanket? Why kill someone for a blanket? I don't understand!"

"It's the bilagáana way, Ernie. Mr. Soliday stole my father's necklace and there's nothing I can do, either. It's gone. It was the piece my father loved most, made by the famous silversmith Slender Maker and decorated with turquoise beads—and he gave it to me. But now it's gone and there is nothing I can do but move on. You've got to move on, too."

"Can we tell someone about it—the tribal cops or something?"

"What tribe? Soliday is the cops for us Indians. Don't forget those grave markers in the white man's garden of crosses. It's not that hard to kill an Indian, more like swatting a fly. Do you worry about swatting a bothersome fly? No, you don't—after all, it's only a fly. Well, Ernie, we are the flies on Soliday's back and he's about to swat us both."

The two boys sat looking at each other, their faces forlorn, thinking of their plight. Finally Ernie, his eyes filled with tears, laid his head back down on the bed and stared into space.

"Marvin, what can we do? What can I do?" he asked, his voice cracking.

"Ernie, I've given this a lot of thought and prayed about it in the box. There is only one thing I can think of to save us both. You need to disappear and you must write a letter to Mr. Soliday—one that will keep him happy and not want to bring you back here to kill either you or me or both of us.'"

"What can I write that would stop this crazy bilagáana?"

"You say this: 'I appreciate everything you have done to try to help me, but I am unable to live in this strict school, no matter how hard I try. I wish you the best; you were a great teacher and schoolmaster.' Then you say, 'Please keep my old blanket as a gift for all your help. I want you to have it.'

"Write it in English and sign it, and then write 'go in beauty' in Navajo so anyone who reads it will know it's really from a Navajo. I'll give the letter to Mr. Soliday and tell him that I tried to convince you not to leave, but that you just couldn't deal with school anymore and a relative took you far away to Chinle, Arizona. Mr. Soliday will think you are Arizona's problem now and hopefully leave you alone."

"If I do what you say, the blanket is his and I gave it to him—for nothing."

"You are trading the blanket for your life and freedom—and that isn't nothing.

"Here's the plan, Ernie. You go to Gallup. My Uncle Freddy lives there and he'll help us. I'll contact him today somehow and you can escape. Once you are home, tell your parents to hide you at the family summer camp high in Beautiful Mountain. It's cold there now, and no one will think to look for you in the mountains. If people ask, have your parents say you're in Chinle.

"Don't let your folks cause any trouble. Tell them you're sorry but you lost the blanket somewhere. Otherwise I'll be in the box again, and this time I won't get out. If the plan doesn't work, I'll have to try to escape myself. If I disappear or die, tell my parents what happened and that I love them—and that I'm sorry about losing the Slender Maker necklace."

Ernie was stunned that their lives were in such danger—but Marvin took charge, tearing a sheet of paper out of his notebook.

"Write it, Ernie, just like I said…."

Ernie protested one last time: "But my grandmother's blanket will be gone. Her grandmother had it at Bosque Redondo, and it saved her from freezing to death when she was in prison and during the Long Walk. I wouldn't be here if it weren't for that blanket. How can I just let him have it?"

"Ernie, you're right—you wouldn't be here if it weren't for that blanket. Now that blanket is going to save another Navajo life—YOURS!

"Write, Ernie, write…."

CHAPTER 14

THE INCREDIBLY RIDICULOUS PLAN

Marvin had devised a plan to save Ernie, and the time for action had arrived.

Ernie wrote the letter just as Marvin had directed him to; hopefully, the contents would satisfy Soliday. By giving Soliday clear title to Ernie's family blanket, Marvin hoped the headmaster would forget about the weaker boy. Taking the white man at face value, he seemed decent enough—but there was always the possibility that once he got Ernie's letter he might track him down and punish him for truancy. Marvin hoped Soliday was more about greed than about a real hatred of Indians—a scarier scenario that cut more deeply.

To protect himself from Soliday's anger, Marvin had written a note of his own in which he said that Ernie Yazzie was speaking Navajo and was a disruptive element in the boys' dormitory. Marvin read that letter out loud to his friend so that there would be no secrets between them, and he told Ernie that he was turning the letter in at noon on Monday no matter what Ernie decided to do.

If Ernie did successfully escape, Marvin's letter would prove that indeed Ernie was a bad apple, that he just didn't fit into the white man's world, and that his disruptive behavior had nothing to do with the way the headmaster's ran the school. Soliday had tried, it implied, but some Indians just can't be tamed. Soliday would have the blanket and Marvin's letter, and it might be enough for him to be willing to let Ernie go.

But, if Ernie got caught before he reached the reservation and was brought back to Two Trees, the outcome would be very different. Soliday would throw Ernie in the box and punish him severely as an example to the other children. He would also read Marvin's letter to all, and Marvin would be seen as a traitor among his peers. Soliday would have both documents, and the evidence would indicate that Ernie was a bad seed who had unfortunately succumbed to health-related problems shortly after coming out of the disciplinary box—another little cross in the growing garden.

Making contact with the outside world from Two Trees was almost impossible for Marvin, even if the call was to nearby Gallup. The only phone at the school was in Soliday's office and no regular trips were made to the town except by the staff, most of who lived on the premises. But Marvin's Uncle Freddy worked as a mechanic in Gallup and the garage had a business phone. If Marvin could get to Soliday's phone, he could talk to his uncle.

Uncle Freddy's heart was pure. He was a good man, but he had fought the alcohol demons his entire life; hopefully he was doing well and was at work—not at his favorite bar. Freddy was a traditional Navajo. He would help if Marvin could make contact.

The garage was open Monday through Friday and was easy to find. Today was Friday, so if Marvin couldn't reach Freddy during business hours, he would have to wait until Monday—and by then both he and Ernie could be back in the box. Still, it would be difficult to make an unauthorized phone call during working hours. Soliday usually worked in his office in the morning, ate his sack lunch at noon, made the rounds of the school at 1 p.m., then returned to the office by 2 p.m., where the radio would be playing his favorite country station.

Marvin had a sudden inspiration as he thought about his ordeal in the box. It was a plan so ridiculous it might just work. He remembered sitting in the musty box a stone's throw from Soliday's office as a song by Patsy Cline came drifting through the air. It was the number one song in America, the announcer said. Marvin had memorized the announcer's words and they hammered in his mind like nails in a coffin; they were there for eternity.

The boy had become compulsive about writing down the events of the day, no matter how trivial or extreme the details. The notebooks were Marvin's personal history class, filled with facts he actually cared to remember. The memorization process had transformed Marvin's developing brain into a storage locker of relevant life events, accessible at any time by his photographic memory.

No twelve-year-old Navajo would have heard of Patsy Cline, much less know "I Fall to Pieces" was the name of her song. But Marvin knew both her name and the song, and this gave him the inspiration for a plan to outsmart Soliday.

Marvin stole a piece of Mrs. Pingry's stationery and, in carefully printed letters wrote, "Mr. Soliday, I will be in Gallup this afternoon. Patsy Cline is coming to town to sign "I Fall To Pieces," her latest album. She will be at the Richardson Trading Post from 1 to 2 p.m. today. If you can come, I'll see you there, Mrs. P."

Having a famous music star show up at a trading post in Gallup was ludicrous, but the idea was so crazy it could get Soliday out of his office for a while. The headmaster loved music, especially the high, twangy voice of Patsy Cline. The radio was never off, and he often was seen humming along to songs.

Marvin knew that Mrs. Pingry took from 1 to 2 p.m. to work on her class's homework and lesson plans and was rarely around during that time. That was also Soliday's time to walk the school grounds—but not this day. Marvin would put the Pingry note in the headmaster's mail slot and, hopefully, he would take the bait and go into town to meet Patsy Cline.

Marvin planned to have Ernie hide away in Soliday's old Studebaker's trunk. Ernie would have to hold the latch closed for the fifteen-minute ride into town, but once Soliday was parked at Richardson's Trading Post, Ernie could slip out and find Mickey's Garage. The plan required Marvin to warn his uncle that Ernie was coming before the boy showed up on his doorstep. There were a lot of "ifs."

At 12:40 p.m. Marvin stuck the folded note in Soliday's mail slot, then headed toward the white man's office. He climbed the massive cottonwood that towered over the box—the same tree that helped him survive by sending him a limb to make a weapon and start a fire. Right on schedule, Mr. Soliday left his office and walked to the mailbox—then unexpectedly walked back toward his office, stopping under the cottonwood whose yellow fan-like leaves dotted the ground beneath it.

Marvin held his breath and hoped Soliday would not look up—or that he would dislodge some small stick that could fall and hit Soliday. The boy watched as the headmaster opened the letter, then reread the note as the leaves blew past his unflinching face. Soliday turned the note over as if he were looking for some hidden message on its backside, and even fingered the letterhead to see if it was legitimate.

Marvin almost lost his footing when an enormous gust of wind hit the cottonwood. Soliday's letter flew out of his hand, but the bilágaana grabbed it before it was gone forever, looked at the paper one final time, and started to sing "I Fall to Pieces"—a magical sound coming out of the hardest headmaster in the Indian school system.

At that moment, Marvin knew he had him, and he almost giggled out loud as he watched Soliday return to his office, turn off the radio and grab his keys from a small Acoma pottery ashtray. Soliday got into his mint-green Studebaker with Ernie safely hidden in the trunk and headed into Gallup. Marvin couldn't help smiling to himself as he watched the car leave the school grounds in a cloud of red dust; now there was plenty of time to make his call to Uncle Freddy.

Sliding down the tree, Marvin snuck into Soliday's office and called the number for Mickey's Garage that his father had given him before he left Toadlena. Marvin had memorized the numerical sequence in case of an emergency—not an impossible task for a boy with a photographic memory, even though he was unaware of his ability at the time.

Marvin had only used a telephone once before, in Shiprock, when his father showed him how the machine worked. No one Marvin knew had a phone; his own home didn't even have electricity much less phone service. Lifting the phone receiver by himself felt odd. He put the cold black plastic case with the rabbit-stick-shaped handle next to his head, then concentrated on remembering how his father had worked the machine. He entered the first number in the rotary dial and watched in awe as the numbers rotated backward, making an odd clicking sound as each digit returned to its original position. It was exciting and frightening all at the same time.

Finally, there was a buzzing noise that sounded like a dying rattlesnake, then a loud ringing at the other end.

A voice answered: "Mickey's Garage. This is Floyd. How can I help you today?"

"Hello, Floyd. Is Freddy in?"

"Let me see if he bothered to make it in today…" Floyd's response made it clear that Uncle Freddy was still having problems.

"Hello. This is Freddy."

"Uncle Freddy, it's Marvin—Marvin Manycoats, your sister's boy…."

"Marvin, it's good to hear from you. Why are you calling me… you in trouble or something?"

"Sorry to do this to you, Uncle Freddy, but Ernie Yazzie, a friend of mine and a Bear Clan brother, is in trouble. We are both boarding here at Two Trees, and I need your help. Ernie's going to be coming over to the garage in about a half-hour asking for you, and I need you to hide him and get him up to his folks' place tonight. They live about 10 miles from the base of Beautiful Mountain. They are traditional and won't be expecting you, but they should be back from the summer camp by now.

"Can you help him? It's important!"

"Marvin, are you OK? Are you in trouble too?"

"No, Uncle Freddy, but if you don't help Ernie, I could be in big trouble. I'm OK, but I've got to help my friend, or he might be in serious danger. A white man here at the school, the headmaster Mr. Soliday, is after him...."

Freddy knew about boarding schools and how they treated Indians—and he realized, from his own experience, that this Soliday was one of the bad ones, an evil coyote spirit that all children should hope to avoid.

"I understand Marvin. Don't worry, I will help. If you get in trouble, leave word for me. If you have to run away, I will help you. If I'm not here, I sometimes go to the Black Bend, a bar on Route 66. I'm trying to be good, Marvin, and haven't had any booze in nearly two weeks—but I'm weak when it comes to the white man's spirits."

"I know it's hard, Uncle Freddy, but Ernie needs you today. I need you today...."

"Don't worry; I won't let you or our Bear Clan brother down. You better go, Marvin. I know you are taking a chance talking on a phone. Get back to your studies, and I'll take care of everything."

The other end of the line went dead. Marvin quickly exited Soliday's office and got to his English class just as it was starting. The old woman with the large hearing horn cupped to her ear never noticed he was missing—something Marvin thought was a good sign.

CHAPTER 15

NO ERNIE

Soliday's Studebaker roared back into the school parking lot at 1:55 p.m., just as Marvin's English class was being dismissed. Marvin could hear the screen door on the office slam, followed by static from the overhead speaker filling the crisp fall air.

"Mrs. Pingry, please come to my office NOW."

The words were sharp; even the static couldn't blunt Soliday's angry tone. As the boys were heading en mass for religious class, Marvin couldn't help shivering—not from the cool October breeze, but because he knew the black-hearted Soliday was peeved and that he was the source of the man's anger. Friday was usually the easiest day of the week at the school because there was no irrigation class that day, which meant no hard labor. Marvin had never wanted to be out in the fields working, but today was the exception: the farther he was from the school and Soliday, the better.

Marvin took a seat near the back of the class where he could see the drama play out through the multi-paned windows.

"Click, click, click..." Mrs. Pingry passed the class window unusually quickly. She, too, could hear the irritation in Soliday's voice and she was worried. Marvin watched in terror as her thin lips became a single line. Marvin understood her body language even though the rest of the class was oblivious to the drama that was about to unfold. Mulling about, waiting for the religion teacher, the children were all talking about how much they hated the white man's gods.

Night fell and it was safe to say Ernie was gone—but where to? All the boys were worried about their friend's disappearance and the questions were flying.

"Where is he? Do you think he's in the box like you were? Did he get sick and go to the hospital? Why did Mr. Soliday call Matchstick Woman to his office?"

Marvin finally said, "I will go and talk with Mr. Soliday..." and the room fell silent. No one wanted ever to visit Mr. Soliday, especially not when a student was missing.

Marvin had Ernie's letter in his back pocket, along with his own letter accusing Ernie of speaking Navajo, and headed over to Soliday's office, his rattlesnake charm around his neck and tucked under his shirt. He needed all the protection he could get. Walking the thousand yards from the boys' dorm to the headmaster's office gave him some time to think of his friend's newfound freedom.

"Ernie should be home by now," he thought, "and there will be a celebration, with fry bread and mutton stew cooking on the stove. He will be so happy and hugging his mom and dad...."

Thinking of his own continued imprisonment saddened Marvin. To cope with his pain, he repeated in his head, "Ernie is saved and back home." He hoped Ernie was safe, because in a few minutes, Soliday would know that Ernie was missing. By tomorrow, Ernie would be hiding high up on Beautiful Mountain and, like his ancestors, he would never be caught. He would have no more of the white man's schools.

Soliday's silhouette was visible through the window. The dark-hearted man never seemed to leave his office; he was like an evil chindi watching and waiting for a weak person to haunt. The wooden clock above his desk read 8 p.m.; he had usually left by this time, but not tonight. Marvin hated the idea of telling Soliday that Ernie had gone missing, but he knew he needed to bring the matter to the headmaster's attention now, or Soliday would be looking for a co-conspirator, someone to blame for not reporting Yazzie's disappearance earlier.

He could hear Soliday turn down the radio when he knocked at the door.

"Come in, and it damn well better be important!" Soliday barked. "Why are you here, Marvin? Have you got something you want to share about Mr. Yazzie, or are you just wanting a good night lullaby?"

Looking at the man who had tried to kill him in the box made Marvin's heart race. "Well, sir, yes… I kind of do have something to report on Ernie."

Marvin gripped his letters tightly and plopped into the chair across from Soliday without asking if he could sit. If Soliday had been more perceptive, he would have noticed Marvin's plop was one of defeat, not exhaustion.

Pausing to get his words just right, Marvin said, "Well, sir… Ernie has broken the rules. He has been talking Navajo in the boy's dorm. This morning he would only speak to me in Navajo. When I asked him to stop, he refused and he told me he was thinking about running away from school. I didn't take him seriously."

"Excellent, Marvin. I'm glad you have finally come around to right side of this equation. I guess a little box time helped you see the light. Have you written down what you just told me about Mr. Yazzie?"

"Yes, sir, I wrote it down, and I put the time and date on it. I also signed my name to the paper in case you need the information for his file."

"Now that's the kind of Indian soldier I like, helping make a better society for all of us... and that includes you, Marvin. Now what's this about running away?" Soliday was smiling at the ammunition against Ernie that he was holding in his hand.

"Sir, I'm afraid...."

"Yes, what is it, Marvin? More stuff about Ernie?" Soliday was practically drooling at the thought of more daggers he could use to shred Ernie's reputation.

"Well, kind of... Tonight, when we went back to the dorm for study time, I looked for Ernie to talk to him about not speaking Navajo, and he was nowhere to be found. I searched everywhere and no one had seen him. I know he was in English class, but I don't know where he went after that. I found an envelope on his bed... It's addressed to you, sir."

Marvin held up a cream-colored envelope, written in black pen in a child's script: "Mr. Soliday, Headmaster, Two Trees Indian School."

"Hand the letter to me, Marvin. Did you read it?" Soliday glared at Marvin, looking for any sign the boy could be lying.

"No sir, I was afraid to open it. Your name was on the front, and I figured with Ernie missing only you should see it...."

Soliday snatched the envelope from Marvin's hand and ripped it open. His eyes danced back and forth as he read the contents. The headmaster's stern face melted into a smile—a sizeable and very revealing smile. Marvin knew then that he had been right: Soliday's anger toward Ernie was because of the blanket, something he had wanted the whole time—and he now had ownership of the weaving free and clear.

When he realized Marvin could also see and read his victorious smile, Soliday's face regained its stern expression.

"Marvin, it seems that Ernie has not only broken the school rules by speaking Navajo, but that he has also run away. I want you to read the letter that you saw me open right in front of you, and then write down exactly what you read. And make sure you say that I had never seen the letter till this very moment."

Handing the letter to Marvin, Soliday asked, "This is Ernie's hand, correct?"

"Yes, sir."

"And you did find the envelope on his bed?"

"Yes, sir, I did...."

"No one else has seen this and you had not opened it?"

"Yes, sir."

"Fine. Write all of that down—that you found the letter on his bed and that the writing is in Ernie's hand, which you recognize, and that you did not open the envelope but gave the document to me and watched me read the letter."

Marvin pretended to read the letter for the first time and made the appropriate sound of surprise at the part about the gift of the chief's blanket. Soliday handed Marvin a pen and paper, and the boy began writing down, verbatim, everything that the headmaster asked him to say. Once he finished, he looked over the document and gave the paper back to Soliday to read.

"Is this ok?"

Soliday's eyes darted from line to line, and the evil smile returned, this time unconcerned about what Marvin might think. The blanket was finally his for the taking. He didn't know where Ernie had disappeared to; all that mattered was that Marvin had handed him a smoking gun, and whatever happened to Ernie Yazzie from this point on mattered little in Soliday's eyes. He would make a halfhearted attempt to locate Ernie, but the boy's return was not important tonight, or on any other day for that matter. What had started off as a bad day of being tricked into thinking he could meet Patsy Cline had turned out perfectly. He was rich. A rare old chief's blanket was now his property. He had a receipt giving him ownership of the weaving and Ernie was missing—hopefully for good.

The cemetery wouldn't be getting any new graves at the moment—unless Marvin changed his tune. Everything at the Indian school was good for now, and Marvin would survive to see another year.

CHAPTER 16

THE NEW SAL LITO

Bloom couldn't believe his good fortune: he was to be the new manager of the Toadlena Trading Post for the next four months. An opportunity to make money to shore up family finances was a rarity on the rez.

By the time Sal returned from his worldwide vacation, Rachael's hózhó curing ceremony would be complete and, hopefully, her wrists and shoulders would be healed enough for her to start weaving again. "Happy wife, happy life," Bloom liked to say—and this new scenario upped his own happiness quotient.

"Got good news!" Bloom announced excitedly, letting the hogan's screen door slam like he was a teenage kid announcing his arrival.

"That was quick. You must have borrowed a helicopter to get up that mountain and bring back all our winter firewood that fast," Rachael said, knowing there was no way Bloom could have completed the task.

"Oh, yeah, that. I didn't get to cutting wood today, but I have plenty of time; it's like summer out there. But I do have some news you will like…." Bloom smiled at Rachael, waiting for her reaction.

"OK, you've got me interested. You're clearly excited and it's not about our piñon firewood—so spill the beans."

"Sal and his wife are going away for four months on a world cruise and I'm going to take over for them." Bloom expected an equally excited response from Rachael, but none came forth.

"You know that there is a lot involved in running that trading post, right? It's not just selling rugs and eating a pickle in the morning." Rachael had grown up at her grandmother's side at the post and had seen firsthand the chores and responsibilities that came with the position. "You're going to be a lot busier than you think, Mr. Indian Trader."

Bloom's smile faded as his bubble of happiness deflated a bit.

"Hell, it can't be that hard, Rachael. Sal is damned near eighty with arthritis, and he doesn't seem to have much trouble handling the day-to-day work."

"Yeah. But eighty also means he has a half-century of experience at that post, and he eats Motrin like candy. Sal makes managing the post look easy, just like you do when you close a big sale to some hotshot billionaire in Santa Fe. It doesn't look hard, but we both know better."

"Well, he's going to pay me $15 an hour and we'll split any of the profits I make on rug or jewelry sales, which should be plenty."

"What about profits on the grocery and wool sales? Will you get any of that?"

Bloom hadn't even thought about that part of the business: it seemed more for show than a vital part of the post's business plan. The rugs and jewelry were where they made the money—or so he assumed.

"No, we didn't discuss that part, other than Sal said I had to restock and keep the books straight."

"That means going to Farmington or Gallup twice a week and picking up lots of provisions. It may not look like that little store has much merchandise, but you will find out differently once you start stocking those shelves. I single-handedly wiped out all the Big Hunks for two weeks running when I was twelve; Sal was ready to kill me."

"What's a Big Hunk?"

"Oh, you do have your work cut out for you. A Big Hunk is like white taffy. It's the best-tasting candy bar on the planet, but old guys like you shouldn't eat it 'cause it could pull the gold fillings out of your teeth. Big Hunks are simply delicious. Boy, did you miss out as a kid."

"I thought I was your Big Hunk."

"You are—and you're even tastier." Rachael gave Bloom a wicked smile and an elbow in the side.

"So there is some grocery stocking involved. What else is so time-consuming?"

"Weavers bring rugs in nearly every day, and you have to buy them or at least try to. You have to look in Sal's log to see what they were paid before, and make sure the rug is the same size, quality, and tightness of weave; then you negotiate the deal. Just because Sal's gone, it doesn't mean the rugs will stop. There will be lots of folks looking for a little loan. You're the new kid in town, and they'll figure you for an easy mark. Did Sal talk to you about this part of the deal?"

"He said that there would be some out-of-pocket expenses, but that I could put them down on the credit sheet and get paid back once that weaver's rug sold."

"Yeah. There will be lots of out-of-pocket expenses, and you have to wait for a rug to sell, so you can get behind the eight ball pretty quickly. Why do you think it took old Sal fifty years to be able to take a vacation? This post is run as much for love as money, I'm afraid."

"Well, he's paying me a wage and he said any of the rugs I buy will be all mine. I can keep all the profits on those and 20 percent of the profit on any he owns."

"How much did you get for that second mortgage on the gallery again?" Rachael knew the answer, but wanted Bloom to realize the magnitude of his financial commitment to the trading post.

"$350,000. Why?"

"You are now in the Toadlena/Two Grey Hills business and you're going to be buying a lot of rugs. I suggest you send quite a few of those rugs to your Santa Fe gallery to give them the most exposure. The post gets tourists, but not enough to absorb all the weavings you're going to be acquiring. Sal probably figured he could go on vacation for four months, if he didn't have to buy any rugs for a while."

Rachael smiled, but not humorously. "It looks like I may need to come up to the post to help you sell to keep our heads above water."

Bloom was starting to take offense. Did Rachael think he couldn't handle a job he had been doing for the last twenty-plus years? But she continued to pile it on.

"I'm going to have to work with you so you can learn to say 'No.' It's way harder than you think. And don't forget you have bathrooms to clean, a wood stove to keep stoked, general maintenance of a hundred-year-old building with a bad roof, and tours to give to any tourists that drop by. And Bloom—just so you know right from the get-go—I will clean our bathroom at home, but those public ones are strictly your territory.

"October is the biggest month around here, so get ready," she continued. "You may wish you had just gotten the wood instead. But hey—I'm looking forward to the extra cash—oh, wait—I mean Toadlena rugs.

"My hózhó ceremony isn't free, either. Great medicine men like Johnson want to get paid, and don't think Preston won't get his cut. There's no discount for relatives, I'm afraid. So buckle up, my love—you're in for quite a ride!"

Bloom's good mood vanished as he realized he was in far deeper than he had expected. Sal was a good salesman—a better one than he, or so it appeared.

CHAPTER 17

FIRST DAY ON THE JOB

Bloom wasn't entirely sure what all his responsibilities would be, but he learned about the bulk of his duties over the next week. Sal filled him in on the tasks that would arise on a daily basis, with Bloom shadowing Sal so he could learn his rhythm. After being in the retail business for twenty-five years, Bloom figured he could surely wing any parts they didn't touch on. After all, a sales gig—even one in a foreign country like the rez—was still a sales gig.

Sal had tutored his replacement in as many of the intricacies of the position as he could, and today was Bloom's first official day on the job by himself. He knew how to write checks, find outstanding bills in the ever-growing charge book and, most importantly, had a list of all the people he should handle with care and those he should show the door. He understood how the stove, generator, refrigerators, and safe worked. The roof was a mess, as Rachael had warned, but there wasn't anything to do but keep the tarps tight on the top and hope that nothing happened while Sal was gone.

The trader had given Bloom strict instructions on what foods to buy for the post, and warned him that "the Navajo want what they want to eat, and you'll be making a big mistake if you mess with my shopping list."

The post was one of the only places to buy groceries for nearly sixty miles. There was the store at the Shell station at the corner of N19 and Highway 491, but they never did anything on credit. Otherwise, people had to go to Shiprock, Farmington, or Gallup, and they didn't offer credit either. Most of the locals preferred Shiprock as they had relatives in that area and it wasn't such a big city.

Bloom figured one of the first things he would do when supplies got low was to buy more healthful foods; he was aghast at all the candy, Skoal tobacco tins, and SPAM that filled the shelves. "They just buy what is offered," he told himself. "Some fresh vegetables and a few organics will do well."

Bloom was very confident he could manage the job. The post was like any other business, he thought, albeit one that sometimes required an interpreter. The memory of his first day at Bloom's so many years ago flooded in as he opened the door for business. He was re-energized to be in sales again. He told Rachael not to worry about him and to just do what she needed to do to heal: he would let her know if he got into difficulties.

The first customer of the day was Hastiin Manycoats. Bloom understood that he was a regular and liked to come up each day to check on mail that he had forwarded to the post and buy an ice cream bar or two—unless it was near the end of the month and money was tight. Marvin was in his sixties, but didn't seem that old. He was vibrant and looked strong. Bloom wondered why Sal called him Old Man Manycoats; maybe it was some unique way of saying he was wise.

"Yá át ééh. You must be Hastiin Manycoats. Sal warned me about you," Bloom teased; unfortunately, Manycoats didn't seem to get the joke

"Why would he say something mean like that?"

"Sal didn't really say that. I was just making a little joke," Bloom said sheepishly. Maybe the man was older than he looked.

"Why would you want to play a joke on me? I'm a vet, you know."

"I'm sorry if we got off on the wrong foot. Let me start over, I'm Charles Bloom. I'm going to be running the post while Sal is on vacation. And thank you for your service."

"What's wrong with your foot? And Sal don't take vacations."

Bloom was completely flustered at this point. "No, no, Mr. Manycoats; you don't understand...."

Manycoats interrupted him: "I understand. It's you that don't get it. I'm joking just like you were, only we Navajo have a better sense of timing it seems." Manycoats was tickled with himself and started laughing, as he climbed into his roost in the antique barber chair.

"You got me! Please don't tell my wife; she will never let me live this down. She has always said she has the best lines in our family."

"Who's your wife?"

"Rachael Yellowhorse. You might have known her Grandmother Ethel, or her late brother the painter." As Bloom said Ethel's name he remembered he shouldn't have mentioned the dead, so he avoided giving Willard's name.

"Yeah. Her grandmother was a great weaver. I was away from the rez most of the time she was working at the post, but I remember meeting Rachael and her brother for the first time when they were kids—it was June 20, 1990, a very hot day.

"I heard her brother was a great artist. Too bad about him passing so young, but that's what happens if you leave the rez. I was lucky I made it back, and you're lucky you got a good Navajo woman to keep you straight."

Bloom thought it strange that Manycoats could remember the exact day he had met Rachael when she was a kid, but he was older and maybe that was just his way of proving to himself that he still had all his faculties intact.

"I agree. I am lucky. We have two kids. You may see them around the post from time to time. Sal tells me you go up the mountain to cut wood. Any chance I could pay you to bring some down for me? It would make my wife happy...."

Manycoats' eyes lit up: "How much you going to pay me?"

"I don't know—what is the going rate?" Bloom was ever the negotiator.

"Well, I've heard that in Santa Fe you can get piñon for about $230 a cord split, but a lot of that wood has beetles and gets a funny smell, and they pop when you burn it. I can do it for $100 a cord split, that's a long bed truck worth of wood."

"Sounds fair. Rachael tells me we will need nine cords of wood, three for our house, and six for the store. You can use the mule if you want—it will make the job a lot easier."

"You got a mule? I didn't hear no mule out back."

"No, I'm sorry—it's not that kind of a mule. It's an ATV," Bloom began....

"Ha! That's twice this Navajo got you..." Manycoats started to chuckle again.

Bloom's face turned red and he hoped Manycoats wouldn't share this joke with Rachael either.

"I can tell I'm going to have to watch you, Mr. Manycoats," Bloom said. He had liked the man from the get-go.

"Call me Marvin. My friends do, and I can tell we will be friends. You will, in fact, be my only white friend—but that still counts in my mind." Marvin hopped off his perch, headed over to the icebox and pulled out a chocolate ice cream bar.

"Put this on my tab if you would, friend. It looks like I've got credit now—unless you want to give it to me free as part of the wood deal." Marvin was gauging how generous Bloom would be.

"It's on the house, but I would like to get the firewood soon. My wife has given me marching orders."

"I understand orders, no problem. I'll get started on that firewood today. And I don't need that mule. I've got a strong back, a good wheelbarrow, and a four-wheel drive truck. I like the exercise; it will keep me alive till I'm ninety, like my dad. He was a great silversmith, in case you didn't know."

"No, I didn't know he was a silversmith. I'd love to see some of his pieces. Do you have any?"

"Wish I did, but I'm afraid there's none left. He's been gone for a long time now, and he sold his jewelry to feed his kids, something a lot of us Navajo do—so I don't have those heirlooms no more."

Marvin said the words "no more" so sadly that Bloom realized there was some untold history there—but today wasn't the time to ask additional questions. Bloom could find out about Manycoats' backstory when he got to know the man better.

CHAPTER 18

"I'VE GOT TWO WRISTS"

The Navajo Nation has its own communication system, and phones are not a part of it. The word was out that Sal had left the Toadlena Trading Post in charge of Rachael Yellowhorse's bilagáana husband, and every weaver in the eastern part of New Mexico seemed to be heading in Bloom's direction.

Sal had warned Bloom that his pocketbook would get too thin if he bought rugs from outside the Toadlena basin, and advised him to stick only with the Two Grey Hills weavers. Sal's rug log would help Bloom decide whom to buy from and what to pay. The best weavers had a red star next to their names, and those were the artists whose rugs you had to be sure to purchase.

"Great weavers make only so many rugs," Sal said before he left, "and you don't want to lose even one of those rugs to another trading post." Sal assured Bloom he would buy back any of his star weavers' rugs when he returned from his vacation if need be—and warned him not to overpay.

Watching Rachael, who was a master weaver, at close range had given Bloom a good sense of what a quality rug felt and looked like. The same criteria applied to every rug: a tight weave with good symmetry, an intricate design using lots of different natural colors, handspun yarn, and size—the bigger the rug, the better. Some weavers had led long, productive lives and won enough accolades to command a premium price; they were the starred weavers in Sal's book.

Bloom was shocked at the number of people who used the post as a kind of second home: kids came in after school to get candy; old men showed up to tell stories and get candy; and, of course, the weavers came to sell their rugs and get free candy.

The weavers were special, and Bloom never had a problem handing out free food. Sal had told him that giving away groceries was fine, as long as they didn't lose money on the store overall; the old trader wasn't concerned about making much profit from food.

Darlene Brown, a star weaver who was pushing eighty, was sitting in a corner of the post. She had come in with her older sister Thelma, who wasn't a weaver but was keeping Darlene company, while she waited to bargain with old Sal.

Darlene lived summer and fall high above the Toadlena Trading Post near a bubbling spring in the Chuska Mountains; her hogan had no electricity, running water, or plumbing. Her truck had broken down, and Thelma, who lived near public housing, had finally found a ride to get her sister so she could bring her rug in to sell.

Rachael had often talked about the quality of the Brown family's rugs. Rachael's Grandmother Ethel was a contemporary of Darlene's mom, and her daughter took over where her Grandmother had left off, producing magnificent tapestry weavings.

Charles wiped his sweaty palms on his pants as he watched the Brown sisters waddle their way through the parking lot. Bloom recognized the Grandmother from her photos in *The Master Weavers* book; he was surprised at his nervousness; he had bought and sold millions of dollars of art over his lifetime, but this was different somehow. A great weaver was headed his way with a major rug that Sal would expect him to buy. If for some reason he couldn't get the deal done with Darlene today, it was possible that not only this rug but also subsequent rugs could be sold to one of the competing post owners—not an ideal outcome and a weak start to his tenure as the post's new Indian trader. Bloom was very competitive and didn't like the idea of an excellent Toadlena weaver leaving the fold.

He went back into the office and looked up the last rug Sal had bought from Darlene about a year ago. He had paid her a total of $8,500 for a tapestry-weave textile that measured 3 x 5 feet, with a count of 80 wefts per inch. Darlene was not a big borrower and owed the post $1,000, which included advances for new tires, groceries, and a trip to Tuba City to see her son, who also had been in need of money according to Sal's notes.

Darlene was outfitted in her finest blue velvet skirt and shirt, with a large, chunky turquoise nugget necklace hanging around her dark brown neck. She looked right out of a scene from a 1920s John Huston movie. For all Bloom knew, Darlene was old enough to have been an extra in one of those movies when she was a kid.

The two elderly women struggled to open the heavy front door while holding onto their canes and the rug. After two failed attempts, they finally walked in—and Bloom was at the ready.

"Yá át ééh, Darlene," Bloom said in his nicest voice. "Looks like you brought me a weaving. I can't wait to see it."

Darlene and Thelma looked at Bloom quizzically, then whispered to each other in Navajo before Darlene replied: "Yá át ééh. Where's old Sal? And who are you?" Apparently, the Navajo communication system had bypassed Darlene's mountainside hogan.

Bloom explained that he was filling in for Sal, but had the full authority to buy her rug and pay her what Sal would have paid. She agreed to let Bloom see her weaving and Darlene, Thelma, and Bloom headed back to the rug room to discuss price.

Marvin Manycoats, who seemed to be a fixture in the post, was sitting back in the barber chair taking in the theater, his head turned so his good ear could catch all the action.

Once comfortably situated on the overstuffed couch, Darlene gently pulled her rug out of its flour-sack carrying case and plopped the beautiful textile on Bloom's lap, both women watching for his initial reaction. He smiled as his fingers caressed the fine handspun yarn, his enthusiasm for the tapestry weave was evident. The design was exquisite, with small rows of intricate circular motifs encompassing the entire border—a Brown family trademark. The rug had an elaborate central diamond design with what appeared to be twelve different natural colors. The weaving was magnificent, and everyone in the room knew it.

Bloom wished Rachael were next to him to see such a masterpiece, fresh off the loom. With any luck, he would buy the weaving and bring it home to show her tonight.

"Looks like a wonderful tapestry weaving. How much do you want for the rug?" Bloom got right to the point without making small talk—a rookie mistake. The sisters expected a bit of foreplay, especially on their first date.

Bloom had reviewed the log, so he knew what Sal had paid for Darlene's last rug and mistakenly figured this would be a short negotiation. The weaving was similar to the previous one, and he assumed she would come in close to that number.

"I'm thinking $12,000 would be about right," Darlene said without any hesitation. Bloom was taken aback; this was not the number he was expecting.

"Well, it's a very nice rug indeed, but I know that Sal paid you $8,500 for the last rug. I looked at the picture he took of you holding the rug and read his notes. Don't you think the two are pretty similar in quality?"

"No, this one is better," Darlene said as Thelma nodded her head in agreement.

"Why is this one $3,500 better?" Bloom countered.

"Because I'm selling it today for $12,000 and you ain't Sal. You know he likes to talk about my rug for a while before he gets down to doing business," Darlene replied matter-of-factly.

Bloom could feel his palms sweating again and put down the rug. The negotiations were going in the wrong direction, and he hoped the back-and-forth banter was her way of breaking in the new kid. He would have to rethink his tactics.

"Well, it looks like you have a debt of $1,000 on the books. How about I pay you $9,000 for this rug and we take off half of what you owe, so you get $8,500—the same as last time—and pay down half that advance?" Bloom figured this offer would get her attention. It was better than what Sal would have offered, and Darlene would know this.

There was a pause while Darlene thought about it. "OK, I want $13,000 for the rug, and you can take the whole $1,000 off my debt. How does that sound to you?" Darlene parried with no change in her facial expression.

Her response flummoxed Bloom; he had never had someone increase the price on the initial offer and wasn't sure what to do.

"Darlene, we both know that's not going to happen—no matter how much I like this rug, which I do. Sal would not be pleased if I paid so much that he couldn't make any money. How about $9,000 and we leave your bill alone?"

"How long do you think it took me to make this here rug?" Darlene asked, peering into Bloom's blue eyes for an answer.

"I would guess around eight months, including the preparation of the wool. That's very fine yarn you spun and lots of nice shades."

Darlene smiled when she realized the bilagáana understood more of what went into her rug than she thought he would.

"Yeah, that's pretty close; you know more about us Navajo weavers than I thought."

"I'm married to Rachael Yellowhorse, Ethel Sherman's granddaughter," Bloom said. He sensed an opening and hoped that saying Rachael's deceased grandmother's name wouldn't be too impolite.

"Oh, I like you better than I did a few minutes ago," Darlene said, cracking a smile for the first time as her sister gave her a "that-a-boy" look.

"So how about my offer of $9,000 with no pay-off on the credit line," Bloom said, trying to close the deal

"I don't like you that much," Darlene said. "But thanks for the offer. Tell Rachael to come by and see me if she gets up on the mountain for firewood. I'd like to hear how she's doing.

"I'll need a $10 loan," she continued. "You can add it to my credit line with Sal. I'm low on gas and need some fuel so I can go to that other post. That guy likes my rugs too, and we can talk for a long time."

Darlene rolled up her rug and put the weaving back in its Blue Bird Flour carrying case. The two women grabbed their canes and headed out of the back room toward the post's front counter to collect the loan.

Bloom started to panic; he was close to blowing an important purchase from one of Sal's stars. He stopped the Grandmothers at the jewelry case: "Wait, Darlene. You don't have to go to another post. I have one more offer for you."

"OK, Rachael's husband. What you offer this time?"

Bloom scrambled for something that would seal the deal without having to overpay, which he was precariously close to doing. Then he saw his kicker. A kicker in the art world is that little something extra that sweetens the pot just enough to close the deal. In Darlene's case, it was sitting in the small, upright circa 1900 jewelry case next to the women. It was filled with Fred Harvey Navajo bracelets that had been made in the 1930s for tourists who came in looking for a piece of the past, and many of the bracelets had beautiful old natural turquoise stones.

"How about I give you $9,000 for the rug, NO payment on the credit line, $200 in groceries for FREE—and you can pick out one of those bracelets for your wrist."

Darlene looked Bloom squarely in the eyes and, without a moment's hesitation, said, "I have two wrists."

Bloom realized he had been outmaneuvered at every point in the negotiation and started to laugh. "Well, you're right Darlene. You do have two wrists. I'll remember that next time I've got to buy one of your rugs."

Darlene chuckled as she stuck out both arms for Bloom to start trying on bracelets.

"You got a deal, Rachael's husband." Darlene decided she liked this new post trader.

✽ ✽ ✽ ✽

Bloom couldn't wait to tell Rachael about his day and the two wrists story, knowing she would love to hear how the great Santa Fe art dealer was bested by an eighty-year-old weaver. Bloom knew this was red meat for Rachael, who never let him forget a mistake, but he didn't mind sharing the joke. He understood he had lots to learn; buying a piece of art from a rich Texan who was downsizing was very different from buying a weaving from a Navajo woman whose life depended on her rugs.

Bloom carried the rug into the house in a trash bag—its new carrying case—and placed the sack on the dining room table. Then he waited for Rachael's response.

"Thought you would enjoy seeing what I was able to buy today. I might make an Indian trader yet."

"I hope you're not buying trash now and thinking it's modern Navajo art," Rachael teased. She knew it had to be something special.

"No, I'm not into the contemporary mindset at the moment. This is much better."

Bloom smiled as Rachael pulled the magnificent rug from the Hefty bag and slowly stroked the wool before her eyes filled with tears and she ran back to the bedroom. The quality and beauty of the weaving brought out her grief about her inability to weave for the foreseeable future; no matter how much she wanted them, Spider Woman's gifts were not within her reach.

Bloom went into the bedroom to console his wife, wondering if he would ever truly understand the mindset of a Navajo weaver. His timing was way off—and the two-wrist story would have to wait.

CHAPTER 19

"I NEED SIX DOLLARS"

Each day had its challenges, but, overall, Rachael's level of happiness had increased since she returned to Toadlena; her injured shoulders and wrists wouldn't allow her to weave yet, but she was learning to live with her new routine.

The first week back was dedicated to getting Willy situated in preschool and adjusted to his new environment. The Tohaali' Community School was only a stone's throw from the trading post—one of many reasons Rachael loved being home. Willy was being taught in both Diné and English, which also pleased Rachael; she wanted her children to be able to learn the native language that was rapidly being lost to enculturation and migration.

While Willy was in school, Rachel and Sam would spend time with her nearest neighbor, whom she had known since she was a child. A widow,

Mrs. Bennally was a retired tribal government worker who now wove rugs full time. Ruth, her only daughter, lived with her periodically.

Ruth suffered from an acute form of obsessive-compulsive disorder that she controlled by counting pebbles as she sold newspapers at the Shell station and Community Post Office on Highway 491, just east of the Toadlena Trading Post. She would stand in her staked-out corner, the *Navajo Times* in one hand, and squat down to pick out anything that was out of place in the surrounding gravel. The small anthills dotting the property were not immune to Ruth's obsession either; each grain of sand was lined up in neat rows.

In New York City, her work would have been called "a revolutionary and new form of creative rock art," but on the rez she was just another sad, crazy Indian. Her mother had hoped her ability to concentrate so intensely would lead her to weaving, but the disorder only applied to certain activities: weaving, unfortunately, was not one.

Samantha Yellowhorse, Rachael, and Charles Bloom's youngest child, was the surrogate granddaughter Mrs. Bennally would never have. Rachael was not worried about Sam being alone with Ruth as she had known her forever, and she genuinely seemed to love children almost as much as she loved pebbles.

Sam enjoyed nestling into a tiny pink cushion next to Mrs. Bennally, listening to the rhythm of the Grandmother's batten and weaving fork. As the wefts fell into place, Bennally told Sam the story of Spider Woman, who taught all Navajos to weave, and of the Hero Twins, whom Spider Woman protected—all of which entranced the toddler. Rachael desperately tried to be part of the moment by helping to spin a noodle of a long, stable brown fleece that had been carded, but even that task hurt her still-swollen wrists. Rachael was frustrated, but at least Sam would be around an active Navajo loom listening and learning, as she had with her own Grandmother Ethel.

In the afternoon Rachael ran to the Tohaai School to pick up Willy and walk the half-mile with him to the trading post. Once there, Rachael lent a hand behind the counter while Willy raided the candy bins and ran from one room to the next, invariably landing on the large, worn out couch in the rug room and playing with a stack of plastic cowboys and Indians.

If Willy were behaving, Rachael would leave him with Bloom and run the five miles home to fix dinner and pick up Sam. If the post were too busy, she would stay there and work with Bloom, then help him close up at 6 p.m. She might prepare something to take home in the post's humble kitchen or just eat light that night.

Bloom, too, had found his work rhythm: Open at 9 a.m. with at least a couple of people waiting on the porch to buy groceries, one whom invariably was Marvin Manycoats, who liked this new version of Sal Lito. The old barber chair in the middle of the post was Marvin's throne, and he would sit for hours soaking in the conversations, not speaking, but always nodding his head and often laughing out loud as Bloom went about his day. It was an unwritten rule that the chair was Marvin's terrain in the morning. He seemed harmless enough, and Bloom liked having the company, especially on days when things were slow.

A few of the post's Navajo visitors had no cars and either walked or hitchhiked to the store, often asking Bloom for a ride back to their homes, seemingly oblivious to the fact he was working. Not having transportation in the twenty-first century seemed amazing: you simply called Uber or Lyft if you needed a ride. But not on the rez. And you couldn't depend on Google maps, which would as often as not point you to a dead-end location. Bloom had to tell tour groups not to use Google maps—which they invariably did—then called for help when they ended up on the side of a mesa or miles off track.

Almost all the locals came to the post for supplies, food, or to sell something. The number of tourists in October averaged between two and eight, depending on the day, and they usually came in small groups. Rachael's presence was as helpful as it had been in Santa Fe when she worked at Bloom's weaving her rug. She could sell; business was never better than when a master weaver was on deck. Having Willy and Rachael around seemed normal and, when Sam was older, Bloom could see his daughter working at the post as well—a family business of sorts. For the first time, Bloom could picture taking over the old post as a possibility, something he would never have considered a year ago. Santa Fe had always been his home, but somehow the rez was starting to feel right.

Bloom enjoyed the Grandmother weavers, none of whom admitted to speaking English and came in with their daughters—though almost all understood well enough when they didn't get the price they'd hoped for their latest gift from Spider Woman. This part of the negotiation would suddenly slip seamlessly from Navajo to English, starting with the words, "not enough money" followed by, "I got a big grocery bill too."

Sal had a complete history of what he had paid for rugs in the past. Many of the weavers knew precisely what to expect and were happy with their offers; a few wanted to see if the new boy in town understood the ropes and tried to push the price on their rugs to retail level, waiting to see his reaction.

Bloom, who had been in retail for most of his adult life, didn't mind this part of the negotiation; he knew that haggling was part of doing business on the rez. All the weavers and their families soon figured out that Bloom would be fair and was not someone they could take advantage of. Word on the rez travels fast, and the temporary flurry of price gouging dropped back in line with the older price structure. And Bloom started a new tradition: he would throw in a candy bar or ice cream cone with each rug he bought, and he always took a photo of the weaver with the rug, as Sal had instructed.

A month had passed and the leaves on the aspen on the Chuska Mountain were entering their final death throes. The store was running low on supplies, and Bloom decided it was time to update the food list. The addition of some organic fruits and vegetables was in order, as well as switching from Blue Bird Flour and regionally grown pinto beans to more cost-effective brands he could order in bulk from Amazon. He also made a unilateral decision not to sell any more Skoal chewing tobacco, because he felt it was not in his customers' best interest.

"If they want to poison their mouths," he thought, "they can take that urge down the street to the Shell station"—a decision that turned out to be a big mistake!

Within four days of Bloom's new and improved store inventory, the vegetables were starting to rot and not one bag of the Amazon flour or beans had sold, even though they were considerably cheaper. Flour was usually the post's biggest seller, with a couple of bags turning over every day.

The Grandmothers started coming into the store asking for small loans of $6 for miscellaneous needs, which turned out to be Skoal. The Shell station didn't keep any credit sheets and wasn't about to lend anyone money.

After a week, grocery sales had dropped by half, and Bloom learned that one of his weavers had taken her rug to another shop, where she had a better chance of finding the supplies she wanted and could buy them on credit.

Marvin watched the drama unfold for a week before he felt obligated to speak up.

"You know, Bloom, Sal tried to give us Navajo better choices to pick from back in the first week of November 2001, and it worked out for him the same way it's working out for you. Maybe you should go back to the old groceries; we don't like change much."

Bloom was beginning to wonder if Marvin had some weird kind of photographic memory, because he always included dates in his conversations and seemed to be accurate in every other way.

"So you think I won't be able to convince the Toadlena community to embrace a more healthy lifestyle? You know I'm just trying to make a positive change in their diets and save them money too," Bloom protested.

"Nope, it won't work. We Navajo don't care about a time schedule or what is best for our pocketbooks or diets. We just want our flour and pinto beans to come from Cortez, Colorado, not the Amazon. You're barking up the wrong rainforest tree."

Bloom considered his options, and then asked Marvin for his opinion.

"Any suggestions?"

"Well, I would give the Amazon flour and beans away because you are not going to sell them unless some bilagánna gets lost and winds up in your store. Maybe do some kind of raffle to get the local folks back in and cut your losses. If you think that getting rid of Skoal will stop the Grandmothers from dipping, you haven't figured us out yet. You're just being like that mule in your backyard," Marvin teased.

"Makes sense, thanks! I appreciate the advice, Marvin. How come you didn't tell me sooner? You're here every day and knew I was going to fail."

"You didn't ask, Bloom. I figured you were one of those men who needed to crawl for a while, before they could understand how to walk. Once they get the crawling down, it usually don't take them long to start running."

"I won't make that mistake twice!"

"See? You're already walking," Marvin grinned, showing all his teeth. Bloom smiled back, knowing Marvin was coming from a good place, the kind one friend shares with another.

CHAPTER 20

THE BIG RAFFLE

Bloom reordered the Skoal dipping tobacco even though he hated promoting its use, and he put a large, empty glass pickle jar by the Skoal tin display that read: "Fifty cents of each Skoal purchase goes to the American Cancer Society to help fight lip and mouth cancer." Bloom raised the price of each tin by 50 cents and put a dollar in the jar to grease the wheels. He wanted to let his customers know that dipping wasn't good for them and that he was serious about warning them of the dangers of tobacco products.

Bloom might not be able to change minds, but he could at least do something that might make a difference. Skoal was now available at the Toadlena Trading Post again, though a tin would cost more, and the message might slowly sink in. Of course, the Grandmothers, who were the biggest buyers of the dipping tobacco, simply asked Bloom for a 50-cent loan each time they bought a can of Skoal, saying they couldn't afford the extra money, but would be happy to put it on their credit sheet and pay later. Bloom just put two quarters in the empty pickle jar and didn't bother to add the 50 cents to their bills.

There were fifty twenty-pound bags of pinto beans and flour lining the floor behind the counter—not one had sold. Bloom decided the raffle idea was genius, though giving bulk goods from Amazon away didn't seem like a big enough deal. But Marvin's suggestion that he herd lost bilagáana into the store to buy his unwanted groceries got him thinking. Instead of making the giveaway just for the locals, Bloom could canvas the entire Four Corners region and Gallup. That way he might be able to sell some rugs to tourists—the rugs were the real moneymakers, not the groceries.

For the raffle giveaway, Bloom thought he should offer something important—such as an early Navajo squash blossom necklace. Sal had purchased a squash blossom with a box and bow design from the 1930s the day before he left on his world cruise. The tourist from New Jersey who sold him the necklace was visiting Monument Valley and decided to stop at the first trading post he ran across to see if he could sell a piece inherited from his grandmother that he wasn't interested in keeping. Needless to say, Sal bought the piece at the right price.

Bloom calculated that if he purchased the piece from Sal's inventory and deducted his share of the profits, his total cost would only be $500. He knew the necklace must be worth at least $1,500 retail, much more in an upscale gallery. He could get his friend in Santa Fe to do an appraisal to accompany the piece, then advertise the raffle in the surrounding towns and on Facebook, hoping the giveaway would bring in some new buyers.

Bloom emailed images and background information to the appraiser and the valuation came in at $2,500, which seemed a bit high in

Bloom's opinion, but that was the going replacement rate down on the Santa Fe Plaza. Bloom used the appraisal information in his print ads and repeatedly put an announcement and images of the necklace on the post's Facebook and Instagram accounts:

"Win an antique squash blossom necklace from the 1930s appraised at $2,500. Buy $20 worth of groceries, tack, or goods from the Toadlena Trading Post and you're automatically entered to win. Buy any Navajo rug and get five free entries! One grocery entry per day, per person. Drawing on October 31. Big Halloween party with free hot dogs and hamburgers. Winner MUST be present."

Bloom liked to think outside the box. Under his short tenure, more candy had been given away than sold, so he figured he might as well have a party and bring tourists to the post for a monster blowout—all on the house. He bounced the idea off his best friend and wife Rachael, who agreed a raffle was a great idea that would give her a new goal to work toward along with the physical therapy on her arms.

The party would require strategic planning. Rachael predicted five hundred people would show up; the free food would draw a lot of hungry neighbors and no advertising would be needed. The Navajo word-of-mouth communication system would be in high gear and the post's party would be swamped, with or without the squash blossom giveaway.

Marvin was in full agreement with the plans, though he wanted more than a free hot dog and piece of pie. He hoped to win the squash blossom necklace to replace his father's piece, which had been stolen by the whites at Indian boarding school. It was a deep wound that had never healed. "Maybe," Marvin thought, "it would take another white man to bring that full circle."

✳ ✳ ✳ ✳

A large sign: "1930s SQUASH BLOSSOM TO BE RAFFLED OCTOBER 31, WINNER MUST BE PRESENT" was placed in the antique jewelry case. Dozens of Grandmothers came in dressed in their finest velvet blouses and cluster bracelets to try on the necklace. They asked Bloom to take their pictures and to send the images to their grandkids' phones. They all expected to win and, if they didn't, they still wanted a portrait that would make them look like the proud winner.

Bloom's grocery sales quadrupled, just as he had hoped, and all the Amazon commodities disappeared. What he hadn't counted on was that no one seemed to have any money, although they were more than happy to add the groceries to their ever-growing credit lines. The debts rose daily by twenty-dollar increments, with the highest volume of items being sold on credit on October 31. Rug sales were not as brisk as he had hoped; only three rugs found new homes with one group of tourists that visited the post. They couldn't attend the party, so Bloom collected their fifteen raffle tickets and gave the extra chances away to anyone who actually paid for their groceries with cash.

The word on the street was that a white man in Farmington would pay $3 for each raffle ticket—and there was no limit to how many he would buy. Bloom had faced a similar issue at his Santa Fe gallery twenty years ago when he was selling highly sought-after Willard Yellowhorse paintings. One person tried to corner the market, which led to numerous angry clients accusing Bloom of running a sham sale. The controversy ultimately cost Bloom Willard Yellowhorse, his best painter, who left the gallery shortly after the fiasco.

Bloom knew that trying to stop people from cheating was nearly impossible—one of the reasons he had never said there was a limit of one ticket per person in his advertising. The more tickets someone accumulated, the more money they had spent at the post—unless, of course, they were gaming the system by buying tickets on the secondary market.

Bloom had been unsuccessful in getting the name of the white man buying up his raffle tickets. Apparently a Navajo bootlegger named Jackson had started an offshoot business, offering to pick up the tickets from the hogans. He paid the locals $2 a ticket, and when he amassed enough, he would cash them all in for $3 apiece—so having to drive to

Farmington was no longer a barrier for locals who wanted to sell their tickets on the secondary market. They loved the extra money they received by simply increasing their grocery bill at the post. It seemed that everyone won—except Bloom.

Bloom considered asking Rachael to do her Navajo thing and get him the name of the bilagáana buying the tickets but, if he ever wanted to be successful managing the post, he had to be able to understand the undercurrents of the communication system himself. All Charles wanted to do was make a friendly call and set the mystery buyer straight on what he was trying to accomplish for the good of the local people and the post. It wasn't so much about winning the necklace as it was about having a great feast at his expense and running a fair raffle. What Bloom didn't realize was the man in Farmington wasn't the kind of person who liked even odds—or ever played fair.

CHAPTER 21

BENCH SILVERSMITH WANTED

Finding the Farmington raffle-ticket buyer turned out to be as simple as looking at his own public bulletin board. Bloom finally asked Marvin, who seemed to have a hand on the pulse of the community, if he knew who was buying up the tickets. He knew Marvin understood the dynamics of the situation and wouldn't want to screw up a good thing for his neighbors, but he hoped they were good enough friends by now that the Navajo might acquiesce.

"Marvin, please tell me who is buying up all my raffle tickets," Bloom begged. "You know this makes the drawing look rigged and doesn't put the post, or me for that matter, in a very good light."

"I see you are trying to walk," Marvin smiled.

"Yes, I've crawled far enough. I need your help."

"Bloom, I know the man's name but, honestly, you should too—and it doesn't require me to become a snitch." Marvin smiled more broadly.

"OK, what gives, Mr. Mule?" Bloom replied, knowing he would be the butt of a community joke.

"You read, don't you...."

"English and a little Spanish, no Navajo yet."

"If I want to buy a set of used tires close by, or I want to know about an upcoming Squaw Dance, where would I go to find out about them?"

"I don't know, Marvin Manycoats, knower of all. You seem to be a human calendar with the memory of dates and times for everything."

Marvin's smile grew even larger, knowing Bloom was right. "Besides me, where can you read about these community events, let's say within fifty feet of where you are standing?"

Bloom paused as he tried to figure out Manycoats' riddle. He looked around the post and realized why Marvin was teasing him. "Don't tell me! The man's name is on my bulletin board," Bloom said with a sigh of resignation. He was glad he hadn't asked Rachael; this was one he would never be able to live down.

"You are officially on two feet now. Pay the man," Marvin said in his best Fire Rock Navajo Casino voice.

Bloom dropped his broom and went outside. Stuck in the middle of the bulletin board, right under his raffle brochure, was a notice that said: "Hiring bench silversmith, experience required." Underneath that notice was another posting that read: "Three dollars paid for each Toadlena Trading Post raffle ticket, good thru October 31. Contact Billy Moss, Moss Pawn and Trading Post, Farmington (505) 905-7100."

"Wow, that guy has some big huevos," Bloom said as he took down the pinned card and threw the 'help wanted' notice into the always-full, large metal trash can equipped with bear protection that sat outside the post.

"Marvin, do you know anything about this guy Billy Moss, Moss Pawn and Trading?"

"Not much. I remember when I first heard about his pawnshop back in December of 2007. He was offering big prices for old Navajo jewelry and art, trying to get stuff around Christmas when we Navajo need to buy gifts for our grandkids. His reputation is that once you pawn a piece, if you don't pay it back right on time, it disappears forever with no extensions or friendly reminders. Moss is always asking for the old Indian stuff that he buys and puts in his little museum in the back of the store so he can show it off.

"I visited his store's museum once on my birthday in 2014, thought it might be a nice treat for myself to go to a local museum, but it wasn't nothing like the Navajo Nation Museum in Window Rock. It was mainly filled with a bunch of old Nasazi pottery and yucca sandals. We Navajos don't even like that stuff, as I'm sure you know." Bloom nodded his head in the agreement. Rachael fell into this group.

"He did have a few really great old bracelets sprinkled in, and lots of worn-out tack and colored bottles, the same kind I used to shoot at as a kid. I always like to visit museums to see if my dad's or granddad's silverwork might be there. In Santa Fe that Wheelwright Museum has got a few pieces of our family silver on display," Marvin said with pride.

"We Navajos stay away from Billy Moss. I've never met him but rumor has it he can be pretty mean. I don't know that for a fact, it's just what I hear."

Bloom decided he would give Mr. Moss a call and find out for himself what kind of a man he was dealing with.

❋ ❋ ❋ ❋

At a side-glance, Billy Moss looked like a field scarecrow come to life, his taut body displayed under overly tight clothing. He had a small head topped with a large black Stetson, slung low on his forehead. Matching black lizard boots outfitted with silver tips etched with backward whirling logs completed the outfit. Moss spoke with a Texas twang, even though he had grown up in Gallup. His mother, who was from Dallas, was the source of his western accent.

Rudy Moss, Billy's biological father, had gone to prison when the boy was three and died there on Billy's sixth birthday, stabbed in the back. His mother soon remarried a respected district school principal whom Billy disliked for the most part, even though he called him dad. He kept his real father's last name and went by Billy, his mother's preference— not Bill as it read on his driver's license. Moss adored his mom and would have done anything for her. She died at the end of a bottle when he was nineteen. Drinking was one habit Billy avoided; he considered all drunks weak-minded and disliked them intensely.

The Moss Pawn and Trading Post was more pawn than post. There was a sundry array of working saddles, tack, out-of-date electronics, DVDs, CDs, power tools, and hunting rifles. The front counter was the trading post section, with numerous cheap silver bracelets mixed in with a few quality older Navajo cluster bracelets. The jewelry was mediocre; the best pieces were all behind Plexiglass cases in his Museum of the Ancients, located behind a chain to the right of the front door. Recommended admission was $1, though only the occasional tourist would pay it.

Billy's childhood home was a ranch west of Gallup where he learned the joys of hunting for artifacts, arrowheads, and pottery sherds and had time to think and be happy—a place to be away from his toxic family. Most of his museum's holdings had been collected legally on his private land, but Billy honestly didn't care where the artifacts originated as long as they were well priced; he was a collector, not a seller. If the feds ever got nosey he could say that all the Anasazi material had been legally dug on his stepfather's property (now his). He would give them a tour of the dug-up ruins with numerous old excavation holes located next to his boyhood home. Moss had spent his childhood with a shovel.

The Museum of the Ancients was one long narrow hallway fitted with Plexiglass cases containing dozens of old ingot bracelets, a few good belts and a half-dozen lesser squash blossom necklaces from the 1940s. Other cases were filled with a hodge-podge of Anasazi artifacts of all types—Navajo baskets covered in dry corn pollen and Apache

Tuss baskets. The Tuss were dipped in piñon pitch that hardened and served as nineteenth-century water jugs before metal pans were universally available. The museum was meant to show the evolution of the Four Corner region from prehistoric man to the early 1940s.

Moss was proud of his museum and rarely sold off any of the pieces, preferring to use the holdings as his personal piggy bank in times of need. He loved it all. Most of the older jewelry had come in as pawn. Many of the original owners had tried to buy back their pieces when they got some money, knowing their favorite bracelet or necklace was merely sitting in the museum. Moss vehemently refused to sell anything back, admonishing them for selling their pieces off in the first place and threatening to cut them off from pawning in the future if they made trouble.

He took the call from Bloom in the same vein as he listened to the Navajo who wanted a chance to buy back their jewelry: it was a nice idea, but it was not in the cards.

"Hi. Is this Billy Moss?" Bloom asked in his friendliest voice.

"You got Billy. How can I help you?"

"Billy, this is Charles Bloom. I'm running the Toadlena Trading Post while Sal Lito is on vacation. I wanted to talk to you about the 'help wanted' card you left on my bulletin board, the one looking for a silversmith and offering to buy raffle tickets for $3."

"Yeah. How many tickets you give away so far?" Billy asked.

"I would guess around 100, more or less," Bloom replied, as he tried to turn the conversation back to his original question.

"Hundred, you say? That's next Saturday, Halloween right, 4 to 6 p.m. at the trading post, must be present to win, right?"

"Yes, that's all correct. I wanted...."

Billy interrupted once more: "Pretty good odds. If you want to sell me a few more tickets under the table, so to speak, between us trading post brothers, I'm willing to pay $3 a ticket."

Bloom immediately knew what kind of man he was dealing with—one who never fully followed any rules and would steal from you easily and without remorse.

"No, I don't have any tickets to sell unless you want to buy groceries or Indian art. This is a raffle. It is supposed to be that when you buy post goods, you get entered into the drawing and help out the post. But you're not wanting to play fair; you're buying up tickets and trying to game the system," Bloom said sternly.

"Game the system, huh? Are there any rules against buying tickets other than at the post? I sure didn't see no rules saying I couldn't get as many tickets as I wanted. You seem to be on some kind of high horse when it comes to this raffle.

"Does that squash blossom necklace actually come with a $2,500 appraisal or is that just hype?" Moss fired back.

Now Bloom was pissed. "Yes it comes with a certified appraisal, and no, there is no written rule about how many tickets you can buy. I'm just asking you as one post owner to another to make the tables a little more fair for the Navajo."

"I can tell you ain't been a post 'owner' for long if you think we need to be 'fair' to the Navajo. I grew up in these parts and I can tell you that if you give one of your Navajo friends an inch, he will take a mile.

"I'm being more than fair. I'm paying these folks good money for a ticket that most likely isn't going to pay off. As you just pointed out, it's at least a hundred-to-one shot, and they can use that money to go get liquored up. That's what they really want—and you and I both know that. Do you think if they win that squash they ain't going to pawn it to me the next day?"

Bloom's stomach turned; the man was a racist and a cheat.

"OK. If that's the way you want to play the game, I can't stop you. But what I can tell you, Mr. Moss, is that I'm going to let my Navajo wife and all her Navajo relatives know what kind of man you are. Remember you have to be present to win. And don't put any more signs on my post's bulletin board. That's there to help the Toadlena community, not enrich another bilagáana taking advantage of the Diné."

Bloom was surprised he had called Billy a bilagáana, but in this case he was one. He hung up the phone.

Billy Moss slammed down the receiver on his end and yelled, "Charles Bloom, you're on my shit list. You can be assured I will be buying as many tickets as I can get my hands on, AND I will be coming to your party with a few of my hungry buddies in tow."

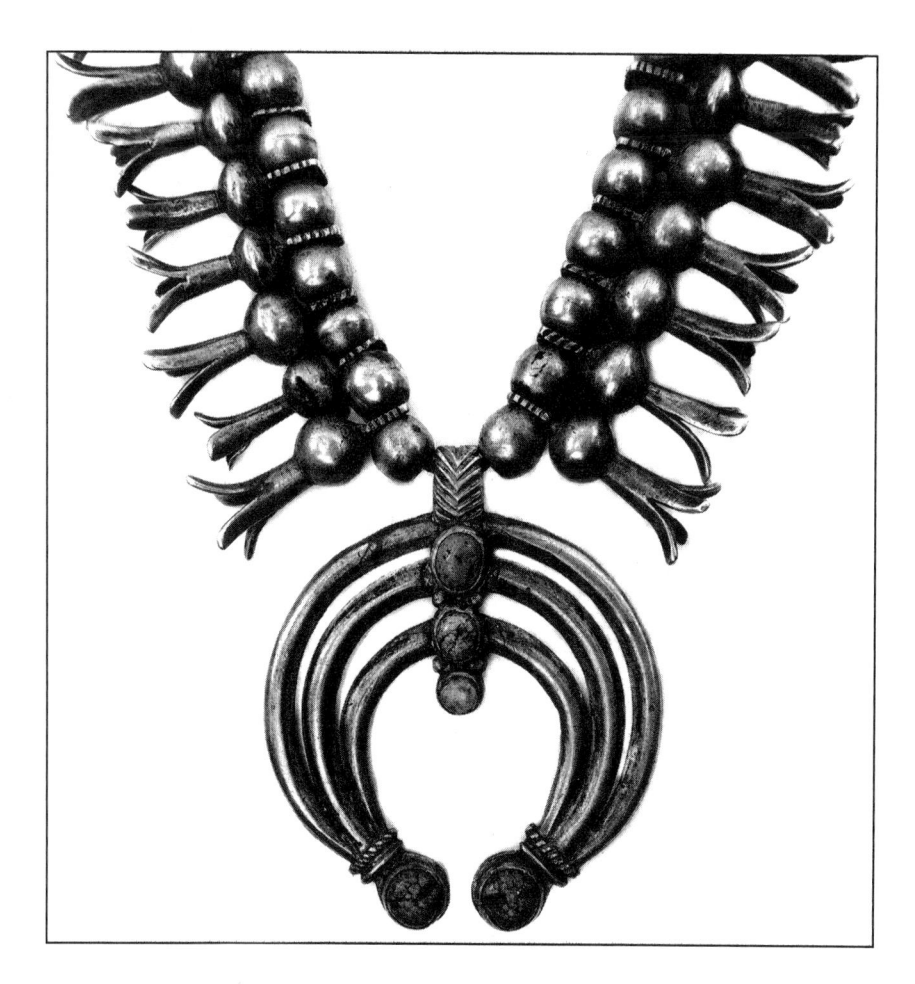

CHAPTER 22

MATCHSTICK WOMAN RETURNS

Billy Moss had a singular mission over the next week: to acquire as many raffle tickets as possible, upping his purchase price to $5 a ticket, $7 the day before the drawing. Second place wasn't an option for him and the more tickets he held, the better his odds. Winning was as much about showing Bloom who was in control as it was about the necklace.

On his own, Bloom decided to increase the odds against Moss by giving away an additional 25 free tickets to any weaver who had brought in a rug in the last six months. He called the additional chances "recognition awards" for being a Toadlena weaver. He wrote down the numbers of each "recognition" ticket he passed out and let the recipients know he would check after the draw to see who had won the prize—and that he wouldn't be happy if Billy Moss ended up holding one of these special tickets. They understood his message and were happy to simply have another free chance to win.

Bloom was still fuming. He was trying to do good for the community and one greedy person—Moss—was trying to screw him. Rachael was less concerned about Billy. In her eyes, he was one of those bad traders who has always been on the fringes of the Navajo Nation; she believed these coyotes got what was coming to them in the end. Jaded by art dealers' shenanigans in the past, Bloom was not convinced that the troublemakers would get their just deserts. In his experience, they were the ones who never seemed to pay any price; they just got rich.

October 31st was warmer than expected, with highs of 65 degrees—perfect party weather. The post's cottonwoods were shedding the last of their saucer-sized yellow leaves, making it feel like both late summer and fall all in one day.

Rachael had spent two weeks preparing for the big day. Bloom ordered an extra four dozen boxes of hard candy, three extra boxes of Big Hunks (on Rachael's recommendation) and a tub of bubblegum. The menu was simple: grilled hot dogs, hamburgers and roasted corn, and an additional $2,000 in groceries.

Marvin Manycoats offered to bring his truck up for trash and grocery duty. Once the party started, he would switch over to the grill. "I've got a soft spot in my heart for hot dogs," he told Bloom as he volunteered to flip dogs—his joke lost on those who hadn't attended Indian school.

All hands were on deck. At her mother's insistence, even Ruth Bennally showed up. Her job was to make sure that all the weavings in the rug room were straight. Ruth greatly enjoyed folding and refolding all the textiles and stacking them by size. The rug room had never looked better, and Bloom thought he might offer her a part-time job.

The party wasn't scheduled to start until 4 p.m., but everything was in place by noon. As Bloom expected, a small influx of tourists came to partake in a real Indian party. By 2 p.m., the post was packed with nearly 150 vehicles, mainly trucks, parked up and down the dirt road leading to the building's front door. A Shiprock farmer had donated dozens of pumpkins for the occasion, and Rachael and the kids spent two days before the party carving pumpkins and lining them around the Post's entrance. Rachael also prepared a half-dozen pumpkin pies, her contribution to the feast.

Ghosts and bad spirits—which are part of the Navajo belief system—did not appear in the decorations, but large cardboard cut-out witches on broomsticks hung from the ceiling between the old tack. Every Navajo knew a real witch would use ground-up bone to cast a bad spell and that the ones with brooms were just there to entertain the kids.

A 1977 Volvo crept up the front driveway and parked in a handicapped space near the entrance. A woman pushing ninety, using her cane as a third arm, opened the front door. Mrs. Pingry looked like a cartoon character with a shock of dyed red and gray hair, the color job having faded a month ago. Her plaid skirt and paisley shirt matched her Volvo's seat cover colors. Hanging from her emaciated neck lay a magnificent squash blossom, the heavy necklace pulling her head toward her chest.

Working her way toward a bench over the uneven post floor, she sat down near the front counter, oblivious to everyone else, and said in her loudest voice to no one in particular: "Hello. I would like to see the squash blossom you are going to auction off today."

Bloom, recognizing a potential buyer, answered the call.

"Well," he said, "we aren't going to auction the piece off, we are giving it away through a raffle. Would you like to get a ticket? One chance comes with every $20 worth of groceries sold, and you get five tickets with any Navajo rug you buy."

"I'd like to see that necklace first, before I commit to buying any raffle ticket," the old woman barked.

"Sure, here it is, right in this case."

The old woman adjusted her 1960s-era glasses and wrinkled her nose. "It's nice enough, got some good age, but it's hard to compare when you got one like this," she said as she jingled her heavy squash with a skeletal index finger.

"Yes, that's one of the finest squashes I've ever seen. It's a real beauty. But ours is light in weight and would be a nice complement to yours on those days when you want something simple and light." Bloom was always selling, even though he knew the old woman's necklace was far superior in every way.

"My necklace is heavy because it's old coin silver, and that means it's valuable, sonny," she retorted, taking umbrage at Bloom's sales pitch.

"Yes, you're right on that point," he acknowledged. "Would you be interested in seeing some of our Toadlena/Two Grey Hills rugs? They're all made right around the post by local weavers."

"What do the cheapest ones go for?"

"A small piece can go for as little as $250," Bloom smiled.

"Ok, let's look at those. Maybe I'll buy one and get five chances for your lesser squash blossom."

Bloom motioned for Rachael to show the old lady some rugs. He could see it would take awhile, and he had neither the time nor the patience to work with this client.

The woman methodically plowed through all the small rugs between $250 and $350, and finally found one she deemed good enough. Each weaving she rejected was quickly folded and returned to its stack by Ruth, who was waiting at the ready.

Rachael walked the old woman to the front counter where Bloom was selling one of the last bags of pinto beans and handing out a raffle ticket when the old lady plopped the rug down in front of Bloom.

"OK, I'd like my tickets and let's make them good ones. Make sure you stir up that raffle jar really well before you pick one. Otherwise, only the old tickets on the bottom will get pulled out, and that won't be fair to me."

"Will do. I'll stir them myself an hour before the draw and again before we pick that winning ticket. I can assure you that you'll have as good a chance as anyone."

Bloom forced a smile as he took down the old woman's information, hoping Moss's cache of tickets wouldn't become an issue. She was just the type to complain and try to return the rug, he thought.

"If you give me a name, address, and email I'll add you to our mailing list and you will get occasional updates on what's happening around the post."

"Mary Pingry. My address is 125 Oak Avenue, Gallup, New Mexico, 87301. I don't have a computer so I obviously won't be getting any email," she added in a condescending tone.

"How did you find out about our raffle?"

"The Lotaburger off 491 in Gallup had a flyer taped up in the window."

Bloom was happy that he had taken a few hours to put up flyers and hadn't just relied on social media to advertise the party.

He smiled to himself: "That's good to know—and you have good taste in hamburgers too. OK. I've got your receipt ready. How would you like to pay for this?"

"I'll pay with a check."

"That's fine. I just need to see your license."

The woman dug around in her purse and retrieved an out-of-date drivers license showing her in better days; the address, though, was the same as the one she had given.

"The total is $262.50 including our Navajo tax."

"I don't live on the reservation. Why should I have to pay a Navajo tax? The Navajo don't do anything for my Gallup roads or police," Pingry said incredulously.

Bloom was used to dealing with individuals not wanting to pay tax, but it was part of the cost of the weaving. He tried his best to lessen the blow of paying the surcharge: "I understand completely, but I have to charge tax. It's the law and I'm responsible for collecting it. At least you don't have to pay the higher Gallup tax rate—Navajo Nation tax is only five percent."

"Only five percent? That's a lot on a fixed income—maybe not to a rich storeowner, but I can assure you that for me every penny counts. I'll go ahead and pay it, but I'm not going to get anything of value out paying an Indian tax and your so-called roads are a mess. Why don't you mention that when you give them my money...."

Pingry made a sour face as she wrote out the check to the Toadlena Trading Post with a shaky hand. Her note on the memo line read, "Indian rug AND TAX." She folded the small textile into a square and placed it in her oversized purse.

"I'll make sure the Navajo Nation gets your recommendation."

"Is there any place I can sit until the drawing besides this hard bench?" Pingry asked.

Bloom wanted to say, "Try your car and maybe turn on the engine and keep the windows up," but instead he suggested the back porch, where there was a nice soft couch and a sweet cat that liked people—"maybe even old crabby ones like you," he mused to himself.

"That sounds like it should work fine. But I'm allergic to cats, so if your animal climbs on my lap I'm going to have to shoo him away."

"Not an issue," Bloom thought. "That cat is a good judge of character and won't want to rest in your decrepit lap." What he said though, was, "That's not a problem. Go have a seat and in a bit, we'll bring you a hamburger and corn on the cob hot off the grill. Good luck with the drawing."

There were days when retail was a challenge, but he wasn't going to let the cranky old woman bring him down. After all, she had bought a weaving, he didn't have to sell the piece to her, and there was one less rug in inventory. Today would be fun and someone would end up with a great necklace. Bloom just hoped it wasn't Billy Moss—or, for that matter, Mary Pingry.

CHAPTER 23

HOW ABOUT A COKE?

The scent of piñon, charred meat and diesel fumes had settled into the Toadlena/Two Grey Hills basin. Laughter bounced off the surrounding hillside as kids ran back and forth. The apple-dunking bucket was a hit; the participants actually did want to grab an apple to eat. Marvin, Rachael, Bloom, and Ruth were handing out hamburgers and hotdogs to an ever-growing line.

Marvin couldn't remember a time when he had so much fun; he had a funny feeling he was going to win that squash blossom necklace and life would get back on track, before he got too old to enjoy what time was left. He was sure his luck was about to change today.

The loud thunder of motorcycles approached from the distance and Billy Moss and two of his shooting buddies parked right up front, partially trapping two handicapped cars in place. Moss was not one to worry about etiquette when it came to lines or parking places. His place was always upfront.

The trio was dressed in their "bad ass motorcycle guy" gear: old-time leather football helmets, dark leather pants, and jackets over worn-out, stained tee shirts. Moss's shirt said volumes about the man's attitude for the day: "The Yankees Suck and So Do YOU!" They looked out of place in the sea of velvet skirts, cowboy hats, and blue jeans as they walked through the post looking to see how the competition did things.

Ruth Bennally greeted Moss in the rug room and asked if he wanted to look at rugs. The trader recognized her from the Shell station where she sold papers, and wondered if she was a part-time employee at the post.

"Nah, maybe later," he said. "I'm here to win a squash blossom and eat till I drop." His buddies laughed, knowing they were going to get a good feed today at Bloom's expense.

"OK, good luck!"

Bloom was so busy he didn't even notice the odd trio come through the back door until the three had cut the line and were in his face asking for two hamburgers each.

"I hear this is an eat-all-you-want party. How about you give me and my boys a couple of hamburgers to start with. We've come a long way and we're hungry." Moss smiled defiantly, exposing two front teeth capped in a rim of gold.

Bloom finally looked up and knew it had to be his unwanted guest.

"Mr. Moss, I'm guessing?"

Moss laughed. "How did you know? You been looking at my pretty face on the internet?"

"No, never bothered. You just look the way I pictured you when I talked to you on the phone."

Moss quit smiling, not knowing how to respond.

"Here's a hamburger and a hotdog. We're limiting them to one per person until everyone gets fed. If we have any left over you're welcome to another. The drawing for the squash will be in 45 minutes. Enjoy the views." Bloom moved on to the next in line.

"Thanks, I will. This looks like a nice place to park and take in the scenery. I need to talk to old Sal when he gets back home to see if he wants a partner in this place. Under the right management—and with a nice little museum—this post could actually make some money."

Bloom ignored his bodacious guest, but a river of anger boiled through him. God, he hoped that man didn't win his squash blossom.

Bloom had completely forgotten about Mary Pingry, and looked around for her. She was still where he had left her, slouched in the corner and hemmed in by an equally old Grandmother who looked much stronger and healthier than the frail Pingry.

"Hey, Marvin, see that old white woman in the corner? Can you please take her a hamburger and a corn on the cob? I had promised I would bring dinner over to her and completely forgot about it—and ask her if she needs anything else. She's a bit cantankerous but she did buy a nice little Navajo rug this afternoon, so she's a new client."

"Sure, boss. Maybe she needs a sugar daddy," Marvin chuckled. He filled a plate with a hot burger, steaming corn on the cob smeared with a knob of butter, a handful of crunchy Lay's potato chips, some sliced garden tomatoes, lettuce, and pickles and headed over to the woman. He thought she looked dead, her neck bent at an odd angle.

"Hi, Mr. Bloom thought you might..." Marvin stopped in midsentence, seeing the necklace she wore: it was his father's Slender Maker piece. He also recognized the old lady, her hair still an off-red color, and in one moment Marvin went from being a sixty-eight-year-old man to a frightened child.

As she looked up at him, he regained his composure and wondered if she had any idea of their past relationship.

"Thanks for the food. Would you mind getting me a cold Coke? I choke easily," Pingry said without making eye contact. Marvin hoped she would choke all right, but not from a dry throat. He pulled up a small homemade stool and sat next to the elderly woman, gazing at his father's long-lost necklace.

"That's a very nice necklace you have there. Do you know who made the piece? I'm not sure I've ever seen one like it."

"Yes, Navajos always compliment my necklace. It was a gift from an old friend years ago. They say the necklace might have been made by Slender Maker and the turquoise beads were added later," Pingry said with pride.

"Yeah, that would make sense. I think you're right. You interested in selling?" Marvin blurted out.

"No, never. I will die with this on; it's very sentimental to me."

"Yeah, it's sentimental to me, too," Marvin thought to himself, "and I like the part where you die with it on—and soon." Rage and fear swelled up from deep within Marvin, as if he had been transported back to the rice fields in Nam. He refocused his mind, knowing he must take advantage of his great fortune. His father's piece was not lost, but was sitting right next to him.

"I understand not wanting to let that one go; it's a great piece. Don't go anywhere. I'll be right back with your Coke."

"Where would I go? And please make it a cold Coke—it's hot out here."

Marvin flashed back to 1961, when Pingry sat in the yellow school bus drinking ice-cold lemonade as all of his friends struggled in the heat. Finding a cold Coke was not what he was thinking about when he went back to the grill station.

Marvin fished a Coke out of the bottom of the ice chest and quickly returned to the porch, handing the wet metal can to Pingry. His good mood had disappeared. Where the woman lived and how he could get the piece back was all he could think about. Mrs. Pingry most likely knew where the squash blossom came from. She was at best complicit, and at worst, a thief of Indian heirlooms. He was at a loss for words; all he could see was his father's necklace.

Finally, Marvin said, "OK. I hope to see you around. Enjoy the party and good luck with the squash blossom drawing." He was surprised by what had come out of his mouth. There was only one squash that interested him now.

Marvin returned to the hamburger station and began doing his own grilling of Bloom.

"Hey, Bloom, how do you know that old white lady? She a customer?"

"She's a first-time buyer," Bloom said, looking back at Pingry, "so I have all her information. She may not buy a lot more, but did you see that squash around her neck? That has to be one of the best I've ever seen. I'd love to get that for the store someday."

"One of the best..." Marvin let his words trail off. Now that he knew Bloom had her contact information, he needed to get it for himself.

"She from Gallup?" he asked.

"Yep, she's from Gallup. I know her neighborhood; I was over there once at Stone Man's house. It's one of those older subdivisions where no structure is newer than the 1950s. Honestly, she doesn't look like the type who could afford the kind of necklace she's wearing. She must have gotten a long time ago or maybe it was a gift."

"Yeah. It was probably a gift. Which neighborhood is that?

"Oak Avenue, on the west side of Gallup."

"I have a friend that lives on Oak. What's her house number? Maybe they are neighbors," Marvin explored.

"I think it was 125, but I would have to check. You can go ask her yourself if she knows your friend. I'm sure she would like some company; the Grandmother next to her doesn't speak any English and I doubt she speaks Navajo."

"I don't think I should," Marvin replied. "She might think I'm sweet on her and I don't need any aggravation at my age. Besides, we still got a lot of hamburgers to cook—I see your three buddies are headed our way for seconds. Guess they don't like the one hamburger rule."

Moss and his thugs were back, wanting more eats. Bloom decided the grill was now closed and laid his spatula next to Moss's plate before the man could demand more food. Then he walked right by the man without acknowledging his presence.

"Who is ready to win a squash blossom necklace?" Bloom roared—and the crowd let out a huge cheer. Everyone but Marvin believed they were going to win. He now had his sights set on acquiring a different squash blossom—and it wasn't the one in the case.

CHAPTER 24

AND THE WINNER IS…

A palpable excitement flowed through the audience when Bloom stood on an old telephone wire spool, still wearing Rachael's cooking apron, and asked everyone to gather around the squash blossom. The necklace was prominently displayed by itself in the antique standup jewelry case, which had been moved from the trading post to the center of the outside dining table for all to view.

"Marvin, would you mind handing me that wonderful necklace so everyone can get a better look?"

Marvin handed Bloom the necklace, which Bloom then draped around his neck. The incongruous sight of a six-foot, one-inch bilagáana dressed in an apron and a squash blossom necklace was not lost on the crowd. Bloom turned from side to side so all in attendance could get an idea at how well the piece hung around the wearer's neck.

A young man at the back of the crowd yelled, "Rachael, it looks like we know who wears the pants in your family...." The crowd—including Bloom—laughed, as Rachael turned crimson, nodding her head in the affirmative.

"OK, let's focus our attention away from Rachael and back to this great old Navajo squash blossom," Bloom continued. "The piece is from the 1930s and done in the box and bow style, with natural blue gem turquoise. Today we are going to give this beautiful necklace to some lucky person. I wish I could keep it for myself—or should I say for Rachael—but you folks wouldn't like that, would you?"

In unison, the crowd yelled, "NO!"

"I just wanted to say that it's been my honor to run the post in Sal and Linda Lito's absence. I'm sure he wishes he could be here, especially when he sees how much candy I gave away." It was the kids' cue to scream for more candy.

"I know I'm a greenhorn, but with the help of all of you, my wife Rachael and our kids Willy and Sam, I think I'm starting to get the hang of things. I promise I'll only carry Blue Bird Flour and pinto beans from now on." The crowd laughed again, knowing Bloom was starting to figure out Navajo preferences that ran deeper than rugs.

"If it's OK with you guys, I want my son Willy to come up and pull the lucky winner. As you know, the winning ticket must be presented by its holder. If we pull a ticket and there is no claim within one minute, I will pull another ticket—so have your numbers ready. One minute is all you have to scream out, 'I won!' Is that clear?"

Billy Moss realized Bloom was pulling a fast one on him; he had at least sixty tickets and they weren't in any numerical order.

"Hey Bloom, that's not fair," Moss yelled in protest. "I can't get through all these tickets in one minute."

"For you who don't know him," Bloom retorted, "this is Billy Moss, Yankee hater. He's the one who bought all those tickets from your friends and neighbors who come and support this post by buying groceries here. It looks like he wants that squash badly.

"Well, Billy, I will let the folks who support this post decide if one minute is fair or not."

Moss and his buddies were desperately trying to put the tickets in some kind of order when one of his goons dropped a handful and they all scrambled to pick them up.

"So, all for one the one-minute rule say 'Yes' and stick your hand up in the air."

The crowd screamed "Yes" and a sea of hands arose.

"Those opposed?" Only Moss and his buddies yelled out "NO!"

"The one-minute rule has passed, Mr. Moss, so it looks like you'd better get organized fast. Once Willy hands me the ticket and I have read out the winning number, I will start my countdown using my phone's stopwatch. What would we do without our phones?"

The grandmother's in the crowd raised their eyebrows at that, knowing a smartphone was only for teenagers or rich people.

Bloom hopped off the large spool and held up the jar crammed with tickets.

"OK, Willy. I want you to really stir these tickets up before you pull one out—like you do with your mom's overcooked mutton stew."

The crowd laughed, and Rachael turned red again. Willy stirred wildly, moving his hand up and down in the jar.

"OK, Dad. I think it's done, but I'm not sure how good it's going to be." The crowd gave the boy a louder laugh than they had given Bloom as Willy handed his father the winning ticket.

"Here we go. The six-digit number is at the bottom of each ticket. The winner is 651073, and the clock starts now."

Everyone looked at his or her ticket and no one called out "Winner!" Bloom read out the number once more slowly, so the Grandmothers could recheck their tickets. Moss had taken over an entire picnic table with all the slips laid out like a deck of cards and was scrambling to see if he had a matching number when a gust of wind from the east scattered his tickets everywhere.

"Don't touch those!" Moss yelled as the trio grabbed at the slips blowing toward the Chuskas. "I need more time. I'm sure I've got it!"

"10, 9, 8, 7, 6, 5, 4, 3, 2, 1… OK, time is up. It's time for a new draw." Moss's protests fell on deaf ears.

"OK, son—give it another go." Willy again rotated the tickets violently, then pulled a slip from the jar and handed it to his father.

"And the winning ticket is 651001."

Finding a 1001 ticket would be much easier for Moss this go around. The crowd assumed he must have the winner, as the whole valley seemed to be present.

Marvin glanced down at his ticket stub as Bloom started his one-minute countdown. He had been staring at his father's necklace around his old foe's neck and almost forgot he had skin in the game. Marvin had one ticket to his name, the result of buying six cartons of ice cream—and it was the winner.

"Winner! I've got the ticket," Marvin announced to the crowd, not quite believing it himself.

"Well, I'll be," Bloom cheered. "Marvin Manycoats, a Toadlena resident, hot-dog griller and war hero may be our winner, and just barely under the one minute rule.

"Marvin, you made a great splash playing out the clock that way. Willy, go get that ticket from Marvin so we can verify his winning number."

Marvin stood up and Willy retrieved the ticket and gave it to his dad at the same time Pingry recognized Marvin Manycoats' name and realized the man that had served her lunch was her old student at Two Trees—and she was wearing his father's necklace! It was time to get out just as fast as a ninety-year-old could go.

"Willy, read the number on that ticket for your dad." Willy, who had only recently learned his numbers, slowly read out 6-5-1-0-0-1.

"Folks, it's official. We do have a winner! Marvin Manycoats, come stand beside Rachael and me to receive your 1930s squash blossom necklace worth $2,500."

As Marvin headed up to Bloom, Moss yelled out, "That necklace is mine. I've found the first number, 651073, so I have the real winning ticket!"

As Moss tried to make his way through the crowd, he bumped into Mrs. Pingry, knocking her almost to the ground. He looked at her angrily, not recognizing her at first, until he spotted the great necklace around her neck. She kept moving forward, intent on making her escape.

"That's my necklace, Bloom. I've got the winning number."

"Sorry, Billy, but you heard the rules that were approved by the whole crowd. I'm afraid you need to hone your math skills."

Moss was livid, and started toward Bloom to teach him some manners when four huge Navajo men from the housing projects stepped in front of him.

"You got a problem with a Navajo war hero winning the big prize?" the most imposing Navajo asked, stepping close to Billy's face. Moss and his buddies backed off, realizing the odds were terrible and so were these men. He knew the largest man had done serious jail time and wasn't a guy to trifle with unless you were carrying a weapon.

"No problem with you, man," Moss said, taking a step back, then turning and shaking a finger at Bloom—a very impolite gesture among the Navajo. "But Bloom, you and I do have a problem—a big one. You're a cheat and I'm not done with this."

Moss made his way toward his bike through the swarms of bystanders, none of whom would move for him. He and his boys were trapped and Moss started to panic. He grabbed a large plastic tub of bubble gum and tossed its content into the air, which created a mass rush by dozens of kids that allowed Moss and his thugs to retreat to their motorcycles.

By the time he reached the front entrance, though, he found his bike knocked over with a significant dent in the gas tank and the front fender bent out of shape.

Pingry had floored her car's gas pedal, knocking Moss's bike out of her way, and was now out of sight, bouncing down the dirt road toward Gallup. "Next time you won't park in front of an old lady's handicapped space," she said to herself, not knowing who owned the motorcycle, but feeling he got what he deserved.

She was worried though. She had been a fool to flaunt her necklace in public. Billy Moss might be her so-called nephew but, like his stepfather, he was not a man to be taken lightly. Moss might wonder about an expensive necklace he had never seen her wearing before, and Marvin Manycoats had served her a hamburger and a Coke. Marvin had wanted to buy the piece immediately and must have recognized it as his father's necklace. Even a twelve-year-old wouldn't forget it—especially not Marvin, a good student with an excellent memory—of this she was sure.

Pingry had a growing number of concerns, and she would need to make plans if she didn't want to find herself in the cemetery with the white crosses sooner than planned.

CHAPTER 25

A LOST LIFE

Ernie Yazzie saw his life as a failure, and he was angry that he had never amounted to anything. He had been running since he was 11 years old. Indian boarding school had taken his family's wealth and dignity and pushed him into booze.

He felt that not getting a decent education was the source of many of his problems, including never marrying or finding love. He dreamed of having a companion to share his life with, but that ship had passed and he was mad about the outcome. His self-worth was permanently damaged by not going any further than the sixth grade—a hard thing to accept for an intelligent man like Ernie.

His twenties were spent drinking and fighting. Ernie was a mean drunk and looked for trouble. After spending six months in the Gallup jail for a DWI and disorderly conduct, Ernie gave up alcohol for good, never wanting to be locked up and under the control of another master again—especially a white one. Staying sober saved Ernie but pushed him deeper into isolation. Without Marvin's friendship, Ernie would have been totally on his own.

There was a part of Ernie that loved Marvin Manycoats. He would never forget his friend going into Soliday's isolation box to protect him like a brother—but Marvin had also helped mold who he became—a man on the run. Making him write that fake bill of sale to the school headmaster so he could never retrieve his blanket was a never-ending loop of anger and regret running in the dark recesses of Ernie's mind. He tried not to dwell on the past but that damaged part of his mind still festered, with no apparent way to heal it.

Ernie's parents shielded him for five years, until he turned sixteen and was free from the white man's reach. They had done their best to homeschool Ernie so he would not be left behind, but there was only so much they could do, and their sheep, which were always in need of new pastures, were a priority. So Ernie spent most of his time with the family animals and building rock walls—and nothing had changed over the years in this respect. Ernie was never far from the walls—the structural type he built on the land, and the deeply seated ones that held his mind hostage. Even though he felt stupid because of his poor education, he read often and on many subjects, and even followed local politics.

Not long after he quit drinking, his mom and dad passed away and he stopped trying to find a soulmate. He focused instead on hunting wild game, a skill set he had mastered. Years of herding sheep in the backcountry had created superior tracking and hunting abilities; he never lacked for venison, his favorite food, and was deadly with a bow, knife, or gun.

Ernie was sixty-seven years old, but looked fifty. A life lifting stone and herding sheep had made him an impressively sized human, the kind that would scare you if you met him on an empty road. Scrawny as a kid, he had grown into a 6-foot, 4-inch man who needed an extra-large hogan to shelter his massive body. The towering rock walls he had constructed were equally impressive, creating a veritable fortress. Ernie felt a kinship with the earth and rock, which helped fill a void that no human had yet to touch.

He couldn't stop building walls and adding rooms to the hogan even after the first dozen were complete. His compound resembled a revival Chacoan village constructed for one person, using similar architectural techniques and local rock formations. Ernie had seen many ancient Nasazi ruins; hundreds were scattered around his ancestral property, most untouched. He learned from observing the Ancient One's buildings, though he never dug up any houses for stones for fear of the chindi that haunted their deathbeds.

Ernie was traditional in his beliefs and fluent in Navajo. It was clear English was his second language, though he preferred not to speak in either tongue. Many interpreted this to mean he was full of himself, when, in reality, he was a shy man who didn't like anyone to tell him what he could or could not do. His reclusive nature and the isolated hogan near Beautiful Mountain kept him separated from most people, which was fine with him.

Marvin Manycoats was a friend despite Ernie's conflicts about the man's role in losing the blanket. Marvin would regularly make the 10-mile dirt road trip from the blacktop to visit Ernie for no other reason than to talk about what Ernie was building and anything interesting he might have read or heard. Since he had moved back to Toadlena, Marvin had never missed a birthday or a big holiday with Ernie.

Today was one of those days when Marvin made an unannounced visit; without cell phones, all visits to Ernie were by chance. As his truck came over the rise, he could see his childhood friend in the distance, riding on a massive black stallion. Marvin couldn't help but imagine what their Navajo homeland must have been like before the white man's arrival, when all Diné were free to roam the backcountry like Ernie, with no rutted roads or trucks, only horses and sheep.

Seeing the dirt cloud rising above his road and headed toward his compound, Ernie spurred his horse on; he wasn't one to welcome strangers. As he got closer, he realized the truck belonged to his oldest friend, Marvin Manycoats, and he slowed the panting horse's gait to a gentle trot.

"Yá át ééh, Marvin. What brings you out to my place? Somebody die? It's not my birthday."

"Well, not exactly, but I do need some advice," Marvin replied. Ernie immediately noticed the squash blossom around his neck.

"Looks like you finally replaced your dad's old squash blossom. I wonder where that necklace ended up—probably with my chief's blanket on some rich white man's wall and or in his jewelry case," Ernie said, his voice deepening.

"No, Ernie. In fact, my father's necklace ended up on Matchstick Woman's skinny neck. Remember Mrs. Pingry? She has it!"

"Matchstick Woman is alive and has the necklace, the old squash with the turquoise beads? You sure it's yours?" Marvin asked in amazement.

"I'm sure. I saw her yesterday at the Halloween party at the Toadlena Trading Post and she was wearing the necklace."

"I heard about that party when I went into Shiprock for supplies. I don't get out often, but I considered going for the free food, and I figured you would be there, but I'm not much for large groups of people."

"I understand," Marvin said, knowing his friend well. "The funny thing, Ernie, is that I was having a great time at the party, I won this $2,500 squash blossom at the raffle, and I haven't won anything since May 8, 1982 at a cake walk, and this is much better than a cherry and peach cake. But seeing that old red-haired witch with my necklace made me want to do something very bad to her, and I still want to—that's why I'm here."

Ernie understood Marvin's anger; he would kill Stanton Soliday if he hadn't died twenty years ago. "What you going to do to get it back? Steal it?"

"I don't have a good plan yet. Part of me says yes, the other part says it's not worth getting myself in big trouble with the law at my age. I can't prove that the piece is mine, and I'm sure she has lots of history to say it's hers, and who is going to believe me? It was 1961. The laws probably don't even recognize a theft that long ago, especially when something was stolen from an Indian."

Ernie shook his head in agreement; the laws never seem to work in their favor. "Well, if she has your necklace, there is a chance she also has my blanket with that fake bill of sale you made me write."

Marvin looked down at his feet. Ernie's remark stung.

Thinking out loud, Marvin said, "Well, I'm thinking I will go talk with her to see if I can make her understand that the piece is mine. If she doesn't want to listen, maybe I'll go to the Navajo Nation press to see if they can put pressure on her, write some big article."

"Be careful," Ernie warned. "She was a bad person when we were kids, and I doubt much has changed her black heart. But if you do go, snoop around the house. Maybe my blanket is there too."

"I promise I'll look around to see if your blanket is there. Who knows? Maybe by next week I'll have two old squash blossoms around my neck."

"Yeah—or a noose," Ernie retorted.

Both men sat quietly and thought of the possibilities, all of which seemed to carry significant risk—and the potential to end badly.

CHAPTER 26

THE BIG TRADE

Rachael was amazed at the amount of detritus five hundred Navajo could leave in one day—not that the after-party mess was unexpected. Bloom, Rachael, and Ruth all were on trash duty starting at 8:30 a.m. Half of the pumpkins were gone and only a few of those remaining were still intact. Candy wrappers floated in the wind until they caught on juniper branches; the nearby trees now looked as if they were in some weird winter bloom, with their flowers—of course—all above human reach.

The half-eaten hamburgers, bits of hot dogs and mushy buns scattered around the grounds were being devoured by the hungry rez dogs that had found their way to the post from the surrounding houses—and the occasional "CAH" reverberated as the ravens swooped in to get their fair share. The post's resident cat was so full of leftovers that she could barely stand; sprawled on the porch, she ignored the pesky canine and avian visitors altogether.

"Another successful party," Bloom thought as he looked out at the work awaiting his attention.

By 10 a.m. the trio was making serious headway. Ruth seemed to be enjoying the process of picking up trash and organizing the garbage into piles. Bloom was sure he could keep Ruth employed if she wanted a job, which would also help relations with Mrs. Bennally, the Bloom family's unpaid babysitter and longtime Yellowhorse neighbor.

Bloom knew Ruth had some emotional issues and didn't form relationships with men easily. She was past forty and had never been married, but she was a good worker and smart enough to be an asset to the post. Rachael had expressed some concerns as Ruth had a tendency to spend money that came her way on bootleg liquor, purchased from individuals she didn't want around, but she was willing to give Ruth a chance if she could stay sober.

Marvin was usually at the post by 9:30 a.m. and today Bloom was waiting anxiously for his grand prizewinner to make an appearance for ice cream and small talk, but the Navajo was a no-show. Bloom didn't want to admit that he was worried, but he did understand that Marvin had a life of his own—even if it was one that revolved around the trading post.

"He probably went to show all his friends his necklace," Bloom said to Ruth, who didn't seem the least bit concerned.

"Maybe he overate and slept in," Bloom hypothesized, knowing this explanation was far-fetched.

Rachael, who was tying up the last sack of trash, recognized her husband's concern. "Bloom," she said, "if you're worried, drive down and check his hogan. I'm sure he's fine, but if it makes you feel better I'll watch the post." Bloom considered this option, and decided not to be Marvin's keeper.

"No, he's a grown man and I'm not his dad. Marvin will show up when he wants to. If he hasn't come around in a couple of days I'll go check his place out," Bloom said, trying to convince himself that Marvin's business was his own and that he shouldn't care that much.

✳ ✳ ✳ ✳

Marvin hadn't slept well for two nights running. The little sleep he did get was in short fits and always accompanied by a nightmare. In his dreams, he was transported back to Vietnam, struggling to escape the jungle's grip—and when he did finally escape, he was twelve again, trapped in Soliday's box and fighting to survive.

"See what some Navajo boy left? Not a very good silversmith, is he? Ha ha ha—it's mine now!"

Soliday's taunting words had awakened Marvin from his fitful sleep, his sheets drenched in sweat, as they had often been when he was a child in boarding school.

What could he do? There was no evidence the Slender Maker piece was his necklace, no photos or bill of sale, and nearly sixty years had passed. It had been in Matchstick Woman's collection since 1961, and there were probably dozens of photos of her wearing the piece over the years. The old "finders-keepers" rule judges liked in this part of the West would come into play. He had limited options, and those were what kept Marvin at home, thinking out the possible ways he could get his father's necklace back and making notes about how to proceed:

> 1) Talk to Matchstick Woman, see if she might understand. She's old, maybe she has no one to leave the piece to.
>
> 2) Break in and take it, like Soliday took it from me.
>
> 3) Hire a professional to take it.
>
> 4) Take care of Matchstick Woman in some other way.

The fourth option worried him. He was a decorated war hero. Was he also capable of taking out an elderly woman for a piece of jewelry? How she obtained the necklace from Soliday was also not clear.

Maybe Soliday and Pingry worked as a team and those crosses in the cemetery were part of her sick legacy. Could she be a thief and a killer of children? If this was possible, then anything Marvin had to do to get the necklace back was also a possibility.

Talking to Ernie the day before brought the painful school experience to the surface. Ongoing deep-seated anger about the loss of his family's blanket and signing the bill of sale under duress was still current history for Ernie Yazzie. Marvin knew he would do it all over again if confronted with that exact situation. Ernie wasn't in that room with Soliday; he couldn't know how deadly serious that deranged man's intentions were.

Marvin would need to travel this road by himself. Ernie was a wild card, one that might go ballistic if he confronted Matchstick Woman, making his fourth solution a reality—especially if she happened to have Ernie's blanket.

This was not something Marvin was willing to risk. Ernie had been to jail once and, if he exploded from his pent-up rage, murder would be a real possibility. It wouldn't take much to kill a woman of Pingry's age, so he would visit Matchstick Woman by himself and see what she had to say. Then he had a brilliant idea.

"What if I trade my squash blossom for hers?" he thought. "She will know it's not an equal trade, but if she believes my story, she might feel that it's the only right thing to do."

For the first time that day he felt as if he had some hope. Winning the squash blossom and encountering Matchstick Woman at the drawing was an omen. "Maybe this was how it was supposed to play out," he thought.

Little could Marvin know there were other forces at play that day—and that the outcome was anything but preordained.

CHAPTER 27

REVENGE

Billy Moss crept back to Farmington after darkness fell, his precious motorcycle's front wheel wobbling through the entire sixty-mile trip. The drive gave Moss time to brood about his options. Bloom was number one on his short shit list. The trader had humiliated him in front of many of his own Navajo clients, not to mention his two buddies. And, on top of it all, Bloom had cheated him out of a $2,500 necklace. Men got killed over much less than that.

A list of reasons he should destroy Bloom were running through Moss's mind.

"I had the winning number and Bloom changed the rules at the last minute. On top of that scam, his SON pulled the winning ticket—and who won the necklace? Marvin Manycoats, who is a friend or employee. I saw Manycoats cooking hamburgers and laughing with Bloom. They were close. And Bloom was the only one to actually see the winning number; the whole thing was probably one big scam."

By the time Moss parked his motorcycle, he had concluded the raffle was rigged and someone was going to pay. What would be the best way to screw with Bloom's business? He would start with Ruth—she was low-hanging fruit, and would no longer be selling rugs for Charles Bloom. Moss had other plans for Ruth.

Next order of the day was to retrieve the raffled squash blossom from Manycoats. If he could, he would destroy the Navajo. Bloom clearly liked the man, who was probably part of the ruse. This would hit at the heart of Charles Bloom. Finding out where Manycoats lived wouldn't be hard; figuring out how to get his squash blossom back would take some planning.

The third person on his shit list was a tangential causality of the Halloween party—Mary Pingry. As it turned out, Moss had a long history with the old woman. She had been his stepfather's serious girlfriend back in the day, and had even become his aunty—a childhood relationship that had endured through adulthood, though the two weren't as close anymore.

His stepfather had once blabbed, when he was stumbling drunk, about how he should never have given Pingry that necklace. He had made a big mistake because it was worth a lot, made by Slender Maker, the celebrated silversmith. Moss had chalked the talk up to a drunk's bravado and regret about the pieces that had gotten away—something Moss could understand being in the pawn business.

Moss had never seen Pingry wear a squash blossom, but even a glimpse of it through the crowd told him the piece was magnificent and old. Maybe the old man had given her an early Slender Maker necklace after all. He would conduct a reconnaissance mission and find out what he could about the necklace. There was a hole in his museum collection and he had plans to fill his early necklaces category—not just with one squash blossom necklace, but two! It was only a matter of logistics and ruthlessness, characteristics Moss didn't lack when it came to acquiring Indian artifacts.

✤ ✤ ✤ ✤

Ruth Bennally was at her usual place near the front entrance off the Highway 491 Shell station and the Highway 16 cutoff to Toadlena, papers in hand, rocks at the ready. The piles of small pebbles displaced by truck tracks over the last couple of days were being aggressively reorganized into rock pile arrangements to Ruth's liking, and she was ignoring a customer wanting to buy a paper.

"Hey, Ruth, I want a paper," Moss yelled for the second time from the front seat of his new Ram pickup truck. He had watched her sort through rocks before when he had stopped for gas; she was perfect for the job he had in mind. Ruth didn't seem to recognize him even though most everyone at the party had watched the slow dismembering of Billy Moss at the hands of Charles Bloom.

"That's $2."

"How about I give you $5 and we talk for a minute or two?" Moss offered.

"Well, OK. What you want to talk about?"

"Hop in, I'm not going to bite. I'm Billy Moss. I own the pawnshop and trading post in Farmington. You probably heard of the place?"

"Yeah, I heard of it. Never been there though. I don't got no truck, so I pretty much stick close to my house."

"Well, how about you come work for me? I think you have a special talent a man like me can use."

"What's that?" Ruth asked. Moss now had her full attention.

"From what I gather you really are good at detail work, sorting and the like. Let's say I gave you a group of small rocks to sort. I'm sure you could do that task, couldn't you?"

"Oh sure. I like to do that. It makes me feel good. Don't know why, it just does."

"Well, turns out I got thousands of little rocks that need sorting. I'm looking for someone special and it takes a fine eye and lots of patience to do this task. Turns out not many people, even very smart ones, can do this job."

"Really?" Ruth said, excited to hear he put her in the "smart people" category.

"Most definitely, and I'm going to pay you $10 an hour, meals, and drinks included. It'll be hard to beat that offer—it's way better than selling papers or folding rugs up at the Toadlena Trading Post. What do you say, Ruth?"

"OK, sounds good. When do we start this job?"

"How about right now? I'm going to take you to a special place where you can get started. It's not that far from here. In fact, I've already put you on the clock. Here's $10. Go inside and get yourself a Coke and sandwich and we'll get started."

Ruth grabbed the money and hopped out of Billy Moss's truck. He had plans all right—and none of them ended well for Ruth Bennally.

CHAPTER 28

WHERE'S RUTH?

Rachael's anxiety was building. Her hózhó healing ceremony was only weeks away; she was ready to return to weaving and the sing was an important part of that process.

Watching her young daughter assisting Mrs. Bennally at her loom gave Rachael hope that Sam might channel the gifts of Spider Woman. Her daughter would mimic the actions of the weaving comb as it methodically beat of the weft, and she would point at Bennally's loom to add more yarn and offer a color choice. The small balls of yarn she handed the Grandmother as possibilities were often the correct ones.

Sam's interest and aptitude made Bennally feel complete. Her daughter Ruth was not given the gift of weaving, though she did have other unique talents, even if others didn't recognize them. Ruth could work on a task to the point of forgetting to eat or drink. She had compassion for animals and the less fortunate, although her empathy could cause problems, such as drinking with others who begged her to join their drunken party. Ruth desperately wanted to be a part of something, even if that something would destroy her self-respect.

Mrs. Bennally was worried. She hadn't seen or talked with Ruth in two days. This was not unheard of—especially if Ruth went on a drinking jag—but she had hoped that the trading post might be a new refuge for her daughter under Rachael's and Bloom's watchful eyes. Bloom had mentioned to the mother that he thought Ruth would do a great job in the rug room and cleaning up, but then her daughter went off the radar. She had checked her usual haunts, including staking out the Shell station, but no one could remember seeing Ruth recently.

Finally, she told Rachael of her concerns when she came to pick up Sam after helping Bloom close the post.

"Rachael, I haven't seen Ruth in quite a few days and I'm starting to worry. I know she's a grown woman but you know she can be like a child at times. You haven't heard from her, have you?"

Rachael looked at the old woman with a worried expression on her face. "Sorry, I haven't. In fact, Bloom asked me the very same question yesterday. He really appreciated all that Ruth had done for him at the party and was wondering if she might want some part-time work."

"Oh, that's so nice of you. She's a good woman you know, not lazy, except for when she's running with that bootlegger crowd. I'm afraid that's where she is now. Maybe you could ask around and see what you can find out. I'm her mother so no one is going to tell me anything."

"I can do some checking around for you. I'll drop Sam off early tomorrow morning and see if we can't run her down."

"Thank you so much. If you find Ruth, tell her I love her and I'm not mad—even if she's drunk. I don't care, I just want her to come home so we can try again."

Rachael smiled sympathetically. Having raised her brother's child, Preston, like her own son, she remembered all too well those times he didn't come home when he was supposed to. She could only imagine what days without speaking to Ruth must feel like for Mrs. Bennally.

What Rachael couldn't know was that Ruth's predicament was about to get much worse than she could ever imagine.

※ ※ ※ ※

Tommy Jackson lived in a small traditional hogan near public housing a few miles from the Toadlena Trading Post. The beaten-down dirt driveway was littered with beer and wine bottles—a welcome mat of sorts for his clients. Liquor is illegal on the Navajo Nation, but it is common practice that people drink there—often in excess. Rachael knew Jackson's history and where he lived, and she thought if anyone knew where Ruth was, it would be him.

Jackson was a longtime bootlegger and alcoholic who supported his drinking habit by serving as the go-between for the liquor stores in Gallup and Farmington and the local population. He had lost his drivers license long ago to a plethora of DWIs, so now he would hitchhike into town, drink, buy numerous 40s, and stuff his backpack with his inventory to distribute at a small profit to the less industrious alcoholics on the rez.

In a different world, Jackson could have been a successful entrepreneur, building a thriving business by meeting the needs of the people around him, but this was the rez, and the best Jackson could hope for was to skim some minor profits off sure deals—like selling raffle tickets to a buyer you knew would pay for them or booze to longtime fellow drunks.

Poverty was a huge barrier to entering the business world, and many Navajo dropped out of school before finishing their education. Jackson had a ninth-grade education. Jobs on the rez were scarce even for those who completed high school, mainly limited to working for the government, farming, ranching, retail, arts and crafts, or bootlegging. Most Navajo men look younger than their chronological age, but not Tommy Jackson. He looked every minute of his forty-two years. He had known Ruth since grade school and had been her primary source of alcohol for most of her life, a fact Rachael knew.

The bootlegger's dirt road desperately needed grading. Two separate trails had been forged by drinking buddies trying to avoid the monstrous potholes in the central track, and the house was no better. Jackson had been left the place by his mother, who also drank heavily. There were no more Jackson family members to inherit the house, so he simply let it go.

Assuming he would be sleeping off last night's festivities, it was midmorning when Rachael showed up at Jackson's front door. She knocked loudly on the crooked screen door. No answer. She banged again, this time yelling for Tommy to come to the door. Finally, the 6-foot, 3-inch 265-pound man lumbered to the door. His size was impressive by any standards, but it didn't seem to faze Rachael in the least; she had dealt with his type before.

"Tommy, this is Rachael Yellowhorse. You know who I am, right?" Rachael stared up into the sleepy giant's bloodshot eyes.

"Uh, huh. You Preston's mom, right?"

"Yes, that's right." She was actually Preston's aunt, but most around Toadlena equated her role raising him to mom.

"What you want, Rachael? Last time I seen you was at Willy's smiling party. That was some fun, but would have been better with beer." Jackson smiled knowing he was pushing Rachael's buttons; at least his long-term memory was still intact.

"That's right, Willy's five now, time goes fast." Talking about the subtleties of time seemed funny to Rachael's Diné sensibilities, but Tommy would understand.

"Time is a bitch out here on the rez that's for sure," Tommy replied.

"Tommy, I'm looking for Ruth Bennally. You happen to see her in the last few days? I've got a job for her and, well, she hasn't been around.

I was expecting her. Do you think she on a bender?" With an alcoholic like Tommy, being straightforward was the best strategy.

"No, I haven't seen her. She's been pretty good lately, not hitting the bottle like before. If you want, I can ask around—maybe the competition been filling in for me."

"I would appreciate that, Tommy. Here's my number if you find out anything. Do you have a phone?" Rachael handed him one of her old business cards from Bloom's.

"Yeah, I got a phone. I need it for business." Tommy smiled widely, showing that one of his front teeth was missing. "That's a fancy card, Rachael. Nice to see someone on the rez is doing OK. You need any drinks?" Tommy had to ask even if he already knew the answer.

"Not for me. I hear it's illegal out here."

"Yeah, I heard the same thing." Tommy laughed and let the screen door slam shut.

※ ※ ※ ※

That evening Rachael got a call from Tommy Jackson. Ruth had not been drinking with any other bootlegger, but she had been seen at the Shell station last week, getting food and heading off with Billy Moss in his truck, and she hadn't been seen since. Apparently, the two appeared to be friendly toward each other, smiling and such. Jackson hypothesized that Moss offered her a deal she couldn't refuse; maybe they were shacking up together or something along those lines.

Rachael thanked Tommy and told him he could come by the post and her husband would give him a couple of fresh sandwiches for his efforts. Tommy promised he would let her know if anything else turned up; free food was always a good incentive on the rez.

Rachael was worried. Billy Moss was not a happy camper. When he left Toadlena he had been threatening to her husband. Her inner voice was screaming that something was amiss, and all signs pointed toward Moss Pawn and Trading Post, Farmington, New Mexico.

CHAPTER 29

DINNER TALK

Rachael's pacing from pot to oven and back was starting to wear on Bloom.

"Rachael, everything will be fine. Preston will eat a peanut butter and jelly sandwich if that's all you have. You need to chill," Bloom grumbled.

"I know, I know, but I haven't seen him since August and now he's got a real job AND is going to assist Hastiin Johnson with my sing. This is the first time he's come to visit us as a real man, and I want everything to be just so."

Rachael's eyes started to well up with tears. Bloom got up from the dining room table and went over to her.

"Honey, I know this is important, but he's only twenty-two. My guess is that he will be late, so there is plenty of time to get everything prepared. Do you know if he's going to stay here or with Hastiin Johnson?"

"He didn't say. He said they were going to go over the medicine for my ceremony this weekend, and that he needed that old gourd that I love so much—you know, the one I dragged out to Santa Fe and back. I guess it's part of my treatment."

A loud smack of the screen door signaled that Preston was home.

"So much for plenty of time," Rachael muttered, giving Bloom her, "I told you so" look.

"Preston, you're early. Dinner's going to be another thirty minutes."

"Hi, Aunty Rachael. How's it hanging?" Preston was needling Rachael as he usually called her Mom.

"Aunty, huh..." Rachael said, waiting for a proper greeting.

"OK, how about patient Yellowhorse?" Preston giggled.

"You brat!" Rachael bear-hugged the skinny young man who was no bigger than he was last year.

"Tell me first off why you aren't eating—and second how's the job and the shadowing of Hastiin Johnson going?"

"I'm eating lots of PB and J, with ramen on the weekends. There is no time to cook with real work and medicine man apprentice duty, and you can forget dating. But I did manage to make something for your jewelry case, Bloom." Preston smiled as he pulled out a heavy ingot silver bracelet with a triangle-shaped, high-grade turquoise cab.

"NOW THAT'S AN ENTRY," Bloom said, eyeing the bracelet.

"I went old school on you, thought it might do better out here at the post than the fancy Santa Fe digs. What do you think I can retail the piece for?" Preston said, utterly forgetting Rachael and the smell of his favorite mutton stew.

"I'd say $950. It's a nice piece and you can net $600." Bloom said, slipping the bracelet on his wrist. "And it fits! That means I can sell it," Bloom smiled.

"Intel has some retooling in my department so they offered me a three-week vacation, unpaid of course. I jumped on the offer, so guess what? I'm here!" Preston said gleefully.

"That's great. You can either have the couch or bunk with the kids. It's your choice, but I would recommend the couch—more room and less noise," Rachael advised.

"Couch it is. This will give me time to work on your treatment and maybe knock out a bracelet or two if I can find a bench that will lend me some tools. All my stuff is back in Albuquerque."

"I'm sure we can find you some tools and see if you can't bring in more money making jewelry than at that old chip plant. You're a great silversmith—don't you ever forget that."

"Thanks, Mom, but in two years, I will be making close to $80K, and I don't think I can make that much beso, even if I'm the best silversmith at Bloom's."

Rachael thought about his argument. "True enough, but remember it's a great skill set to have once you start a family, extra money and all that."

"OK, enough with the family talk. I don't even have a girl yet, but I understand where you're coming from. Lots of my shoes came from Grandmothers' rugs."

"Tennis shoes, Christmas gifts, my first truck—yes, lots of things," Rachael agreed.

The family sat down for a delicious meal, and after the kids were put to bed, the three of them discussed the goings on around the post, including all of Bloom's early mistakes. Preston couldn't believe

Bloom was so green that he would try and switch out the Blue Bird flour. "Rookie mistake," he said.

Preston was proud that Bloom had stuck up for the Navajo and let the white trader feel like crap for a change. He didn't like Moss, even though he had never met him.

Rachael got around to talking about her meeting with Jackson and information he had come up with.

Bloom was not pleased. "Rachael, you can't go to a guy like Tommy Jackson's house alone. That's just not safe and I'm not happy," he said in a stern voice.

"I can't, huh? Let me tell you, Charles Bloom, I've handled a lot worse than Jackson. Don't forget I'm from here; they know me and are more afraid of me than you!"

Bloom shriveled in his chair. He knew when she called him Charles Bloom he was in trouble and Preston knew it too. Both the men in the family squirmed.

"OK, you're right. I'm sorry. It's just that I would be crushed if anything else happened to you. Please promise you will let me know if you plan on doing something like that again."

Now it was Rachael's turn to feel bad. Her husband was still traumatized by her ordeal in Santa Fe last August when she was almost killed—so her visit to Jackson had direct consequences on him too.

"I'm sorry. I promise I will let you know next time. But, on the bright side, I did get some information about Ruth: the last person she was seen with was our friend Billy Moss."

Bloom's faced soured. "Not that guy again. What do you think he's up to? My guess is it has to do with us. He's got it out for me now and maybe he thinks Ruth works at the post or, even worse, maybe he knows Mrs. Bennally is our sitter."

Preston had listened to the entire discussion and decided it was time to add his voice to the conversation.

"How about I go up to Farmington and find out what he's up to. Maybe I'll see Ruth there. I know what she looks like; I drank with her back in my wild unemployed days."

It was Rachael's turn to make a sour face. Bloom chimed in before Rachael could say anything.

"That would be great, Preston. He doesn't know you, so you can go snoop around. I know he's looking for a bench silversmith—maybe tell him you're looking for a little extra work."

"No fricking way, Charles Bloom!" Rachael exploded. "I'm not having Preston acting as a spy. You don't know anything about this Moss guy."

"First you want me to get married and have kids," Preston countered, "and now you're saying I am a kid. Which is it, Aunt Rachael? I believe I'm old enough to handle this—and it's my idea, not Bloom's."

Rachael didn't like the Aunty Rachael jab this go around either, but realized she was in the wrong. Preston was a man and she had to let him go. After all, the meal she had fixed tonight was to celebrate the fact he was now a grown-up.

"You're right. I'm sorry, again... but keep me in the loop. That man Moss could affect this whole family and not in a good way."

"I promise I will stay in touch, and I'll be careful," Preston said. "By the way, Bloom, I'll need my bracelet back. I need something to show the guy that I really am a silversmith. Who knows? Maybe he can get me more for this piece."

Everyone laughed as Bloom reluctantly dropped a sure sale into Preston's front pocket.

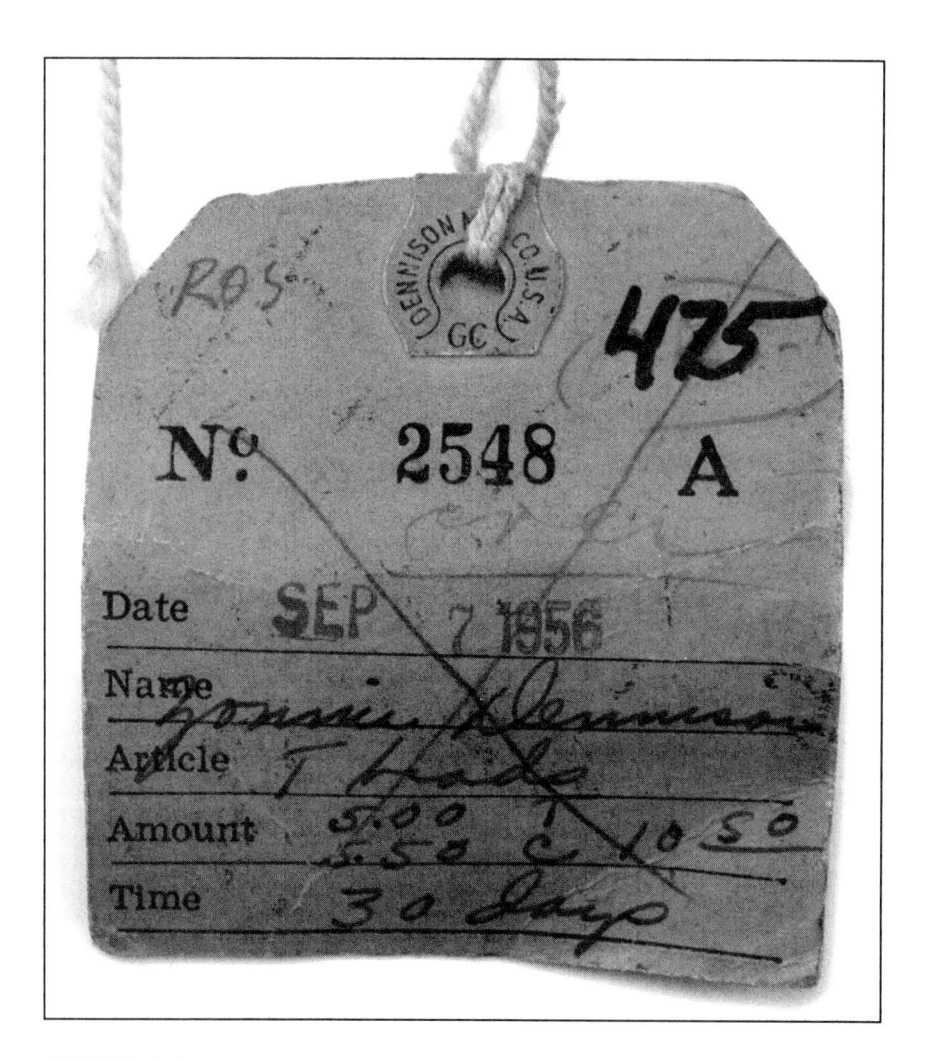

CHAPTER 30

NO ONE IS THE WISER

Moss Pawn and Trading Post looked like an old Western movie set, complete with a dilapidated frontier-style wagon, two large Mexican grinding stones, and a badly weathered oversized teepee. The turquoise luster on the sign had faded to gray in the harsh northern New Mexico weather. Parking was generous—as were the ruts that had become a permanent fixture in the landscape.

Stores like Moss's dotted the outskirts of the Navajo Nation, looking to take pawn from poor Indians in need of fast money. The inside of Moss's post was filled with worn-out saddles, tack, out-of-date electronics and the obligatory turn-of-the-century oak display case filled with not-so-old pawn jewelry.

Preston walked through the front door and waited for his eyes to adjust to the dark interior. Two older women were looking at DVDs and speaking in Navajo about the poor selection. There appeared to be only one store employee, and no sign of Billy or Ruth. The person behind the counter was a middle-aged white woman with a prominent belly peeking out from under a tee shirt that read, "I've seen better days." Her crookedly pinned yellow nametag read, "Jane. Ask me if you need help."

"Yá át ééh. You looking for anything in particular?" Jane asked in a sharp western twang, barely making eye contact with Preston. "Got something to pawn?"

"Well, I heard you might be hiring a bench silversmith. I'm pretty good with the metal and could use the extra work."

"Yeah, Mr. Moss is looking for a good man to work the back bench. Can you repair as well as make jewelry?" Jane was now fully engaged.

"I can do about anything if I have good tools and supplies. You want to see one of my bracelets?" Preston pulled the heavy ingot piece out of his front pocket and handed it to Jane.

"Wow, that's nice. If I hadn't seen your maker's mark, I would have thought it was an old bracelet heading for the Moss museum." She pointed toward the museum with her lips in Navajo fashion.

"It's not old, just the kind of jewelry I like to make. Your museum looks nice. Mind if I take a peek?"

"Sure, just lift the chain. We usually charge a dollar, but seeing how you might work here, I'll let you in for free." Jane knew anyone rarely paid, but saying they charged a fee made the Moss museum like a Santa Fe gallery instead of a vanity display in a two-bit pawn shop.

"Nice pawn. Lots of good old jewelry, the kind they like in Santa Fe, huh?" Preston asked as he stuck his nose close to the Plexiglass displays. Jane came out from behind the counter and stood near Preston, trying to get a read on the man.

"Yeah. Billy don't sell this museum stuff, though plenty of folks have tried to buy it in the past. We just can't find the old material anymore; all the Navajos done sold it off years ago. They tell me the heyday was back in the 1960s. If I could go back in time, I'd buy up everything," Jane said.

Preston thought he wouldn't buy Navajo jewelry. It would be better to go after San Francisco property or an Andy Warhol painting.

"Where did all the old Nasazi pieces come from? You know we Navajo try to avoid this stuff."

"Oh, I know. Most of the Navajo just look at the jewelry and baskets. I don't know where Billy gets all that crap. He inherited a small ranch near Gallup, and I know some of it came from there. My guess is it just comes from all over; you can't spit without hitting some kind of ruin around these parts."

Preston nodded affirmatively, knowing she was right. On Rachael's land alone there were a half-dozen untouched Anasazi ruins. The Navajo avoided these places and would never consider digging for pots, knowing they would be angering the chindi.

"You know when Mr. Moss will be back?"

"Billy should be back by noon and here until around until 5 p.m. If you want, you can leave the bracelet and I'll show it to him. Give me a cell number where he can reach you and you can come back in to talk."

Preston knew better than to leave a $950 ingot bracelet with someone named Jane and made a different suggestion.

"How about you take some photos with your phone. That way, Mr. Moss will get the idea, and he can call me if he likes what he sees, and I don't have to come back to pick up my bracelet if he's not interested." Jane's lips turned down, but she agreed and took some photos with her cheap personal cell phone.

On the way out the door Preston stopped and asked, "How many employees you got here? Seems like a pretty big place for just one person to handle."

"I'm the only employee. Me and Billy can handle the load most days. He's got a new girl assisting him with personal stuff, but she don't help with the store."

"So I would only have to make or repair jewelry and not sell anything or take in pawn?"

"Yeah, pretty much. Maybe help out on occasion, answer a ringing phone or such, but you're worth more making jewelry than selling—especially with the quality of the work you showed me."

"Great. I'll wait for Mr. Moss to call."

As Preston walked to his car he considered the possibilities: "The assistant must be Ruth," he thought, "maybe I should have asked Jane her name, but she could get suspicious of such an odd question, so it's better I didn't. I'll just have to hope I get the call back from Moss—then I can press harder."

Preston was hungry and headed into town for a bite.

※ ※ ※ ※

When Billy Moss walked into the shop at noon beads of sweat were visible along his hatband. He pulled a Dr. Pepper from the store's refrigerator and threw the $1 plastic cap in the trash as he plopped down in his favorite chair.

"Jane, I must have walked six miles today. I'm sure glad it's only forty degrees outside. You make me any money? I could use a nice hit; seems like all I'm doing is spending these days."

"Well, you might have to spend a little more. I had a Navajo guy come in an hour ago, couldn't be more than twenty-four years old, looking for work as a bench silversmith. I think he's a keeper."

"Why do you say that? He show you his work? Did he leave me anything to look at?"

"He had one piece, but it was a doozy." Jane pulled out her flip phone and showed Moss the photos.

"You have to be the worst photographer in the world. These photos aren't for shit. How about getting a smartphone? It's the twenty-first century, don't you know," Moss said, not bothering to hide his frustration.

"I noticed you don't have NO phone. How about you giving me a raise or better yet buy us a decent store phone, and you'll start getting good photos," Jane shot back.

Moss ignored her as he usually did. "You sure he made this? It looks like an old ingot piece, maybe from the 1920s?"

"I know, I thought so too, but you can kinda see his mark right here, P.Y. with the little horse emblem next to his initials. That's a new bracelet and he said he made it. I watched how he acted and the questions he asked seemed legit to me."

"Hmmm, who is this kid? You know him or his relatives?" Moss was intrigued by the possibilities.

"He wrote his name down and a phone number. It's a New Mexico area code. I didn't ask his last name. Sorry," Jane apologized, knowing Moss would be pissed.

"Damn it, Jane. How many time have I told you to get their name, phone number, and email, girl."

"I know, I'm sorry."

"Well, I'll give the kid a call. I'd love to have him make me a bunch more of these ingot bracelets, but he's got to lose the initials." Moss laughed and Jane joined in, knowing that they would sell the pieces as old bracelets and no one would be the wiser.

CHAPTER 31

NO SIGNATURE, PLEASE

Preston got the call back from Moss as he bit into a scalding hot barbeque sandwich from the Farmington DQ. He wasn't up to driving to Toadlena just to turn around and come back to Farmington to meet with Moss.

Preston remembered being a kid and thinking that Farmington was such a big city, with so many restaurants and three theaters. A few months in Albuquerque had jaded him. Having everything nearby at a moment's notice made him appreciate his DQ sandwich even more. What was truly important was home and the family that surrounded him at night.

"Is this Preston?" the voice on the other line asked.

"Yes, this is Preston. How can I help you?" Preston knew the call was from Moss, but wanted to sound professional—not an easy job when his mouth was dripping beef juice.

"You were in my store an hour ago and it looks like you're a damned good silversmith. Anyway, you can you come back in and show me that bracelet, and we can talk about you working as a bench silversmith?"

"Sure, I'm just around the corner on Main Street finishing my lunch. How about I come by in, say, thirty minutes?"

"Perfect, that sounds great. By the way, what's your last name? I didn't see it in the paper you left Jane."

Preston hesitated before replying, "Yellowhorse. It's one of those common Navajo last names, kind of like Begay, but you already know that."

"Yes, I do. See you soon." Moss replied.

Billy Moss knew Yellowhorse was fairly common, but it wasn't like Begay or Yazzie; it was more like Tsosie or Nez, and he wondered who the man's relatives were. If he was a keeper, Moss might want to delve more deeply into the kid's past. The trader understood that on the reservation you're dealing with not only the person you hire, but all his or her relatives too.

Preston worried he had hesitated too long before giving Moss his last name. He hadn't thought this part out, and being a successful spy took some forethought. He decided he would give the man his dad's family's lineage if he wanted more names. If Moss did find out that Rachael was his mom, he would deal with the Bloom fallout by saying, "A kid needs to work regardless of who his parents are, don't you think?"—at least that was Preston's plan for now.

This second time he walked into the Moss Pawn and Trading Post, there was no Jane, just Moss sitting in his chair sharpening a huge hunting knife. Moss figured the kid had to be Preston, so he laid the blade on the table, stood up and introduced himself.

"Nice to meet you, Preston. Have a seat."

"Thanks. Nice place you got here. Love your museum; you got some great jewelry in there."

Moss smiled. The museum was his baby and he liked that the kid could recognize quality.

"Thanks, Preston. I do love the old pawn stuff and I must admit those photos of your bracelet that Jane showed me say you're not too bad, either. You do know that as a bench silversmith you make minimum wage and I get all the pieces, right? But I do provide the materials and tools," Moss said, looking to see if the kid understood the position.

"Sure, I know that's the case for most silversmiths, but you've seen my work and you and I both know you will do great with my jewelry. It takes me a while to make one piece, but these are not your average-grade bench bracelets."

Preston handed over his bracelet for Moss to evaluate. "I would think that is a $950 bracelet, don't you, Mr. Moss?" Preston asked as Moss looked at the piece carefully, examining the backside for the small telltale lines of cracking silver that said the piece was made out of ingot using old-style silversmithing methods.

"Ingot, huh, with cold chisel stamp work?" Moss looked up for the first time.

"Yes, that's right, old style. But I can do more contemporary pieces too...." Preston offered.

"No, I like this work just fine. It might go for $950 in Santa Fe but out here it's $650 tops—and that's still damned good money for a bracelet."

"Well, we agree to disagree, but the main thing is it's good work, right? Better than what you'd get from your average bench silversmith?"

"Yes, you're right, Preston. It is better—so what are you proposing?"

"How about you pay me minimum wage and when a piece sells, I get 15 percent of the sales price. You will still make a lot of money and it gets me some extra cash that I can use now." Preston watched for Moss's reaction.

"It's more than I have ever paid a smith, but I must admit you're not average." Moss stuck out his hand to shake on the deal. Preston responded and Billy squeezed his hand hard—not in the Navajo weak-grip way, but like a white man showing who was the boss.

"Follow me and I'll show you where you can work. Can you start tomorrow?"

"Sure, I can be here when you open, or even little earlier if you need me."

"Great. Tomorrow at 10 a.m. is fine."

Moss gave Preston a tour of the back of the store. He would have a large, hand-wrought mesquite table to use as a workbench, all the necessary tools and a large number of old stamps and dyes. It was more than adequate. Preston noticed a back room that looked like a bedroom, and headed over to see what was there.

Moss stopped him just as he was about to look in.

"That's just an old guest room I sometimes use for friends who've had too much to drink. Your work area is limited to this large back room," Moss said, trying to divert Preston's attention. It was clear that someone was living in the room. The bed was wrinkled, clothes were folded in the corner, and a stack of gum wrappers were piled near the dressing room table. It was the wrappers that intrigued Preston; they were neatly arranged in pyramid fashion, something Ruth Bennally would do.

Preston wondered if she were living in that room. "OK," he said lightheartedly. "I'll keep to the workroom, but if I get drunk I know where I can flop."

"No drinking here. You do that on your own time," Moss replied, not getting the joke.

"And by the way, since you're making the jewelry for my store, I don't want any of your silversmith initials on the pieces. I'll give them the Moss Trading Post stamp later. You know, promote my own brand," Moss said with a sly smile on his face.

Preston knew the crooked dealer was going to try to sell his pieces as old pawn, and he had no intention of putting a trading post stamp on the bracelets, but that was OK. Preston wouldn't be working there long enough to complete a single piece or get a paycheck. Both men had their own agendas—but only one would work out as planned.

※ ※ ※ ※

Bloom's workday was particularly lucrative. Sales always made Bloom happy and today he was beaming. The Western art patrons from the Smoki Museum in Prescott, Arizona, had visited. The small but energetic group had listened intently as Bloom discussed the story of the post and its weavers and he sold four expensive rugs and a nice row bracelet. A good day's work.

There was no doubt that Rachael was the one who made the rug sales happen. She could talk about the time it took to weave a Toadlena/Two Grey Hills rug, and the energy and skill needed to prepare the wool and spin and card it before even beginning to weave. After making the sales, Rachael felt her job was done and she went home early to spend time with Sam and Willy and give them a lesson on caring for sheep.

There had been no word from Ruth Bennally and her mother was getting worried. Rachael was worried too; she did not like Preston playing spy with a man like Moss.

Over a meal of leftover lamb stew and sourdough biscuits, Preston told Rachael and Bloom the story of Moss, the empty bedroom that looked lived in, and the pyramid of wrappers piled in the guest bedroom. "And they don't stamp the bracelets with your mark," he added.

Bloom now despised Moss and warned Preston to be very careful with the man. If he would fake jewelry, he might be willing to do anything for money.

Bloom wondered if it were time to call in the local tribal police to look into Ruth's disappearance, but Preston convinced Rachael and Charles that he could handle the situation. Working there for a few days, he should be able to find out something about Ruth. "Not to worry," he joked. "She isn't missing—she just hasn't been found yet."

Bloom encouraged Preston to complete a bracelet and leave it at the post so Moss couldn't come back and say the silversmith hadn't kept up his end of the bargain. He also suggested Preston engrave the back of the piece so it was clear it was a new bracelet. Preston didn't like the idea of giving one of his bracelets away for nothing, but agreed with Bloom that since he was there to help Ruth, his payment would come in the currency of good karma.

Rachael's stomach hurt thinking about the whole scenario. She hoped Preston was right that Ruth was safe and that working for Moss wasn't putting her son in any danger. She decided to keep a close watch on the situation and considered making her own visit to Moss's place if need be. She had tended sheep as a young girl and knew how to sit for long hours, watch for trouble, and act if needed.

CHAPTER 32

ANT BEADS FOR THE TAKING

Two days had passed since Marvin's unexpected visit to Ernie with news about Matchstick Woman and the Slender Maker squash blossom. In his dreams, Ernie had flashed back to his Indian school days: once again, he was escaping in the trunk of Soliday's car, then running and running with nowhere to go. Today he decided he had to visit Matchstick Woman—not to socialize, but to get some answers.

Marvin had given him the address, so this would be a one-man operation, like hunting a mountain lion. Go in and look around. If his blanket were there, he would take what belonged to him; if not, so be it. If the old lady were around, maybe he could make her talk. He hoped that seeing Matchstick Woman wouldn't trigger some deeply repressed well of anger that would make him strike out. That was a chance he was willing to take and a possibility he couldn't predict or control.

To formulate a plan, he needed to think—and the best way for Ernie to think was to build a new wall. He needed a fresh supply of flat rocks to carry out an idea he had for a rock fireplace that required lots of smaller-sized stones, the kind most easily found around Indian ruins. There was a ruin hidden in an isolated slot canyon just out of view of his property that had the materials he needed: a large cluster of Nasazi ruins and a few scattered early stone Navajo hogans embedded in the south-facing canyon ridge, all in different stages of disrepair. The canyon was relatively deep and, unless you knew the where the entrance was, you would never notice the spot formed by an ancient spring that still ran on occasion.

Having spent years herding his mom's sheep when he should have been in school, Ernie knew the area well. He decided to ride his horse out to the ruins and scavenge rocks. Once he had built up a sizable pile, he would bring the truck down an old cattle trail to take them back to his hogan. The two days of hard physical work would help him focus his mind—something he needed to do before he went to see his old teacher.

A faint haze of dust on the horizon where none should be on a calm autumn day put Ernie on alert. There were a few trails and rough dirt roads in the area, but rarely did anyone come this way, so the dust meant danger to Ernie. He went into stealth mode as he made his way close to the entrance to the canyon and slipped off his horse, tying him up near a grassy area with a seep of water bubbling up through the cracks, a gift of the good summer rains.

Ernie's body became one with the canyon wall as he made his way to a vantage point, looking for anything out of place, when he saw the origin of the disturbance—fresh tire tracks, motorcycle tracks to be specific. A dirt bike had more than likely gone in, and not just once: there were numerous tracks all made by the same bike, going in and out. "Must be pot hunters," Ernie guessed.

Pot hunting on Indian land is rare, because the federal and tribal laws against the practice are severe, so the people who commit these crimes could be dangerous, and might rather kill than get caught. Ernie crawled the last hundred feet along the tracks until he could see over the edge of the rim. Cross-legged on the bottom of the canyon floor sat an intensely focused Navajo woman, in what he could only reason was a trance. There was no motorcycle in view.

"Maybe she's not human," Ernie thought, but as he watched it became apparent the woman was mortal, and attractive too. Her body was sideways and she wore a baseball hat, the long flowing black hair beneath it touching the ground. There was a bowl and a large milk jug of what looked like water positioned nearby. The woman's hand occasionally dropped something into a small bowl, though she never shifted her erect position. Ernie could not figure out what was happening, so he crept closer until he reached a point where he could see the woman's face and get a closer look at her actions.

She was Navajo, in her forties, with a pretty face and a slight build. She was sitting at the base of a substantial dormant ant bed, picking what appeared to be small rocks out of the pile—a strange sight in the middle of the desolate Navajo Nation. Ernie watched her machine-like movements in amazement as she methodically worked through a small section of fine pebbles, found something, picked that something up, then dropped it in the bowl with an audible ding.

Ernie scanned the surrounding area, but he neither heard nor saw anything out of the ordinary—no one else was there, just a lone Navajo woman on his land, picking through ant beds for who knew what. Ernie was sure this was some kind of sign; maybe Changing Woman had reappeared as a human and was trying to give him some guidance about how to deal with Matchstick Woman and Marvin. Perhaps he should avoid the old woman altogether and listen to the Holy People.

After forty minutes of watching, Ernie decided he had to address this Navajo woman, but do it quietly, in a non-confrontational way, on the off chance she was a chindi rather than a human so he wouldn't anger the spirit. He knew there were things that one could not explain on the Navajo Nation, and this might be one of them. When he was within twenty feet of her, Ernie came out into the open with his hands to his sides and his palms out, showing they were empty.

"Yá át ééh, I'm Ernie Yazzie. Everything OK?"

The woman looked up. Amazingly, she didn't scream or get upset—she just answered as if seeing people in a remote slot canyon was an everyday occurrence.

"Yá át ééh, I'm Ruth Bennally. You want some water?" She pointed with her lips toward the water jug.

Ernie was surprised the woman had not jumped when he had spoken. Maybe she was a spirit after all.... "OK, that would be nice," Ernie responded, slowly walking over and sitting by the water jug, watching the spirit do her work. He took a long drag of the cool water from the old plastic milk carton.

"What you doing out here? Kind off the main road, don't you think?"

"Oh, I'm working," she said cheerily. "Billy Moss has me picking out these little beads hidden in these ant piles. It's fun AND I get paid. There are so many of these beads, I will fill half this bowl by tonight when he fetches me."

Ernie looked at her ever-growing collection of turquoise, bone, and shell Nasazi beads, and decided that she was indeed a woman—if a very unusual one.

"Don't you worry about the Old Ones and chindi, handling things from the dead?" Ernie asked, wondering why a Navajo woman would do such a thing.

"No, not really. I don't feel any spirits from these rocks. If I did, I wouldn't do it. Seems fine to me. It's as if the beads ask me to find them and bring them back to someone's neck. There are some very cool ones, too. Take a look at this group I found this morning."

Ruth picked up a couple of beads in the shape of miniature birds, rich in artistic merit. Ernie didn't touch the artifacts, but he did take a look. She was right; they were beautiful and a man who works in stone could appreciate the artisan's abilities.

"Yeah, those are neat. Never seen anything like them. How long you been doing this work?"

"Oh, not long—a week, maybe less. Time has kind of stopped. I pick beads all day, which makes me feel good, then I go back to Billy Moss's place and I eat, drink, and go to bed. I guess I'll keep going till Billy tells me to stop, or I run out of ant beds, though that doesn't look likely."

Ruth moved her lips from side to side, pointing out the dozens of old and active ant beds. "You work for Billy too?" Ruth asked, her eyes probing Ernie's face.

For the first time in many years, Ernie felt a rush of adrenaline as he looked back into a woman's eyes. He liked both the looks of this woman and her straightforwardness; there was nothing but truth in her voice and face.

"No, I live in a stone hogan on the other side of this ridge. Beautiful Mountain is in my backyard."

"How did you get here? You walk?" Ruth asked, realizing she hadn't heard any vehicular noise.

"My horse—he's a quarter mile over there behind that grandfather juniper."

"Oh, I love horses. Can I take a look?" Ruth asked with the innocence of a child, putting down her bowl and standing up.

"Sure, come on. I'll introduce you. He's a great animal. I call him Neal the Real Deal. You can ride him if you want. He's more friendly than I am, that's for sure."

Ernie was surprised by both his generosity and his easy revelation of his demons. His cheeks turned red hearing himself admit his shortcomings.

"You seem friendly enough to me. I would love to ride him. I can use a break. The sun will be late in the horizon before Billy comes to get me."

The two strolled as if on their first date, talking and getting to know each other as Ernie retrieved Neal. Ruth was a natural with horses, even an animal of Neal's size, and rode the stallion bareback along the mesa ridge, her long hair flowing in the wind.

For the next three hours Ernie watched the methodical Ruth clean ant bed after ant bed, forgetting about his own rock pile. The two had made an instant connection, something neither had experienced in years.

✤ ✤ ✤ ✤

Matchstick Woman had been forgotten for the moment and for the next three days Ernie came and sat with Ruth as she collected prehistoric beads and amulets for Moss. They talked about their life experiences and failures, and how hard things could be when you were alone in life. Each recognized the other's pain and shortcomings. It became evident they both had significant issues, but in each other's presence their faults seemed to vanish into another dimension, a place where damaged people could prevail and maybe even find a semblance of happiness.

Ruth cautioned Ernie that Billy Moss could have a disagreeable temper and wouldn't like her spending time talking rather than working because she was getting paid by the hour. Ernie wanted to confront the man who was breaking federal laws on his ancestral land, but he craved Ruth's presence more than judging what was right or wrong. So Ernie left each day an hour before the sunset and promised to come back midmorning to sit, talk and share the meal and sweets he brought with him.

From a safe distance, Ernie watched the dirt bike retrieve Ruth. The man never took his full-face helmet off, so he couldn't get a good look at him. Moss would bark something and Ruth would hand him the bowl, which he would then carefully empty into a cloth-lined Mason jar. Ruth would leave the collection bowl under a large snakeweed bush; the empty water jug was picked up to refill for the next day. Moss never got off his bike.

By the end of day three, Ernie realized he had two pressing issues to deal with, both involving white people. Matchstick Woman in Gallup had been his priority before Ruth arrived on the scene, and now Moss in Farmington was apparently taking advantage of the woman and exposing her to jail time, even if she didn't realize what was happening. He had to decide which problem was the most pressing and how far he would go to correct the wrongdoing, with the thought of the white man's jail always in the back of his mind.

It was time for action regardless of the consequences, although if Ernie had known that Pingry and Moss were interconnected, he would have rethought his strategy. He didn't know it yet, but his plan was seriously flawed—and death was looming over the mesa for all those involved.

CHAPTER 33

BACK TO GALLUP

The north wind was blowing as the first blanket of snow fell on the Chuska Mountains. Marvin grabbed his favorite green knit hat before leaving his hogan. "An early snow, maybe a bad winter...." he speculated as he looked up at his boyhood mountaintops. He took the heavy snow as a sign that he, too, was entering the later part of his life cycle, with very few days left in his future. He needed to make the most of the time that remained, and it seemed if as signs were all around him, warning him of things to come.

Tomorrow, he would make his unannounced visit to Mrs. Pingry to see if she might be a reasonable person. His plan was to trade the necklace he had won for his father's squash blossom—an even swap of sorts. Marvin was programmed to remember people, dates and times; he didn't need to reference his childhood notebooks to recall the events leading up to the illegal confiscation of his necklace; those memories were indelibly etched in his gray matter. A verbatim account of how Stanton Soliday became the new owner of his precious family piece might be more powerful if recited from the heart than if read from the pages of a twelve-year-old's diary—which Pingry would assume he forged. Marvin would go to Gallup with protection, however. A witching rattlesnake rattle might help jog Pingry's memory; the powerful necklace might not be enough, the truth would be his strongest weapon.

Marvin's conviction that he was the rightful owner of the Slender Maker necklace would make him sound believable, but the story would be better with Ernie standing next to him, backing up his version of the 1961 events. But Ernie didn't seem to have any interest in getting involved unless his blanket was in the mix, so Marvin would go it alone on this trip. He hoped he wouldn't need more trips or muscle to convince the old lady that the necklace was rightfully his.

It took a couple of cranks to get Marvin's 1987 Ford pickup running. This was only the second time he had used the vehicle in the last two weeks and he hoped it was the cold and not his alternator going bad. The truck's tires were totally worn and long overdue being traded out. Regardless of how things went with Pingry, he would come back home with some fresh tires, celebrating a new start in life.

Marvin arrived in Gallup and went directly to Shannon's Tire Shop on Maloney Avenue. It was a family-run business, and Marvin had bought tires there once before. They had given him a reasonable price and treated him with respect. He knew Wal-Mart might be cheaper, but local was better in Marvin's mind.

A white man in his mid-forties ran the front counter—the same person who had helped him last time. He was probably the owner. The man's strong jawline told of a long lineage of white ancestors, though his accent betrayed a Navajo sensibility. Marvin told him he needed four new tires, not the most expensive ones but something that would last awhile as he might not be buying any more. "Sam the Man"—as his nametag read—offered Marvin a cup of coffee and a fresh donut as he went about getting Marvin what he had requested. In short order, he had found the appropriate tires, changed out and pitched the old treads, balanced the new ones, and rung up the sale.

"Hastiin Manycoats, that will be a total of $652," Sam the Man said.

Marvin started counting out the cash from his silver money clip. "How about $650 even?" Marvin smiled, showing all his teeth.

"Sure that's close enough. We appreciate your patronage. It's hard to stay in business these days with Wal-Mart and Amazon breathing down our necks. By the way, if you have any problem with your tires, or if you want us to check the air, we always do that for free," Sam said, making it clear he owned the shop and wanted to let Marvin know his business mattered, and that he made a smart decision to buy from Shannon's Tire Shop.

"That's good to know. That's why I buy from you guys and not the other Sam," Marvin joked, referring to Sam Walton, the founder of Wal-Mart. Sam the Man didn't get the joke, which was not unusual—Marvin was smarter than most. The shop owner filled out the receipt and asked Marvin if he would like a copy.

"Yes, I do want a copy. It's always good to have a receipt for things— you never know when it might come in handy," Marvin said, wishing he had one for the squash blossom he was about to try to pry from Matchstick Woman's boney fingers.

The receipt listed the four new tires, the warranty and the fact he had paid the tax, all in cash. Marvin signed the white copy and the owner gave him the pink copy, which Marvin folded up with his money and put back in his front pocket. Receipts were important in the white man's world—for old chief's blankets and maybe for new tires, too.

※ ※ ※ ※

125 Oak Avenue was an average slump-block home at the end of an unremarkable cul-de-sac. The now dead, knee-high summer grass was scattered with waist-high thistles, their purple flowers long gone. Only skeletal seedpods remained, the front yard saying volumes about the owner's living conditions. A 1977 Volvo sedan

was in the garage, visible through a small side window. The car's hood was dust free, but the wheel wells had a lining of telltale red rez dirt: Pingry was home.

Marvin rang the doorbell and waited. Two minutes went by with no answer. He rang again, and could hear someone rattling around inside.

"Hold your horses... it takes me a while to get there," Pingry yelled as she cracked the door open and peered out. Seeing Marvin Manycoats, his rattlesnake tail talisman dangling from his neck, she tried to close the door, but Marvin stuck a boot in the jam.

"I know you recognize me and want to run, but I'm only here to talk, Mrs. Pingry. I don't want any trouble."

The old woman could hear the voice of the child she had wronged so long ago, and she had no choice but to let him in.

"OK. No trouble. My nephew is coming over shortly, and he might not like the fact you forced your way into my house," she said with a quiver in her voice.

"No force, just talking," Marvin said as he entered the dark room. The drawn mustard-yellow drapes allowed a single beam of sunlight to filter through a back window, the rays highlighting dust particles suspended in the stuffy room. Marvin couldn't help but remember being trapped in Soliday's box, the sliver of light streaming in through the roof. The hairs on his neck stood up.

The two sat down on a couch that had been new in 1959, its salmon-colored upholstery still vivid, preserved by the room's dark interior. The living room had two yellowed Remington prints whose color now matched the living room drapes. Family photos were scattered randomly, but nothing of any value was visible. The Slender Maker necklace was not around Pingry's neck. Marvin, on the other hand, had his newly won squash blossom hanging just underneath the rattlesnake rattle.

"What do you want from me, Mr. Manycoats?" Pingry asked, already knowing the answer.

"You have something that is very precious to me. That squash blossom you wore at the Halloween party was mine, stolen from me in October 1961 by Stanton Soliday when I was at the Indian boarding school. You remember me, don't you?"

She acted as if she were thinking.

"How about the rattlesnake body on the plate that matches this tail, the day was October 3, 1961. I'm sure that must ring a bell." Marvin shook the tail, which still made its TTTTTRRRR sound, for emphasis.

There was no doubt she had never forgotten that incident. It was as if she had a fear of snakes and been shocked by how well Marvin had done in the box. He had not been an ordinary child, and was undoubtedly a very strong-willed man.

"Oh yes, now I remember. It's been a long time, but I don't know anything about a stolen necklace."

Marvin told the story that had been in his head for decades. He went into great detail, leaving nothing out, telling her about the necklace's history and how he lost the heirloom, giving specific dates and times—and Pingry quickly realized she was in trouble.

Soliday had given the piece to her to entice her into a sexual relationship that soured after a year, upon which Pingry left the school system to avoid Stanton Soliday's grip. He had asked on two occasions for his gift to be returned to him, but she had argued that the necklace was hers, and said that if he tried to take the piece she would turn him into the authorities, and Soliday relented. That was more than fifty years ago. In Pingry's mind the necklace was hers—but she still had to be careful.

"OK, let's say for the point of argument it was your family's necklace at one time. It's been in my possession for most of my life and no court is going to buy this story. I mean fifty years... Come on, Mr. Manycoats."

"I understand your position, but you know I'm telling the truth, and I have an idea that might work for both of us."

Marvin offered the squash blossom he had won in trade for hers and, if she made the swap, promised he would never bother her again. He would also put the transaction in writing. His new necklace might not be the worth as much as the Slender Maker, but it was still valued at $2,500, and she wouldn't have to worry about the law—or Marvin Manycoats—knocking on her door in the middle of the night.

Pingry weighed the options. She was old and wouldn't live much longer anyway. Her so-called nephew was actually Soliday's stepson and no real relationship to her. He did visit on occasion and had helped when she needed it—but what did she owe him? It was her decision after all.

Because she didn't have any children, Billy Moss was the sole beneficiary of her estate. Hopefully, he hadn't noticed the Slender Maker squash blossom around her neck at the party and, even if he had, he would still get a lovely necklace either way. With Marvin's trade, she could wear the squash blossom necklace in public and not be worried about its history or value—and she knew in her heart it was the right thing to do. She was lucky Marvin was willing to make a swap and not just demand the necklace be returned.

"OK, I will make the swap. You can have my—I mean your—old squash blossom and I'll take the one you won in the raffle. I want that certificate that Bloom talked about, the one saying it was worth $2,500, and a receipt from you stating that you initiated the trade," she said.

Marvin agreed. "I'll write a receipt now, and will bring the certificate by the next time I'm in town. You have my phone number now, so I'll call you beforehand and not just drop in like I did today," Marvin said. Realizing he was about to get his precious necklace back, he was trying to be as understanding as possible.

Pingry shuffled to her bedroom, where she pulled the necklace out of an old jewelry box, along with a pen and a piece of her Indian school stationery. Marvin took the opportunity to look around her place once she left the living room. There was no sign of Ernie's blanket, nothing of value, in fact, but the midcentury modern couch. Ernie would be disappointed.

The old woman came back clutching the necklace and the notepaper in her hand. "Well, let's do this thing. You hand me yours, and I'll hand you yours," she said with the first glimmer of humor. Marvin smiled, catching the joke.

They traded necklaces, each hanging one around the other's neck. Marvin stuck his rattlesnake necklace under his shirt; it had done its job, and Marvin now could return the rattle back to Mother Earth. He smiled when he sat down on the couch to write out the receipt, remembering how he had stolen a piece of that letterhead to help Ernie escape. It was the circle of life.

Once he was finished, he let Pingry read the document. She reminded him to date the letter, which he did, although Marvin would never forget the day or time he got his necklace back.

He handed the receipt back to Pingry. "Perfect," she said. "I guess we're done here, Marvin."

"I do have one more question, Mrs. Pingry. I know you don't have to answer, but it would help me if you could..." Marvin asked.

"Well, you haven't been shy so far. What's the question?"

"Ernie Yazzie had a great old chief's blanket when he arrived at the school. I'm sure you remember Ernie. He was a classmate who ran away from Two Trees on October 5, 1961, and his blanket ended up in Soliday's office before it disappeared."

Pingry considered the request and decided she didn't owe Soliday a damned thing, but she did owe Marvin Manycoats more than she could ever repay, so she let down her guard for once and answered truthfully: "I remember that. He took the blanket just like he stole your necklace. I'm not sure what happened to it after that, but my nephew

Billy Moss might. He lives in Farmington and knew Soliday very well, so he might know where some of the pieces ended up. Talk to him. It's a place to start. I wish you the best of luck."

The old woman paused for a moment, looked down at her feet, took a big gulp and looked into Marvin's face, her eyes watering. "I know it doesn't count for much of anything at this point, but I'm sorry, Marvin. I really am. What we did to you Navajo kids was inexcusable. At the time, I thought I was helping, but I realize now that I was a part of the problem, not a solution."

"It was a long time ago, Mrs. Pingry. Maybe this trade will help put both our minds a little more at ease and make our next road easier to travel," Marvin said, his father's necklace finally back where it belonged. He stroked the turquoise cabs for the first time in half a century.

Pingry remembered she was expecting a visit from her nephew in less than an hour, and she didn't want to have a confrontation between Marvin and Moss, especially with the Navajo wearing the Slender Maker necklace, so she hurried Marvin on his way.

"OK, Marvin, we're square. Good luck with the rest of your life. You can just put the certificate in the mail. I trust you."

When he left, she sat down on the couch trying to decide how to handle the other half of the equation: Billy Moss.

CHAPTER 34

DON'T EVEN ASK

Billy Moss's multi-strand necklace of prehistoric beads would be complete in less than a month, thanks to Ruth's unusual ability to sort through the anthill mounds built over ancient ruins. In the process of building their small piles of rocks, the industrious insects also pull out fine prehistoric relics buried deep in the ground. Beads that would never have been uncovered without a shovel and strain roll neatly down the sides of the anthills. Self-sorting selection without digging is nature's way of hunting artifacts.

Moss ignored the fact that he was on Indian lands and breaking National Graves Protection and Repatriation Act laws. There were federal laws dating back to 1906 to protect both federal and Native antiquities. The beaded necklace would be displayed in Moss's growing museum, so it wouldn't be for sale. The trader reasoned that he was not stealing artifacts, but instead saving and sharing them with visitors to his Museum of the Ancients. Without his intervention, he rationalized, the beauty created by the Anasazi jewelers would be lost to a bunch of ant piles. He was certain many dealers and collectors would agree with him.

Once Ruth had completed the necklace, he would give her five six-packs of beer and send her back home, telling her not to say a word or she would find herself in deep trouble with the law. After all, she was the one who pillaged the sites, not him. Ruth would return to the Shell station back on the booze and be forgotten. Bloom wouldn't hire anyone who was drinking, and with that much free alcohol and money in her pocket, word would quickly get back to Bloom that Ruth was hitting the bottle again.

The magnificent squash blossom Moss had seen on Aunty Pingry at the Halloween party had been on his mind him all week. That necklace was a significant piece; it certainly looked like the silversmith Slender Maker's work. He was now convinced his stepfather, Stanton Soliday, had given her the necklace while he was in love with Pingry when Moss was just a kid. She had never worn the necklace around her nephew and he had known the woman his entire life, so she was hiding the precious squash blossom for a reason. The question was why—and he planned to find out.

She was old and would be easy to manipulate. He would get the answers to his questions and then acquire the necklace one way or another—and waiting for her to die of natural causes wasn't one of them. The opportunity to add a Slender Maker necklace to his museum was a drug he could not resist. Besides, it was a family piece—his.

The time of reckoning had arrived for both squash blossom necklaces. Bloom owed him the grand prize from the raffle, which Moss was convinced was rigged to make Marvin Manycoats the winner. Mary Pingry had his family's piece, and she would return it to its rightful owner, the only person in the Soliday lineage left alive—him.

Moss called his Aunt Pingry on the store phone. He didn't believe in cell phones, which he felt could track his every move. In his line of work, it was better to work under the radar; when it came to modern technology, you never knew who could be listening. A prominent sign in his Museum of the Ancients read, "Don't even ask if you can take a photo!" A small round face with crossed-out eyes emphasized the point.

He was expected at his aunt's house around noon. She had asked Billy if he could mow her lawn while he was there, as the yard had not been touched all summer. Moss said he would be happy to clean up her front yard, knowing he wouldn't do it. It could go another season—if she managed to live that long. The twelve o'clock appointment was perfect; he had already dropped Ruth off at her job site and gotten back to the post in time to orient Preston, which meant, "go make jewelry." He hoped to have time to drop by Manycoats' hogan for a chat on his way back to Farmington.

Preston showed up at 10 a.m., just as the trading post opened. He was ready to work and Moss felt comfortable about the kid—he had a positive energy and the talent to make him some serious money. Preston figured he could get some ingots pounded out for a bracelet as well as do a little snooping when his so-called boss left. Jane, who ran the counter, wasn't very bright and was more interested in the small black-and-white TV hidden behind the old-fashioned cash register than in watching what went on in the back of the store.

Moss left, saying he would return around 4 p.m. Preston took a break after spending an hour-and-a-half hammering silver. The back of the building had a long, 8-foot x 40-foot room housing the Museum of the Ancients. A door at the end of the hallway led to the workbench area, then to the guest bedroom; behind that was Moss's office and a storage room for boxes, cans, and the like. Another door at the rear of Moss's locked office was secured with a heavy padlock.

A sign in front of the office read: "Knock first. If no answer, go the f*ck away!"

Preston slipped into the guest bedroom and looked around. He found a small-sized pair of pants and a tee shirt from Newcomb High School,

Class of 1993, in a dresser drawer. The bathroom had a few toiletry items, including a hairbrush with some long black hairs that looked Navajo, a toothbrush that was still moist and a tube of toothpaste without a top—but no more definitive clues as to who was living there.

Preston went back to work. It was clear someone was living in the guest room, a Navajo with a slim build, probably a woman. Hopefully, it was Ruth Bennally. He assumed whoever was living there was coming and going at odd hours, before the post opened or after it closed, which meant that either the guest had a key or someone was opening and closing the doors for her. It appeared that Preston might have to make a bracelet for Moss since he hadn't yet learned enough to solve the mystery.

※ ※ ※ ※

The Green Monster, as Billy Moss referred to his custom mint-green-colored Harley motorcycle, was now drivable again, thanks to some tweaking. Though the dents and paint loss were a constant irritation, he didn't have the time to send it to the shop. Seeing the bruised bike made him even more determined to get even for losing the raffle drawing to Manycoats—that necklace was *his* as far as Moss was concerned.

As fate would have it, the trader rolled into Aunty Pingry's driveway thirty minutes after Manycoats' unexpected visit and departure. Pingry hadn't moved from the couch. She was still deep in thought about all the bad things she had done in her life and wondering what she could have done differently.

"Ding-dong" rang the 1960s doorbell. "Damn it, now Billy's here. What an old fool I am." She took the raffle squash blossom off and shoved it, along with Marvin's letter detailing the swap, deep under an orange couch cushion. She did not want to have a confrontation with Moss.

"Hey, aunty, how's my favorite relative been? I saw you down at the Toadlena Trading Post on Halloween, didn't I?" Moss already knew the answer and was just waiting to see how she would respond.

"Yes, I was there. Sorry we didn't get to talk. I wasn't feeling well and had to leave suddenly."

"What a shame that Bloom fellow screwed you out of the squash blossom necklace. As far as I'm concerned, Bloom's not in the white man's corner," she said, appealing to Moss's racist leanings.

"Sure was a damned rip off. I'm not done with Bloom or his Indian shill, the guy that won. Marvin Manycoats was working for him. Can you believe that Bloom had his own kid pull out the winning ticket and came up with some cockamamie one-minute rule, like we were dropping food on the ground and then counting." Moss's eyes dilated with anger as he relived the moment.

"Yes, it's not fair, but things have a way of working themselves out," Pingry offered.

"Speaking of squash blossoms, aunty, you had a great old necklace on that day. I don't remember seeing that before. Is it a new acquisition?"

"Oh, it's just something I've had for a long time. It's not a big deal," Pingry said nervously.

"Huh. Looked pretty good to me. Mind if I take a look? You know how I am about old Indian jewelry; I can't get enough."

"I have it locked up down at the bank. Can't take a chance with that kind of thing in Gallup. People around here love to steal Indian jewelry for booze. I'm sure you understand, working at a pawn shop near the reservation."

"That's true enough, but I'd really like to see the piece—so which bank do you have it in? I'm assuming I'm still your only heir, so it's going to be mine someday anyway. I should know what's in your safety-deposit box in case something happens to you. Can't even trust banks these days. I sure hope it's not that Wells Fargo on Aztec Avenue after all the shenanigans they pulled with fake accounts and the like."

"It's not at Wells Fargo, you are still my only heir, and my fortune is all yours." Pingry let out a weak laugh as she raised her arms and waved them around. Both knew she had an outdated house, a 1977 Volvo, and not much else.

"So how about I drive you down to the bank? We can go take a look." Without waiting for a reply, Moss grabbed the Route 66 key ring out of a plastic bowl near the door and headed toward the garage.

"I'll pull the Volvo out of the garage; it probably needs a wash after being out on the rez anyway."

He moved before Pingry could speak. Paralyzed by not knowing what to say, she sat unmoving on the couch, her legs on top of the hidden necklace.

Moss entered the dank garage, walked to the rear of the building, and pulled a string to open the door. As he walked toward the driver's side to back the Volvo out, he noticed the back bumper had a series of dents, all covered in mint-green paint—his Green Monster's custom paint job!

"What the hell," he said, bending over to take a closer look.

"Damned if she wasn't the one to run over my bike," Moss said in disgust. Shaking his head as if to say, "No way she did this," he backed the car out and let the engine warm up as he pondered the condition of his motorcycle under the overcast November sky.

Moss left the car running, slammed the door shut, and went back through the door he had come through. Pingry was still motionless on the couch, an antique silver squash blossom dangling from her frail hand. Moss stopped, looking intently at the necklace.

"OK, what gives Aunty Pingry? That's my necklace, the one that Navajo stole at the raffle. How come you have the piece?" Moss was confused, and still angry about seeing his motorcycle paint on her bumper.

Pingry asked Moss to sit next to her and told him the story of what had happened in 1961 and the years since then. She told him how his stepfather had stolen the necklace to begin with, and that it didn't matter anymore, as she now had a lovely necklace, free and clear, that would be his after she died.

As the old woman slowly told the story, her voice sometimes cracking, Moss's anger began to grow. What an incompetent old fool she had become!

"So, let me get this straight. My dearly departed stepfather stole Indian art from Navajo children in the 1960s and you told that Navajo Marvin Manycoats—who, by the way, stole MY squash at Bloom's—to ask ME about his friend's blanket AND you gave away a Slender Maker necklace that you had owned for nearly 60 years—a necklace I will point out that would also have been mine someday—and you did ALL this today. Is that about right?!"

Pingry was starting to squirm. The talk had not gone as she had expected and she was now afraid of her nephew, who was no longer sitting but pacing back and forth in front of her.

"Well, I know it sounds kind of crazy, but I honestly think I did the right thing. You can have this squash blossom now..." she said, trying to hand the necklace to Moss. "You don't have to wait till I'm gone. It's yours today—go ahead and take it."

No longer pacing, Moss did not take the necklace, but stood menacingly close to the old woman.

"Was anybody else over here beside Manycoats?" Moss asked, trying to assess the situation.

"No, no... just Manycoats. I've only talked to him and, of course, you. He came alone."

"When, aunty, when were you going to tell me about hitting my Green Monster motorcycle? Let me answer for you—never!" his eyes narrowed into small slits; he was seething with anger.

"What? I'm not sure what you're talking about…."

Pingry stood up and tried to back away at the same time, realizing she was in serious trouble. She caught her foot on a throw rug and, without her cane for support, tripped, falling backward. She hit the ground with a THUD and an audible SNAP as her right hip disintegrated on the hard oak floor.

"Ah, ah… my hip. I broke my hip!" she yelled, gripping the squash necklace tightly in her hand. Moss took a seat on the couch, considering his options as the old lady writhed in pain.

"Call an ambulance. I'm badly hurt. Please call for help, Billy," Pingry implored.

Billy took a cushion off the back of the couch and said, "Here, let me help you, aunty. Try to breathe more slowly. Let me put this pillow under your head in case you hurt your head too."

The old lady weakly lifted her head and he placed the pillow on the ground under her neck.

"Let's see your head. You may have cracked it wide open, something worse than breaking a hip."

Moss slipped on his motorcycle gloves and wrapped his hands around Pingry's neck as if he were going to feel for an injury—then, with one violent twist to the right, broke her neck in multiple places. The old woman went limp; there was no more pain, only gurgling noises.

Moss violently snatched the couch cushion from under her neck as if he were doing a dinner table trick. With another THUD, her fragile cranium hit the floor, a small rivulet of blood immediately forming around the base of her skull. She wasn't quite dead, but she would be in a few short minutes. As far as Moss was concerned, one problem was solved and, for his efforts, he would receive a house, a car, and the return of squash blossom necklace number one.

There would be no waiting for Pingry to pass naturally, or visiting her in the hospital as her hip healed—especially when he could blame her death on the thief who stole an old woman's valuable heirloom. Moss smiled as he thought of the irony of the situation, the revolving squash blossoms all coming home to roost in his museum's display case.

Moss went outside and moved the still-running Volvo back into the garage. He wiped his fingerprints off the car door and steering wheel and moved his motorcycle from the front of the house to the inside of the garage. He had a workable plan to frame one Marvin Manycoats for the old woman's death; all he had to do was make the house look like a robbery gone bad and not leave any evidence that he had been there.

Back in the living room, Moss opened her purse and poured the contents out, then quickly went through the drawers, leaving them ajar. He found the white jewelry box where Pingry must have kept the necklace and chuckled, leaving the box in place to be discovered by the cops. It was perfect.

He found an old scrapbook that hadn't been touched in 20 years. On the third page, he found pay dirt—a photo of Pingry, dated October 23, 1971, with her Slender Maker necklace proudly displayed around her neck. He slipped the photo out and put it in his front pocket. He discovered Marvin's phone number on a piece of paper next to the couch and took that too.

He gently pried the squash blossom necklace that was still in Pingry's hand out of her grip, and carefully cut the necklace's old string with his knife, removing the silver beads that she had squeezed in death and returning them to her palm. He then placed three beads under the couch; they were barely visible but still easy for the police to find. He then pocketed what he considered the plunders of war.

The scene was set: There had been a robbery; Aunt Pingry's Slender Maker necklace had been stolen, an empty jewelry box testifying to its existence. A struggle ensued and the old lady grabbed the trading post necklace hanging around Marvin's neck. In her desperate fight, the old string broke and the beads went flying. In his rush to leave the scene, Marvin missed a few crucial pieces of evidence—the three beads bearing Manycoats' and Pingry's prints. When the cops started snooping around, they would discover that the beads also happened to match those on the necklace given away at the trading post. Five hundred people could testify it belonged to Marvin Manycoats.

Satisfied with the scenario he arranged for the cops, Moss looked out the window to make sure the coast was clear, retrieved his bike from the garage, and left the scene. He knew the next part of the story would require a visit to Marvin Manycoats, but not at his hogan as he initially planned. His spontaneous murder of Pingry had changed his rat-trapping method.

Moss had not uncovered the note detailing the terms of the necklace swap that Manycoats and Pingry had signed. Tucked deep under the cushions, it could be another piece of critical evidence, if the cops bothered to look that hard. If it were to be found, it would sink the false murder scenario and shine the light of guilt on Moss himself.

CHAPTER 35

BROKEN MATCHSTICKS

Ernie was tired. Thoughts of his lost chief's blanket were floating in his subconscious and sleep continued to come in uneven spurts. Today he slept late, 9 a.m., unusual for a man who woke to the morning sun and his roosters crowing. The time had come to visit Pingry and find out what happened to his blanket. He knew that Marvin had the same intention and might beat him to her, but his friend's plan seemed a long shot. It was never good to trade with a thief, no matter how old she was.

Whether Marvin would indeed ask about his family's blanket at the old witch's house was also not a sure bet. Ernie wouldn't blame Marvin if he didn't look for it; he was focused on recovering the Slender Maker necklace that he knew Matchstick Woman had.

Ernie felt he, too, must do what he could to pursue his own interests. Visit the old lady, scare her, even rough her up if need be, and find that blanket. If Marvin hadn't visited Pingry yet he would try to retrieve Marvin's necklace, too, so at least one of them could sleep well at night. The old feelings from his Indian school days had raised their ugly heads once more, but as of today, there would be no more running.

Ernie rarely left his rock enclave and didn't much like driving. Neal, his black stallion, was his preferred method of transportation, but Gallup was over an hour's drive by truck, so he had no choice. A 1995 street map of Gallup would help him locate 125 Oak Avenue.

Ernie arrived at an uninteresting house in a quiet cul-de-sac at midday. He cruised by slowly to see if there were any signs of life; nothing set off alarms in Ernie's head, so he was sure the coast was clear. He doubled back to a nearby liquor store and parked his car off to the side. He figured the liquor store was good cover for a Navajo his age, even though he now hated alcohol and considered it part of the white man's curse on his people.

He quickly walked the one-and-a-half miles back to Matchstick Woman's neighborhood and bushwhacked his way through a tall stand of dead thistles. Ernie could see the old woman's house and stopped to watch it. Hunting prey came easily to a man who killed to eat; Pingry was merely a different kind of meal, one to fill the soul rather than the belly.

Ernie sat motionless for five long minutes; still no activity. He stood up when the garage door opened and a white man pulled out on a green Harley motorcycle. He appeared to be a bilagáana wearing a leather helmet, complete face scarf, black down jacket and blue jeans. The man guided the bike out through the garage door, which he then closed manually. The back of a car was partially visible in the garage when the door was open. The man looked around, then accelerated out of the neighborhood. Marvin wasn't sure, but something about the way the man left on his bike made him feel like he had seen him before, though he couldn't place where.

Ernie sat in place as if he had shot an elk and was waiting for the beast to bleed out. After forty-five minutes with no signs of life, he eased himself up from his squatting position; his stiff knees were slow to start moving.

"Age is catching up with me," Ernie thought as he worked his way over to the house. "I only hope Matchstick Woman is in there."

He had seen the man close the garage door by hand so he figured it would be the most accessible entry point. There would be no quaint discussions of right and wrong—he wanted his piece back and, if she had the blanket, she WOULD give it back.

Ernie listened intently before he breached the garage door. The Volvo looked like it had been to the reservation recently; caked red dirt lined the wheel wells. Ernie felt the car's hood with his cold hand—"slightly warm," he thought, "the car must have been used in the last hour." He didn't discover anything else of interest in the garage.

Ernie turned his attention to the interior of the house. The handle turned smoothly; the garage door was not locked. He eased his massive body into the house. A hunter, Ernie smelled something he recognized—fresh blood! The hair on the back of his neck stood up and he pulled out a large skinning knife for protection. When he got to the living room, he saw Pingry on the floor, apparently dead. Looking around, he went over to her withered body and felt her neck—no pulse, "but still warm, like the car. She hasn't been dead long," he thought.

For the next five minutes, Ernie methodically searched the house to see if anyone else was there, half expecting to find Marvin's body. All the drawers and cupboards were ajar; someone else had been looking for something. There were no signs of a Navajo necklace, but in a lower drawer of the bedroom dresser a small Two Grey Hills rug was hidden under folded bed sheets. The chocolate brown weaving still had the weaver's name attached—Violet Roundhouse—and a $250 price tag from the Toadlena Trading Post. It wasn't his chief's blanket, but it would be a start on reparations. He stuffed the small textile under his jacket.

Whoever that man on the motorcycle was, he knew the old lady was dead; that was a given. Whether she had died of natural causes or by violence was not clear. The way he had driven off, the house being tossed, and no ambulance arriving during the forty-five minutes Ernie had waited outside pointed to the more ominous explanation.

Pingry, the Matchstick Woman who had terrorized him when he was a child, was dead. She looked so pathetic laid out on the floor. She was no longer a threat, no longer able to haunt his dreams. Ernie stared at the crumpled body next to his feet. He wanted to feel some empathy for the woman, but he couldn't find that place in his heart—"another causality of the Indian boarding school," he thought.

Ernie snuck out the same way he had come in—through the garage—and headed back to the rez. If he still drank, he would have gotten a six-pack at the liquor store for the road and downed it all, but he was not that kind of Indian anymore. He had gone from a drunk to an angry person who wanted answers—and one of the few people on the planet who could have helped him was now dead. Ernie hoped Marvin hadn't killed Matchstick Woman, though he thought it was a possibility, or he could have hired the man on the green motorcycle to fix his problem.

"She wasn't worth the risk of a lifetime in prison, even over a family heirloom," Ernie thought, wondering if the outcome would have been any different if he had found his blanket in Matchstick Woman's possession. He wasn't sure he knew the answer; he had built up a lot of anger over the years, but the man who had raced off on the motorcycle seemed like a good place to start.

CHAPTER 36

BLANKET TALK

Moss returned to his house at 3:30 p.m. and devised an alibi for the day; he could say he had worked on accounting, paid bills, did laundry, then gathered up a load of high-grade turquoise and a couple of ingot bars for his new silversmith.

He hoped his motorcycle hadn't have been spotted in Gallup. Covering his face was smart, so even if someone recognized the bike there was no way to identify him as the rider, unless it was on Oak Street—that was the one weak link. The Green Monster was now hidden in a remote work shed, one he used when he traded for hot material that needed to cool down for a while.

If a video camera had filmed his bike, he could say it was missing. He had lots of motorcycles and easily might not notice one was gone—especially a bike that was damaged and not really drivable. Then he remembered the green paint on Pingry's Volvo that could link him to his motorcycle if anyone had seen him at her house. This tie to the crime could be a significant problem, but he had hidden his bike shortly after arriving, wasn't at her home very long, and never saw anyone in the cul-de-sac. It was probably not worth worrying about.

He switched to his 2017 Ram truck and brought in the supplies for Preston.

"How goes it kid? You make me any bracelets yet?" Moss asked as he walked into the room carrying two large plastic tubs.

"I'm getting close." Preston looked up, hammer in hand.

"That's good. Make it in the old style. I went to my house and found a supply of quality turquoise that's ready to go and more silver for you to work with. This should keep you busy for the next month."

Moss set the heavy tubs down next to Preston, who was thinking he wouldn't last many more days as the bench silversmith. Moss could take the tubs back to wherever they came from.

Using the phone number Pingry had for Marvin, Moss called him. Marvin picked up on the third ring.

"Yá át ééh," Marvin said in no-nonsense Navajo fashion.

"Hi, Marvin, this is Billy Moss up here in Farmington. How you doing?"

Marvin knew Billy was pissed that he didn't get the squash at the trading post, and that he and Matchstick Woman were kin. He doubted it was a friendly kind of call.

"I'm doing OK. How can I help you, Mr. Moss?" Marvin replied cautiously.

"Well, I talked to my aunt, and she explained about the Slender Maker squash blossom being stolen from you way back when. She told me about the old Navajo blanket too, and I thought maybe I could help. I'm sorry about all this. I had no idea any of this had happened until today."

Marvin was surprised by Moss's reaction, and felt there might some hope for Ernie Yazzie to get his blanket back.

"Thank you, Mr. Moss. Do you know anything about Ernie's blanket? Maybe who owns it?"

"Marvin, please call me Billy."

"OK, Billy. Do you know anything?"

"Well, truth be known, I would rather talk in person. It's not the kind of thing I like to discuss over the phone. I'm sure you understand. Can you come up to the store tomorrow morning at 11 a.m.? I'll set aside an hour and we can chat."

Marvin thought for a moment and decided he had nothing to lose. "Sure, Billy. I'll see you then."

"Great. Oh, by the way, Could you bring that squash blossom of your dad's with you? It sure would be a treat to see something that magnificent. I'm a fan of great silversmiths, and Slender Maker was the best. I've got a Navajo kid, Preston Yellowhorse, working for me, making some outstanding jewelry; you'll love to see his work."

"OK, I'll see you tomorrow."

Marvin knew Preston was Rachael's kid. It seemed very unlikely he was working for Moss, so it was probably more complicated than a bench silversmith job. He would ask Bloom about it in the morning, before he drove up to Farmington.

Sleep washed over Marvin in a warm wave that night. He had his heirloom safely against his chest and felt good about the transaction with Matchstick Woman; he hoped that tomorrow he would learn more about Ernie's blanket and finally get the peace that had eluded him for so long.

❋ ❋ ❋ ❋

Marvin arrived early at the Shell station and post office on Highway 491. The coffee was still fresh and he bought a small cup for the road. He dropped the appraisal certificate in the mailbox as he had promised Matchstick Woman he would, so all the loose ends were now taken care of. Marvin felt re-energized. Maybe there would be even more good news after he spoke with Billy Moss, he thought as he drove back to his hogan for a frybread before he went to talk with Bloom.

Plumes of sweet piñon smoke were rising from the metal fireplace as Marvin exited his front door, his hunger blunted for the moment. He preferred to walk the five-mile dirt road to the Toadlena Trading Post. Marvin smiled as he inspected his shiny new truck tires as he began to walk. It had been four long days since he had last visited the trading post—a record for a man who liked his routines. The brisk morning air was rejuvenating and the exercise freed up his mind, giving him time to reflect on the circle of life. This morning's meditation was on how the Slender Maker necklace found its way home.

"Walking is the key to a long life," Marvin mused, "and plenty of chocolate ice cream bars make life enjoyable. I would have never won Bloom's raffle squash blossom or gotten my father's necklace returned without buying ice cream, and without exercise, I would not have felt right treating myself to all those delicious treats."

A feeling of comfort enveloped Marvin; he was sure he had found the right road to enlightenment. Today, two ice cream bars were mandatory—anything to help pry open another cosmic window of understanding. His stomach growled in agreement.

Bloom was sweeping crumpled leaves off the front porch as Marvin came into view. Bloom smiled and felt a great relief knowing his friend was OK. He had already decided to go check out his hogan if he didn't show up this morning. Sweeping leaves was just an excuse to watch for Marvin.

"Yá át ééh, Marvin. How does it feel to be the big winner of the annual Toadlena raffle?"

Bloom was already thinking in terms of staying put in Toadlena and becoming a fixture in the community. Sal couldn't run the post forever. There was a good chance the old trader would consider retiring now that he'd had a taste of freedom, and let Bloom take over his lease from the Navajo Nation. The tribe owned the Toadlena building and all the contents related to the building, even though Sal had put a hundred thousand dollars into the place. If Sal decided to retire and no one qualified stepped in to take it over, the post would close after 109 years. Bloom was determined not to let this happen to Toadlena as it had to so many other posts.

"Well, I'm luckier than you think. Turns out I was able to trade up, so to speak," Marvin smiled, pulling the old necklace out from under his well-worn flannel shirt.

"Wow, that's quite a trade. Is that the necklace Mary Pingry had on at the Halloween Party? Looks like someone ended up with the better end of that deal," Bloom said as he examined the horseshoe-shaped central naja closely for the first time.

"Yeah. I went up to see the friend I told you about and stopped by her house. We were able to make a trade. She really liked the one you had in your raffle, so she's happy—but you're right. I got the better end of that stick."

Bloom wondered why Pingry would agree to the swap. She had downplayed the value of the raffle necklace compared to her own, so he thought there was probably something else involved that Marvin didn't want to discuss.

"This looks old. It's all ingot silver and maybe made by that famous silversmith whose work is in the Wheelwright Museum. What's his name? Slim something?"

"Slender Maker."

"Yep, that's the guy. His najas are so distinctive. Is this necklace by Slender Maker?"

"Yes, Slender Maker did all the silver work and made the naja too. The turquoise was a later add-on—great Number 8 turquoise beads and Blue Gem almond-shaped tabs."

Bloom had been so entranced by the silversmith's skills that he hadn't even noticed the turquoise. "You're right. Those are great stones, perfectly graded. Looks like they're bow drilled," Bloom observed, knowing that hand drilling beads was time intensive—which probably meant the turquoise stones were old, the work done before mechanical tools ruled the rez.

"Bow drilled, all right. Can't get stones like this anymore. The Number 8 mine closed a long time ago." Marvin exposed the face of one of the beads, showing the telltale conical hole that proved it was drilled by hand.

"So how do you know the turquoise was a married to the necklace later? Those are old bow drilled stones; it looks original to me," Bloom said.

"Old family secret." Marvin smiled; he wasn't ready to talk about his painful past history.

"OK. You can tell me when you have the time to share your secret Indian knowledge about how the Navajo can tell a marriage of two old pieces was joined to look like one original necklace." Bloom knew there was more than Marvin was letting on but decided not to press.

Marvin bought the first of his two ice cream bars and held court in the antique barber chair, patiently waiting for Bloom to finish his morning chores. Once Bloom was free, Marvin said, "I'm going up to Farmington today to see Billy Moss. I heard a rumor Preston is working for him now. Is that true? I thought his college degree had landed him a good paying job in Albuquerque."

Bloom was always amazed at how fast news traveled on the reservation. He hesitated and considered his words carefully before responding. He didn't know how much to share, and wondered why Marvin wanted to see Moss.

"Preston still has the Intel job, but he has a month off and thought he would earn some extra spending money as a bench silversmith while he was home. Moss had an opening, as you know."

"Working for Billy Moss seems like it wouldn't be something you or Rachael would like too much...." Marvin watched Bloom closely for any facial tell, sensing there was more to the backstory and wanting to get a read on what Bloom's intentions were with Moss.

"Well, you're right. Rachael was not a happy camper, but Preston is an adult, he can do as he pleases. Not much we can do about that."

Bloom tried to change the direction of the conversation. "I guess maybe I should ask you the same question. Why are you going to see Moss? After his outburst at the raffle, I wouldn't think you two would be best friends—and you already traded off the necklace he wanted. He might not like that. I'm pretty sure Moss thinks he should have won that necklace; he didn't seem to be a fan of my one-minute rule." Bloom smiled, remembering how pissed Moss had been.

"I think he probably has cooled off by now. That's one of the reasons I want to go up there and maybe mend some fences. It's time to heal, and this last week has shown me a new way to forgive and forget. I guess I'm going to do some of the forgiving part."

Bloom didn't understand what Marvin was getting at, but realized that there were some cultural bridges he might never be able to cross—and this apparently was one.

"Well, Marvin, like I warned Preston before he took the job with Moss, please be careful. I don't think this is the kind of man I would trust; I'm pretty sure he's out only for himself and takes the law lightly—but hey, that's just one white man's opinion."

"You could be right, Charles Bloom. I will listen to your advice; you probably know more about whites than I do." Marvin still didn't understand why Preston was working at Moss's post, but he took Bloom at his word—including his warning to be very careful when dealing with Billy Moss.

"Let me know how it goes with Moss, would you?"

"Sure, if you give me another ice cream bar on the house." Marvin flashed his trademark smile, knowing Bloom was as much a pushover for giving away food as the Navajo were for ice cream.

"OK. Full report, one ice cream bar on the house."

The men shook each other's hands in Navajo fashion to solidify the deal. Little did they know the final report would be terrifying for everyone involved with Billy Moss.

CHAPTER 37

QUITTING TIME

Preston was almost sure Ruth was living in the post's bedroom, but he needed a definitive sighting and, hopefully, a talk with her to make sure she was safe. The guest room had a small window that you couldn't see through: the inside of the glass pane was covered by a black trash bag that read, for all purposes, "redneck privacy please."

He decided he would get to work by 7 a.m., knock on the window, and see who was at home. If Moss answered, there might be trouble and quitting time would be one shift early. For a fast and hidden getaway, Preston parked his car down the street and walked up a wash behind the post that ran the length of the property. The arroyo was dry most of the year, except when the summer male rains arrived; today it was a perfect highway for his purposes.

Preston worked his way through the thick stand of salt cedar trees and came out near Ruth's window. He broke off a long dry branch shaped like a claw at one end to use as a knocker, hitting the windowpane like birds do when they see their reflection during mating season. The plan was that if Ruth peeked out he would talk to her. If anyone else came to the window—especially Moss—he would drop the branch and run for cover, hoping the trader would think it was an animal or the wind knocking at the pane.

The third time he tapped with the branch a face peered out through one small corner of the plastic sack. Preston recognized Ruth and he popped up smiling, hoping she would remember his face, which she did.

Ruth cranked open one of the small glass panes. "Hey, Preston, what's up? What you hitting my window for?"

"Hi, Ruth. Everything OK? Rachael and your mom have been worried. You haven't made contact with her in a while."

"Oh, I'm sorry... Tell my mom and Rachael I'm OK. Sorry about not calling. I got no phone and Billy don't like people using his store phone for personal stuff. But I'm cool, not drinking, just working."

"You know, Ruth, I've been working for Billy this last week as a silversmith, but I haven't seen you around. What kind of work you doing all day?"

"Oh, that's great you're working here too. I'm about eight miles east of Beautiful Mountain, not too far from Ernie Yazzie's place. I'm picking beads for Mr. Moss. It's pretty fun, easy work—not like selling papers," Ruth said with a smile.

Preston had no clue who Ernie Yazzie was or what she meant by picking beads.

"What kind of beads?"

"Oh, the old, ancient kind, you know—the Nasazi beads, the ones the ants pull up. There are thousands out there. Then at night, I string them up. Here, I'll show you."

Ruth disappeared, then came back to the window with two long strands of turquoise, shell and bone seed beads. At the end of the string hung five large amulets that she had found among the ruins.

"See, this is what I'm doing. Pretty neat, huh?" Ruth was brimming with excitement.

"Yes, those are cool for sure. Well, I'm glad you're fine, but if you would, don't mention that you and I talked to Mr. Moss."

"How come? If you work here too he won't care if we talk—it's not like I'm working right now."

"I think he might care. Better just keep this between us Navajo," Preston said in Diné to emphasize the point.

"Ok, see you around."

Ruth disappeared behind the black bag. Preston realized that what Moss had Ruth doing—collecting artifacts on Navajo lands—was illegal, but at least she was safe and seemed in good spirits. He only had one other question, and that was what was behind that padlocked door in Moss's office. He hoped to get that answer before he left his silversmith position later today. If the opportunity arose, he would investigate further.

Preston felt good as he walked back down the arroyo. He indeed was a spy. "Only one more door to open and my mission is complete," he thought as he stepped out of the trees and got into his car.

Trucks lined the front of the bagel shop off Scott Swamp Road. It was a local favorite with good food and slow service, perfect for killing a few hours before the pawnshop opened. Preston hoped that Ruth would be long gone before he arrived; he didn't want any slip-up on her part. Moss wouldn't appreciate that his grave-robbing secret had gone public. Preston didn't care about such activities, but the authorities would undoubtedly feel differently.

His tenure as a bench silversmith for the Moss organization was quickly coming to an end. The Moss bracelet was nearly finished and, even without the application of an antique patina, it appeared old like vintage pieces that would change hands for $2,000 in Santa Fe during the Martindale summer antique show.

On the end of one terminal, Preston planned to etch a tiny "PY" and "Diné" barely visible to the naked eye. He hoped whoever was thinking of buying the piece would use a magnifying loop and recognize that the piece was a reproduction. Preston grinned, thinking of Billy Moss's reaction to getting caught cheating red-handed.

The finishing touches would be a substantial saw-tooth bezel and a green Cerrillos stone, a replica of the pieces housed in museum collections. Moss would no doubt be pleased with the work. When his shift was over, he would leave the bracelet on the bench with a note thanking Moss for the opportunity, telling him to keep all the proceeds when the bracelet sold, and asking him to send his wages to his Albuquerque address.

Today was going to be big for Billy Moss—a meeting with Marvin and lots of fireworks after. He picked Ruth up at the usual time behind the post, away from prying eyes. The Ram truck was the vehicle of choice for his outing. He had packed three jugs of water, a sleeping bag and some extra food. Moss wasn't sure when he would be able to get back to collect Ruth because of his planned schedule, and he wanted to make sure she didn't freeze to death or die of dehydration in case he didn't return until the morning. He needed many more beads before his multi-strand necklace was complete.

Ruth was OK with this arrangement. She told Moss not to worry; she would be happy spending the night out in the open, even if it snowed, as long as she had a good sleeping bag. In reality, she hoped she might get more time with Ernie, who spent each day with her. She was becoming fond of the gentle giant, and he seemed to like her too.

CHAPTER 38

FALLING TO PIECES

After leaving Bloom, Marvin ambled back home. The twenty-four hours since the return of his father's necklace had been marked by deeply buried emotions bubbling up into his consciousness.

"What was going on with Preston Yellowhorse," Marvin wondered. "He had to be up to more than just making some extra money. He's too talented a silversmith to be working for a man like Moss at a bench and getting paid minimum wage."

He still hoped he could somehow get Ernie's weaving returned so both men's lives could change dramatically for the better. The burden of guilt, which had plagued him all his adult life, could finally be removed.

Marvin entered his hogan and went directly to the only piece of handmade furniture in the home—a 1930s oak bureau—and pulled out a set of well-worn notebooks that had been hidden in his sock drawer. These were his Indian boarding school diaries, the very notes that helped develop his photographic memory.

Marvin realized his ability to recall details was not like that of most people. He could remember specific dates, places, and individuals he had met—that was just how his mind worked—and he felt the journals had played a large part in that evolution. Reading the passages for the first time in ten years brought the sounds, smells, and feelings of Indian school streaming back into his consciousness; Patsy Cline's voice, his crazy idea for Ernie's escape while stuck in a claustrophobic box that stank of urine, the memory of eating sacred raw snake meat, losing his precious necklace, and forcing his friend to gift his blanket to the evil Soliday.

"These are the old images," Marvin said as he rubbed the long-lost squash blossom necklace. "I will have better memories soon." He automatically hid the notebooks under his bed pillow, even though he knew they had done their job.

"Today is a new day, a new life," Marvin said as he pulled his green knit hat over his ears before heading back out into the chilly morning. "Looks like a cold winter, but I am ready for whatever you can throw at me, Mother Earth." Marvin smiled as he looked at the ten-foot-high stack of perfectly cut firewood next to his hogan.

Marvin got into his truck and started the engine, this time with the first turn of the key. "A good sign," he thought. He sat thinking as the cab slowly warmed up, the wind blowing off the first big snow on the Chuska that now was streaming down the Toadlena basin. "Sure glad I got new tires. Hate to hit ice and end up in those Bisti Badlands."

Marvin's usual route to Farmington was on Highway 491, passing by Tsénaajin and Tsénaajin Yázhí and Table Mesa before turning east at Shiprock on Highway 64. He usually stopped at City Market in Shiprock for groceries, which was cheaper than the Toadlena Post, but not as convenient or as much fun. Today, though, he would take the slightly faster route going east on Indian Service Route 5, traversing the Bisti Badlands and turning north on 371 through the off-reservation trust lands. The first section of the hour-long trip was barren; a moonscape of white hills, the name was fitting for a place where not even a Navajo could scrape out a living.

The solitary drive gave Marvin the opportunity to meditate on how he could convince a man like Billy Moss that a rare and valuable chief's blanket was actually the property of a Navajo man, taken from him by Soliday nearly sixty years ago. On the phone, Moss sounded like he wanted to help, but he would need to talk to the man in person and look him in the eyes to know the real story.

As the Ford truck entered Farmington Marvin slowed, then turned left on Highway 64 heading toward Moss Pawn and Trading Post. He passed five pawnshops before he saw Moss's store on the far west side of town. Marvin wondered how a town of forty thousand could support so many pawnshops; you would think the competition would be vicious. Marvin had never used Moss's place or any Farmington pawnshop for that matter; when he was short of money he preferred the Gallup pawnshops, if only because it was an old family tradition to pawn in in that town. Tradition was important to Marvin.

Marvin found the exterior of Moss's Pawn and Trading Post unimpressive. He backed his truck into a space at the front of the shop, a trick he had learned in the military: it was good to be ready to leave if you didn't know what kind of trouble was waiting. Backing in won't waste time or leave you vulnerable. His only sibling, his older brother, Ned Jr., had been killed in a rollover years ago, so Marvin always took his driving seriously—and this was one of those occasions when it would pay to be diligent.

The front door dinged when he walked in and two cameras greeted him—not unusual in pawn stores with high-ticket items. Marvin wondered if the cameras were working or just there for show; Moss seemed more like a for-show type of guy.

Jane greeted Marvin without raising her head. He smiled to himself, thinking, "Yup. She looks like a Jane." He announced he had an appointment to see Billy Moss—and Jane, clearly surprised, looked up from her magazine.

"Must be rare for Navajos to get an appointment," Marvin said, noticing Jane's not-so-subtle reaction.

"No, nothing like that—I just didn't know you was coming. Billy usually tells me when he has an appointment. I'll go get him"

Billy was in his back office, where no one was allowed unless the trader was present. Jane checked with Moss to see if the man indeed had an appointment, which he did. Moss followed Jane back to the front of the shop.

"Yá át ééh, Hastiin Manycoats," Moss said, trying to sound respectful. "How about we go back to my office where we can talk. Would you like some coffee? I just brewed a strong batch."

"Sure, I never turn down fresh coffee. This is cup two already for me—and just call me Marvin."

"OK, Marvin, how do you like your coffee?"

"Two scoops of sugar... I got a bad sweet tooth." Marvin grinned, showing his two front teeth as a joke.

Moss didn't get Marvin's Navajo humor. "Hey, Jane," he called, "can you bring Marvin a cup of coffee with two scoops of sugar?"

Jane wasn't particularly happy about being Marvin Manycoats' waitress, but she did as she was ordered. The two men sat down, Moss at his desk and Marvin across from him. Jane delivered the coffee and promptly left, closing the door behind her.

"I appreciate you wearing that great Slender Maker necklace for me. You mind if I take a photo with my Polaroid camera? It looks so cool and I've never seen Slim's work except in museums."

Marvin had considered not bringing the necklace, but Moss had asked and he wanted to start off on a good footing with the man—though he wasn't keen on having his photograph taken anytime. A Polaroid snapshot sounded better than one of those smartphone pictures that tracked your face and movements. In this respect, Marvin and Moss were on common ground.

"OK, but we Indians charge $1 to take our photos, you know." Marvin thought Moss would get the joke.

"No problem. Around here we charge the tourists $2. Say cheese!" Moss shook the photo to let it dry and looked at the image. Satisfied, he put it in his desk drawer and started his subtle interrogation.

"I'm happy that my Aunt Pingry swapped necklaces with you. I know that piece must be so precious to your family. It was an awful thing to have happen, especially when you were a kid. I didn't know anything about this until yesterday, when my aunt called me. It's just inexcusable."

"Yes, Billy. The experience was painful, and I wish I did have some family left to share the piece with, but I'm afraid it's just me. I am relieved that part of my ordeal is over. I'm hoping you can help me solve another mystery, the one about Ernie Yazzie's chief's blanket."

"I would love to help if possible. What can you tell me about the blanket's disappearance?"

"Last I knew that devil Soliday was selling the blanket to Old Man Springer's trading post back in October of 1961."

Although Moss didn't love his stepfather much, the "devil" part stung—even though the trader's facial expression never changed.

"Can you tell me what exactly happened, how the rug ended up in Soliday's hands to begin with?"

Marvin took a few minutes to tell Moss how he and Ernie lost their heirlooms to Soliday; he wanted to give the man the best chance to help him find the piece.

"Wow, that's an amazing story to say the least. Do you know if there are any photos of the weaving? That would make it a lot easier to identify."

"No photos that I know of. We Navajo didn't have cameras back then."

"How about Yazzie? I'm assuming he's still alive from the way you talk about him. Could he identify the piece? A lot of years have passed and he must have been pretty young when it was taken."

"He's not that far from here—he lives east of Beautiful Mountain. And he would recognize that blanket for sure."

"Does he know that we're talking? I don't want to get his hopes up too much," Moss said, fishing for more information.

"Not yet, but I plan on telling him soon. He will be excited to learn anything about the blanket's whereabouts. Even if there is only a small chance of finding it, he hasn't had any hope at all for a long time. So what can you tell me?" Marvin was ready to hear answers at this point.

"Well, I don't know if you knew this, but Soliday was actually my stepfather. My mom married him when I was twelve. He and I didn't get along well—he was a very tough disciplinarian, as you know."

Marvin understood this all too well, and was now uncomfortable knowing that he was dealing with the devil's kin. He wondered if he had shared too much.

"I did end up with all his papers, which is why I think Aunt Pingry wanted you to talk to me. As it turns out, I think I might know what happened to the blanket. It will take some deep digging on my end, but I'll do what I can to help Mr. Yazzie get what is rightfully his returned to him. Do you have a phone number for Mr. Yazzie?"

"He's got no phone, but he's the last turn off to the west at the base of Beautiful Mountain, a long, bad dirt road that goes on for about 10 miles. You can visit him if you want to, but go slow when you get to the house. If he doesn't know who's coming, he might not be so friendly, if you get my drift."

Marvin was letting Moss know Ernie was not fond of strangers—particularly white ones—and if he knew the bilagáana was Soliday's kid, he would shoot him on sight. Marvin left that part out.

"Thanks for the heads up. That's good to know. I can see why he might not like us bilagáanas," Moss said. Marvin surprised at the man's intuitive grasp of Ernie's state of mind. This white man had clearly been among his people for a while.

As Marvin was getting up to leave, he realized a song was softly playing in the background, one he remembered. It was Patsy Cline's "I Fall to Pieces." A shiver went up Marvin's spine—it was a bad omen.

He looked at Moss and asked, "You like this song that's playing?"

"I do. It's one of my favorites. There is something about that woman's voice that brings me right back to my childhood. How about you?" Moss asked.

"Yes, her voice is memorable. I can see why you like listening to her. I got to go. We'll talk soon."

Marvin had started out the door when Preston walked by heading for the bathroom. "Hi, Preston, how goes the silversmith work?"

Preston forced a smile, wondering why Marvin was at Billy Moss's place. "It goes good. Nice to see you, but I got to get back to the old grindstone."

Preston turned and went back in the direction he had just come from. The ever-observant Billy Moss noticed both the interaction and realized that Marvin knew Preston by name. He had never checked on the Yellowhorse kid's background. Maybe it was about time he did.

Moss decided he would walk Marvin to the door to make sure he took off while he still believed the trader was a nice guy.

"You heading back home?" Moss asked

"Pretty soon. I'm going to do some shopping first. Cheaper to buy groceries in a big city than out on the rez."

Moss noticed the new truck tires, which stood out on a truck like Marvin's.

"Looks like you already been shopping—new tires, not much rez mud yet."

"Yeah, I picked them up in Gallup when I visited your aunt. They cost $650 cash at Shannon's Tire Shop, including service for the lifetime of the tires, but I figure these tires will probably outlast me." Marvin smiled, knowing that at age sixty-eight and not being much of a driver, it was probably true. "Lifetime Guarantee."

"I reckon you're right." Moss smiled back, knowing Marvin had no idea how correct he was.

CHAPTER 39

SHOWTIME

Preston was worried as he went back to his workbench. He had some questions about Marvin's visit; tonight over dinner he would discuss them with Bloom.

"Why was Marvin at Moss's store?" he wondered. "He didn't seem surprised to find that Preston was working for a man Bloom despised. Maybe he was doing some recognizance on behalf of Rachael or Mrs. Bennally, and Bloom wasn't aware it? Or maybe Bloom sent Marvin to make sure Preston was all right."

The last explanation seemed the most likely, but whatever Marvin's reasons for coming there, Moss Pawn and Trading Post would be down an employee by the end of the day.

There were three tasks left on Preston's mental to-do list:

1) Finish the old-style bracelet as promised.

2) See what was behind that padlock—a more dangerous proposition.

3) Write a letter of resignation and get the hell out of Moss's trading post for good.

All to be accomplished by 5 p.m.

Preston decided to text an update to Rachael so she would be in the loop; He knew his mom would worry all day, but he would feel better if she knew what he had found—even if the information was delivered by text, which was not her favorite form of communication.

"Ruth here and safe. Working for Moss, relic hunting near Beautiful Mountain.

"Marvin M. came to Moss's, not sure why. Ask Bloom or you?

"Will quit today, see you tonight for a good meal."

(Smiley face and heart emojis)

Rachael could let Mrs. Bennally know her daughter was safe even if she was doing something illegal. And, hopefully, Preston would have a better understanding of Moss's business activities before he left the premises. If nothing turned up, then Moss was someone else's problem. Preston was done being Mr. Investigator; he was not cut out to be a spy.

Moss appeared unexpectedly to check on his bench silversmith.

"How goes my masterpiece? Sweet piece of Cerrillos turquoise, huh?" he asked, looking over Preston's shoulder and inspecting the work.

"Beautiful stone. Will make a great setting for this bracelet. I'm getting close. I'll finish this piece today, and I should be able to get the next ingot pounded out before I leave. You going to be here for awhile?" Preston asked, hoping Moss would leave so he could do some looking around.

"I may have to go out for a good part of the day. I'll let you know my schedule before I leave. How well do you know Hastiin Manycoats?"

"Not that well. I've seen him around the Toadlena Trading Post occasionally, but that's about it," Preston replied unconvincingly.

Moss knew that most kids, like Preston, didn't hang out around that post unless they went to the nearby elementary school or had friends or family in the area.

"So you couldn't say what kind of guy he is?" Moss was pushing Preston, looking for a reaction.

"No, not really. Never spent time with the guy, though I heard he was a war hero or something like that."

"That's interesting. OK. I'll see you soon."

Moss learned enough to tell that Preston did know Marvin better than he was letting on; now it wouldn't take long for him to figure out the real story behind Preston Yellowhorse.

He opened his out-of-date Dell computer, Googled Preston and Willard Yellowhorse, and in five minutes he had all the answers he needed. Charles Bloom's wife Rachael Yellowhorse had raised Preston as her son. He was a plant and was looking for something. No wonder the talented jeweler was willing to work as a bench silversmith for such low wages.

The trader was even more convinced of Preston's espionage mission when he discovered an entire page on Bloom's Santa Fe gallery website displaying beautiful Preston Yellowhorse bracelets—all sold. There was no way Bloom would allow a relative, who was also one of his artists, to jump ship to work as a bench silversmith. Something was rotten in Denmark, and the stench of corruption started in Farmington, New Mexico.

Moss would set a trap and wait to see what crawled in. Catching rats was his specialty: you just need a tasty morsel, and he had the perfect one. Drowning was Moss's preferred method of extermination. In his mind, Preston was now on all fours—and he hoped the young man couldn't swim.

Today was going to be an exciting day: Moss had laid two separate traps—one for Preston Yellowhorse, the other for Marvin Manycoats—and if everything fell into place, neither would be around much longer.

CHAPTER 40

PICTURES DON'T LIE

Twenty-four hours had passed since his aunt's murder. Moss assumed her body would soon be discovered, so this was the perfect time to capture Marvin Manycoats. Moss looked forward to hanging Bloom's squash blossom accomplice for the murder of Mary Pingry. He told Jane to take the day off, because he wasn't feeling well and might lock up early. There was snow in the air, and it wasn't likely there would be much traffic.

Jane, who had worked with Moss for 15 years, realized that closing early because of the weather was not her workaholic boss's usual routine—but some deals were best done in private, and she figured this was one of those occasions. He didn't look sick to her and, frankly, she would rather not know the details. Instead, she viewed the opportunity to leave early as a great way to get a jump-start on her mountain of laundry and to watch some Judge Judy without being interrupted by customers.

Moss's next move was to leave a phone trail by calling Pingry's house, waiting ten minutes and calling her phone again. Then he practiced his pitch to the cops a few times before he dialed the Gallup Police Department.

"Hi. I need to have someone go out and check on my elderly aunt. I'm afraid something bad may have happened to her. I just had a Navajo guy, Marvin Manycoats, in my store pawning some expensive Indian jewelry, and he had my aunt's antique necklace with him. It's a piece she loves and would never sell."

The officer on the other end listened carefully, taking down Moss's complaint in full.

"He pawns me a very nice old squash blossom, then proceeds to pull out my aunt's necklace, a real beauty of a piece that I know well, and asks me how much I'd give him for this one. He got squirrely when I asked him where he had bought the piece and said never mind—and left not long after that. Before I asked him about where he got the piece, I managed to take a picture of him wearing the squash. It's definitely my aunt's necklace!"

"I understand, Mr. Moss. Have you checked on your aunt today?"

"I called my aunt's phone twice, but she didn't answer. She's ninety years old and rarely leaves her house. I'm sure something bad has happened. This Navajo, Marvin Manycoats, stole her necklace. I know he did. And who knows? It could be even worse than that. I have all his information. Can you please send a police car by her home to see if everything is OK? It's 125 Oak Avenue," Moss said in his most concerned voice, smiling into the phone's receiver as he enjoyed his spurious tale.

Gomez, the female officer who had answered the phone, promised they would look into the matter for him.

One hour later, a detective named Marshall called back with the bad news: Mary Pingry was dead and foul play was a possibility. They wouldn't know for sure if it was a homicide until they got the autopsy results, but all signs pointed towards a robbery: the house had been ransacked.

Detective Marshall asked Moss what might be missing.

"She didn't have much of value," Moss replied. "Just her antique squash blossom necklace in an old white jewelry box in her top drawer. Underneath that, she usually had about $1,000 in cash for an emergency. I'm afraid I was her only relative. Did you find the necklace or the cash?"

"Only an empty jewelry box," the detective said. "We are dusting the place now for prints. Any chance you can come down to the morgue to identify the body?"

"I'll be there in a couple of hours. I'm up here in Farmington, or I would have gone to check on her myself.

"I have a picture of my aunt wearing her necklace. I also told Officer Gomez I managed to get a Polaroid of this Manycoats character wearing the same piece this morning. I'm not telling you how to do your job, but Manycoats should be a suspect."

"He is high on our list as a person of interest. What can you tell me about Marvin Manycoats, Mr. Moss?"

"I can start with what he's driving—a beat-up old 1987 Ford truck, faded yellow with brown stripes. I got his license, too—NM GRN1864. When he began to act squirrelly, I wrote the plate number down.

"I walked him out of my store because I didn't trust him, and noticed he had new tires on his truck. When I asked him about them, he said that he got them at Shannon's Tire Store in Gallup yesterday. This guy didn't have two cents to rub together, so my guess is he paid cash for those tires—with my aunt's money.

"Why would you come up to pawn your stuff in Farmington today if you were in Gallup buying tires yesterday? Seems kinda suspicious if you ask me...."

"I would agree with you, Mr. Moss. We have lots of things to investigate here, starting with Mr. Manycoats' whereabouts. Thanks for the information. I'll see you in two hours; hopefully I'll have some answers by then. It was a great break that he picked you, of all people, to pawn the necklace."

"Yeah, one in a million. I will probably be there closer to 3 p.m., Detective Marshall. I've got to get something finished up here before I can close down."

Moss put down the phone and picked up the Polaroid photo of Marvin wearing his Slender Maker necklace and the 1971 picture of Pingry wearing the same piece. Then he updated Preston on his afternoon schedule—the trader would be gone for about five hours. He told Preston to lock up if he wasn't back by closing, and handed him a complete set of store keys.

Preston smiled and said he would stick around until 5 p.m.; if Moss hadn't returned by then, he would leave the keys in the pot with the plastic flowers next to the front door.

"I'll see you tomorrow if I don't see you later today." Moss smiled and headed out the door.

Preston listened for sounds of the truck, which took off to the west in a hail of gravel, then looked at the handful of keys and said out loud, "Bingo!"

Unfortunately, you shouldn't yell Bingo until you know for sure you have a winning ticket—and Preston's number was about to come up.

CHAPTER 41

A SETUP

Shiprock's monolithic mass was in view as occasional flurries hit Marvin's truck window. The radio DJ gave the temperature at 38 degrees, with a winter storm watch for tomorrow morning. Marvin ignored the warning about severe weather; he had some storms of his own to pass through.

"Soliday's son! I can't believe that Moss is that old man's stepson!"

Marvin was still trying to figure out the implications of that revelation. Pingry had said Moss might know something about the blanket, but she hadn't told him the whole story. He turned down the radio as he talked it out to himself.

"Maybe that tidbit was too embarrassing, or she was afraid I might blow up knowing about that connection. I called Soliday the devil and Moss's expression didn't change. Maybe he did hate the guy—it's not that hard to imagine. Yet he was playing his dad's favorite Patsy Cline song, so there must be some kind of affection there too...."

The whole story was hard to believe, but the circle of life composed of ice cream, exercise, and good fortune that Marvin had recognized earlier could also be at work here, so he didn't dismiss any of the possibilities.

Bloom had warned Marvin that Moss was not a good guy—and watching the trader's bullying at the Halloween party reinforced the idea that this was an angry man. But today he was fine, better than fine. And that song? It had to mean something. Marvin couldn't decide on which side of the fence his emotions lay.

The radio announcer came back on and warned that tomorrow would be a bad day to travel, so Marvin decided to fight the Foodland crowds and load up on supplies in case the storm turned out to be worse than expected—which it often did on the reservation. Then he would head over to Ernie's place. The man had the right to know the full story, Soliday and all.

Marvin parked his car as far from the entrance as possible to get more exercise in case he was homebound tomorrow. As he turned off the engine, "Where the Boys Are," a Connie Francis song, came on. He shuddered, knowing there was danger following him. If he could only decipher what the airwaves were trying to tell him....

The store was buzzing with activity. Normally, Marvin would enjoy the people-watching, but his mind was occupied with thoughts of his friend. He wandered aimlessly up and down the aisles, trying to figure out what the Holy People were telling him. Ernie Yazzie was like Moss: he could be an angry man, and his short fuse had cost him six months in the county lockup thirty-five years ago. Ernie was older and wiser now, but not far below that calmer surface was a man who was still on the edge of exploding.

Marvin was selecting apples when he accidentally dropped one. As the fruit rolled across the ground, the off-kilter movement tweaked something in his mind.

"Maybe Ernie went to Matchstick Woman's house too," he thought. And if he had found out about the Moss-Soliday connection, he might make an unexpected visit to see Moss—and that would not be good.

Going to see his friend became priority number one, and a steaming Foodland roasted chicken and some homemade mustard potato salad would go along way toward keeping Ernie on the right path. Maybe Marvin would even spend the night. Ernie had lots of room, and there were worse places to be snowed in—at least he would have company.

First, though, Marvin had to feel out his friend before he told him about the Matchstick Woman-Moss-Soliday connection. Having a plan made Marvin feel better and, when he rubbed the turquoise his father had interspersed between the squash blossom beads beneath his shirt, he relaxed immediately.

He then asked, in a whisper, for Changing Woman to look after her children tonight—Marvin knew he needed all the help he could muster.

The voice of the Navajo Nation KTNN AM 660 was playing in the background as Marvin grabbed the last hot chicken under the heat lamp. He must be heading in the right direction, he thought: he never got the last chicken.

"We have an updated weather report," the DJ announced. "The storm watch has been upgraded to a warning. It's the first major storm of the season—time to gather up your sheep. Expect accumulations of eight to twelve inches of snow in the next twenty-four hours."

Marvin wasn't worried. He had a four-wheel drive truck and the bad weather was a half-day off. He would check his tool chest to make sure he had his chains in there before heading for Ernie's place.

The lines were long as he stood waiting to check out when an overhead speaker blared. "We have a special in the ice cream section—two for the price of one on all cartons of Blue Bunny Ice Cream."

Apparently, Marvin was not yet done shopping. As he pushed his cart toward the frozen food section, the circle was coming into sharper perspective.

CHAPTER 42

I'M NOT DEAD YET

Finding the turn-off to Ernie's place was easy enough in the daylight when the conditions were good. Marvin made a mental note of the location of the fence and the worn-out tire marking the turn in case he ever had to come back in a storm at night.

There was a fresh set of truck tracks on Ernie's road—something unusual, Marvin thought. Ernie wasn't the type to go out much. He now really wondered if Ernie had paid Matchstick Woman a visit. Marvin's anxiety increased as he pulled up to his old friend's house. The truck was in the front yard, but there was no sign of Ernie or his favorite black horse.

"Ernie must be out riding," Marvin said to himself. He knew that if his friend could see the dust cloud raised by his vehicle, he would come back pronto. Marvin could always count on Ernie's hunting skills to be in full force.

Ernie, who was with Ruth, heard the far-off mechanical hum of an engine and headed to a vantage point where he could see a fine line of dust in the distance, so he knew someone was coming along his ten-mile dirt road. He had spent every day but one talking to Ruth about life and his passion for building rock structures. He hadn't been this social with another human since his mom died.

Yesterday was not a good day. Ernie's hózhó had been endangered by the white woman's trapped chindi. He had discovered the old lady dead and hadn't heard anything about her passing on the radio—a bad sign. He didn't mention his trip to Gallup to Ruth, who seemed oblivious to the fact that he had arrived hours later than usual. When she was entranced finding beads, time seemed to stop for the girl. Ernie understood her obsession well enough, as he felt that way with his wall structures. It was one of the ways they were simpatico.

Ernie scrambled back down the hill.

"Ruth, I got to go see who's coming up my road. It's probably nothing, but I don't like anyone on my mom's land, especially if it turns out I don't know them."

"OK. I'm fine out here. I got good gloves and a hat, and look at how much food and water I have—even a sleeping bag if I need it. Moss told me he might be very late picking me up tonight. You don't need to worry about me, but do come back. If I get cold, I might need a warm body in my sleeping bag."

Ernie and Ruth both blushed; this was a new step and one he liked. He might be twenty-five years her senior, but he wasn't dead yet.

"You can count on it, but I might be a while. I'll see you soon, I hope"

Ernie jogged off, mounted his horse and, in one fluid movement, spurred the stallion toward his compound.

❋ ❋ ❋ ❋

Marvin waited two minutes in his truck—a typical Navajo courtesy—before knocking on Ernie's door. A polite guest waits for the host to straighten things up, especially if it's an unannounced visit. But there was no Ernie and no horse, so after two bangs on the wooden door, he turned the handle. The door was unlocked and he walked in. Ernie would be OK with him escaping the cold.

There was no sign of his friend inside either, though a half-full, lukewarm coffee pot was on the stove. Marvin helped himself to a cup even though he was still feeling the effects of Moss's strong coffee from a few hours ago. He went back out to his truck, brought in the bags of flour and beans he had picked up for his friend, and put his ice cream into the solar-powered refrigerator.

There is a saying on the Rez: A rich Navajo is a bad person because the wealth means he or she is not giving to friends and family. Marvin would never be accused of being rich.

The smell of the roasted chicken hit Ernie's nose at the same time as he recognized the Ford truck, and a rare smile appeared on his face: "Marvin's here."

He slowed his horse from a gallop to a trot, knowing the intruder was an old friend. Ernie wondered if Marvin might have had something to do with Matchstick Woman's death, and he hoped her chindi had not affected Marvin too. Ernie would tread delicately on that subject, considering that he never called the police, just stole Pingry's little rug and left.

"Yá át ééh, Marvin. Where you be?"

"I'm in the house fixing you a nice early dinner. I hope you like hot chicken and potato salad," Marvin teased, already knowing the answer.

"Nah, I hate chicken. I only eat pork now, working on a new religion," Ernie laughed, his mouth watering in anticipation as he dismounted and put his horse in the corral just as the first flurries hit the warm ground. The snow melted instantaneously.

"So you got good news for me, Marvin? Have you found my blanket along with my dinner table?"

"Well, I do have some good news," Marvin said as he met his friend at the front door. Ernie spotted the necklace immediately.

"I can't believe my eyes! The Slender Maker necklace! I remember you wearing that on the yellow squash bus when they hauled us off to Gallup. God, we were scared! This story got to be good!"

The two men headed back into the hogan and sat down at the table, the hot steam rising off the chicken fogging the single windowpane. Ernie tore into the chicken with his hands, gobbling hunks of breast meat. Marvin, oblivious to the poor table manners, followed Ernie's lead. These were lifelong bachelors at their best.

Marvin told Ernie about yesterday's encounter with Matchstick Woman, and didn't leave any details out. Ernie listened intently and tried to talk as he gulped an overly large bite of chicken. It took him a moment to recover.

"So… so… Is that everything? Nothing else about my blanket? What did this Moss guy say exactly?"

Marvin retold the story of his visit with Moss, with Ernie nodding his head in agreement. His head stopped shaking when Marvin filled in one key detail:

"Billy Moss is Soliday's stepson. He says he's got the records Soliday kept and thinks he knows where the blanket might be—so we have hope," Marvin said, looking sympathetically at his oldest friend.

"Soliday's son! Why you waiting to tell me this until now?" Bits of chicken spewed into the air as Ernie responded to this revelation.

"Well, because I knew you might get upset, like you're doing right now," Marvin said flatly.

"I have a right to be angry. That man's stepfather stole my childhood and my dignity. If his son knows something, we need to go see him now and demand to read those records—or I'll show him what a big, mean Navajo who lifts rocks all day can do with his fists."

"Would you calm down and eat some potato salad? There are ways to do this, right ways and wrong ways."

"You mean like making someone sign a bill of sale that was a lie—that kind of right way?" Ernie said spitefully, immediately regretting his words.

"Well, if you say so—but I did what I thought was right. Remember, I was twelve and you were eleven. Those would have been tough decisions for an adult man, but for a scared kid, well…" Marvin's voice started to crack, and Ernie interrupted.

"I'm sorry. You're right, we were scared kids, and we did what we had to do survive. Soliday was a bad man, and we were in a very bad school. People who didn't have to walk our path shouldn't judge us; not all Indian schools were like Two Trees," Ernie said.

Marvin looked at the half-eaten chicken, his appetite evaporating with the steam.

"Well, now I got a question for you, Marvin. Don't take it the wrong way, but I got to ask and you got to tell me the truth. I'm not judging you."

"Go ahead, I don't have any more secrets." Marvin looked up and locked eyes with his friend.

"Did you kill Matchstick Woman to get that necklace?"

"Did I kill her? No! I told you I swapped her my raffle necklace for my dad's. It was a good trade and nobody got hurt."

"You sure about that? You didn't force the trade and things went bad?" Ernie asked once again, looking for any sign his friend was lying.

"No, absolutely not. Why would you even ask me such a question?" Marvin demanded.

"Matchstick Woman is dead. I found her yesterday in her home, dead like a chicken with its neck snapped. Looked to me like someone killed her."

"You saw her dead yesterday? What time?" Marvin was now so distraught his stomach was hurting.

"Not sure. I don't have no watch, but I'd guess around 1 p.m. or so. I saw a man on a motorcycle leave the place just before I went in. I was going to get some answers from Matchstick Woman, but someone apparently got to her first."

"Did you call the police?"

"Nope. I looked for your necklace and my blanket, then I skedaddled out of there. It's not my business. And I haven't heard nothing on the radio about no deaths."

"Did you find anything when you looked around?" Marvin asked his friend, who was looking down at his feet.

"Yeah, a little Toadlena/Two Grey Hills rug. I took it," Ernie confessed, looking up defiantly.

"OK, well, we can deal with that later. What did the man on the motorcycle look like?"

"Bilagáana, medium-sized guy, nothing that would scare me. Nice bike, light-green color with New Mexico plates—I wasn't that close so I couldn't tell you anything else except that he was in a hurry to get out of there."

"A green motorcycle?" Marvin's mind flashed through all the stored images of motorcycles in his mental Rolodex until he recognized an entry—"the Toadlena Post, mint-green, October 31, three men with bikes, one was Moss!"

Marvin now felt so sick to his stomach he was afraid his chicken was going to reappear.

"Ernie, I think I'm in big trouble and I hope you aren't, too. Did you clean your fingerprints off anything you touched at Matchstick Woman's house, like a door handle or wherever you found that little rug?"

"Sure, I touched things. How else would I get in and out?"

Then it was Ernie's turn to feel sick. He had left fingerprints in the house of a dead woman, he had stolen her rug and he had been in jail. The cops would have his old fingerprints on file. Cops liked to close cases, and he would now be a prime suspect—a Navajo with a grudge and a history of violence, in the house of a dead white woman who had worked with the man he accused of stealing his family blanket.

"I think I've been set up, and maybe you have too, Ernie. Moss was asking me questions about where you lived."

"What did you say?"

"I told him where you lived and that you didn't have a phone. I also told him I was going to talk to you soon. That green motorcycle you saw, I believe it's Billy Moss's ride. I remember seeing it at the Toadlena Trading Post. I think Moss might have killed his aunt, but I'm not sure why...." Marvin's voiced trailed off. The chicken dinner was officially over.

The reservation radio station was blaring again, but it was no longer background noise. The two men were unconcerned about the weather reports; they were listening for any news about a white woman's death in Gallup.

As they began discussing the possibilities, Ernie forgot all about Ruth, who would soon have a hungry coyote bearing down on her.

CHAPTER 43

A SERIOUS PREDICAMENT

Preston didn't waste any time after he heard Moss's truck leave the parking lot. Keys in hand, he was ready to find the one that would unlock the padlock on the door behind Moss's office. On his third attempt, the tumbler clicked and the lock opened. When Preston carefully pushed the door open, the smell of gunpowder filled his nose.

"Was it a booby-trap?" Preston wondered, his mind racing as he fumbled for the light on his phone. "Shit! Look at all those guns," he said out loud.

The room was an arsenal of machine guns, bump fire stocks and multiple-round ammo clips. There were bags of gunpowder stacked like flour, and a few weapons he couldn't even identify. The cache of military hardware was not what he expected, and his heart was racing as he considered the possibilities.

An odd slapping sound behind him broke through his thoughts; when he pivoted around toward the noise, there was Billy Moss with a two-foot billy club in his right hand, hitting the wooden stick against a leather strap gripped tightly in his left hand.

"Looks like I've got a Bloom spy in my midst," Moss said with a crazed look on his face, his eyes squinting in the dark room. "You're way out of your league, kid—and I guess you must realize it about now."

"No, you have it all wrong, Mr. Moss. I... I was looking for some tools that I needed... for my bracelet."

"Really? That's the best you can come up with? You better start getting straight with me, or you're going to be on the wrong end of this billy club."

Moss slammed the club down on a desk, the CRACK reverberating through the small room. Panicking, Preston considered grabbing one of the guns on the rack behind him, but he didn't know how to use a machine gun, or how to tell if it was even loaded. He was screwed.

"OK, OK. You're right. I'm not being completely straightforward."

"Start talking and don't leave anything out."

"I wanted to find out about Ruth… Just trying to make sure she is OK. Her mom's a friend of my mom. That's all, we were just worried about Ruth." Sweat was dripping down Preston's back in the chilly back room.

"What did you find out?"

"Well, I talked to Ruth only once, this morning. She told me she was happy and fine, was doing some work for you and not to worry. I was going to let her mom know she was fine tonight. Case closed."

"So you were at the store before we opened?"

"Yes. I came in at 7 a.m. to see if Ruth was here. I talked to her through the back window for a few minutes—that's all."

"What kind of work did she say she was doing for me?"

Preston wasn't sure how to handle this question, so he lied. "Picking through gravel. She said it was fun and she was happy."

"That's all she said? Nothing else, just picking through gravel?"

"Yeah, nothing else."

"Hand over everything in your pockets and give me the code to unlock your phone," Moss demanded.

Preston reluctantly handed over his phone, keys, a pocketknife and his wallet, and gave Moss the phone code—1680, the year the Pueblo Indians overthrew the Spanish in New Mexico.

Moss read Preston's text message to Rachael:

"Ruth here and safe. Working for Moss, relic hunting near Beautiful Mountain.

"Marvin M. came to Moss's, not sure why. Ask Bloom or you?

"Will quit today, see you tonight for a good meal.

(Smiley face and heart emojis)

"Looks to me like you knew Ruth's job description perfectly. You're not being straight with me, boy. That kind of crap will get you in serious hot water—capisce?"

"Yes, Mr. Moss, I do. I'm sorry, but I don't care if you are collecting some little turquoise beads—we Navajo don't like Nasazi stuff to begin with, so take them all. I'm happy if you do, fewer issues for me."

Moss listened. Preston probably didn't care about the relics; that part was true, but the rest of the text showed Preston was snooping for Bloom or at least for his wife. That was a problem—and he had found the guns.

"What else did Ruth tell you? I want every detail, the truth this time."

"That's it. She said that the place she was picking up the beads was twelve miles east of Beautiful Mountain, near Ernie Yazzie's place."

This information stunned Moss. Yazzie's name came up again, and somehow Ruth knew the man.

"What did she say about Yazzie?"

"Nothing. Just that his place was close to the bead site. I don't know Yazzie, and I didn't ask her any other questions about him."

Preston's answer seemed sincere, so Moss changed topics.

"Tell me why you broke into my private locked gun room."

"Well, it was stupid. I was interested that's all. There was a locked door, we Navajo are curious people."

"You ever hear the phrase, 'Curiosity killed the cat?'"

"Maybe, not sure."

"Well, it means you're in deep shit, my friend, and so is Ruth, thanks to your catlike instincts."

Preston knew he was in a dangerous predicament and that there was nothing he could do about it. If only he were a mountain lion instead of a pussycat! The best he could hope for was to land on his feet at the moment of truth. But for now, his balance was off and he was tipping toward death.

CHAPTER 44

RAT TRAPS

Moss ordered Preston to take off his belt, which he then used to tie the younger man's arms to his sides. He removed Preston's shoes and duct-taped his legs together. A dry cloth was shoved into Preston's mouth, which Moss duct-taped closed, taping over his eyes as well.

Preston was pushed down to a supine position on the cold floor and told not to move or he would become Moss's personal punching bag. To reinforce the point that he was not messing around, Moss viciously slapped Preston's right arm with the billy club, causing severe pain and generating muffled cries from the young man. Before Preston could recover, Moss swatted the leather strap across both his legs, raising a colossal welt and releasing another muffled scream of agony.

"You see, Preston, I'm a man who can make your life very painful. I am in complete control of this situation, so I suggest you don't move.

I'm going to leave you alone now, and you better have some answers when I come back that will help me decide your fate. If you're lucky, you will limp out of here under your own power. If you understand me, nod your head."

Preston nodded affirmatively.

Moss, who had placed a "Closed" sign on the front door, slipped out the rear entrance, went back down the dry arroyo, got into his truck and headed to Gallup. He had an appointment to keep and another rat to drown.

* * * *

Detective Marshall was a well-seasoned, methodical cop who understood Gallup's seedy side. He had seen a number of murders in his career, but was still amazed that a minor robbery could cause someone to take another's life. An antique Navajo squash blossom was valuable and, in Gallup, New Mexico, could undoubtedly lead to murder.

Marshall visited Shannon's Tire Shop off Maloney Avenue, and the owner did remember Marvin's visit two days ago. An invoice was retrieved that gave Marvin Manycoats' address and phone number; he had indeed paid $650 in cash, tax included. The time stamp on the receipt was 11 a.m.

Cash transactions were not unusual in Gallup, but this one was larger than average. Marshall's instincts said, "robbery money." The detective assumed Pingry's death was a homicide and dusted the house for fingerprints, which were plentiful; hopefully, a positive match would be forthcoming.

Moss arrived at the Gallup Police Department three hours after his initial call. When Detective Marshall took the bereaved Moss to the morgue for positive identification of the body, Moss played to his audience.

"Is this your aunt?" Marshall asked as he uncovered the broken body for viewing.

"Yes, I'm afraid it is. She was such a sweet lady. Why would anyone want to harm her?" Moss said in a sad, low voice.

"We don't know yet, but we should have answers soon. If robbery is the motive, these cases usually solve themselves in short order."

"I hope you're right. I feel certain that Manycoats is involved in some way. He acted guilty. I'm sorry, but can we go somewhere else to talk?" Moss asked. What he wanted was a comfortable chair; he wasn't the least bit concerned about the body he had identified, but he was in full fake bereavement mode.

"Sure, I understand. Let's go to the medical examiner's office."

Moss followed Marshall to the second-floor office, where the detective poured him a stale black coffee and began the interview. Marshall was not naïve, and realized that everyone involved in the case could be a suspect. Who knew how much money was at stake—the crime could go deeper than a squash blossom necklace.

"Mr. Moss, let me say I'm sorry for your loss. If you don't mind, I'm going to tape our conversation."

"That's fine. I'm here to help. And thank you, this is such a shock. I had just talked to my aunt a couple of days ago. She was such a vibrant lady."

"We found what appears to be a fairly fresh dent in your aunt's back bumper. Do you know if Mrs. Pingry could still drive herself around?"

"I don't know about any dents, but she could drive. She drove all the way up to the Toadlena Trading Post on Halloween—that was the last time I saw her."

"Were you both at Toadlena?" The detective asked.

"Yes, that is correct."

"And I'm assuming she must have driven by herself?"

Moss was starting to worry the detective would ask what he himself drove. Luckily, the cop didn't go down that path.

"Yes, she drove herself, alone. I didn't know she was going to be there; unfortunately, I just saw her for a second. The place was packed—must have been five hundred people. God, if I had known, that would be the last time…."

"So you went for the party, not to see your aunt?"

"Not so much for the party, but for the raffle. The post gave away a nice squash blossom necklace, and you had to be there in person to win. The winner that day was this Marvin Manycoats, and that was the piece he brought in to pawn to me today. Somehow the necklace had been damaged since he received it on the thirty-first. When I saw it today, the string was broken, and I'm not sure, but it seemed like there were a few missing round silver beads. I brought in the pieces. I thought it might be of some help."

Moss produced a plastic sack with the raffle squash in it.

"Why do you think Manycoats would want to pawn two squash blossom necklaces on the same day?"

"I have no idea. The raffle necklace was found money I guess, and for that matter, my auntie's stolen necklace was too. Or maybe he figured since he stole my aunt's piece, he only needed one, so he sold me the lesser of the two for some spending money—and when he saw how much I gave him for that one, he thought he might as well sell both. I'm sure he would have sold me my aunt's necklace if I hadn't started asking questions."

"How did you pay him for the one squash blossom he sold you?"

"He wanted cash, so that's what I paid the man."

"How much?"

"$750."

"Did he sign for the money?"

Moss had not expected this line of questioning and was not prepared for it, but he figured he could make up a bogus receipt later. He had a note with Marvin's writing on it, or he could just write, "paid cash," and do a scribbled signature. Problem solved.

"Yes, he did. I'm sorry I didn't bring that with me, but I do have his address and phone number. I copied those down for you."

"That's good. I would like that information before you leave, By the way, can others verify that Manycoats won the squash and that this is that piece?"

"Oh yeah, lots of people can verify that. I had hoped to win the piece myself and had bought lots of tickets for the raffle. Funny how things turn out. I end up getting the necklace, but the man who sells it to me may have killed my aunt.

"Here are the pictures I told you about."

Moss showed the Polaroid of Marvin and the old photo of Pingry wearing the exact same necklace. Marshall took photos of the images with his phone and announced what he was doing to his recorder before he returned the pictures to Moss.

"I agree they look to be one in the same. Are you sure that your aunt hadn't simply sold the antique necklace to Mr. Manycoats sometime in the past?"

"No way. That was a gift from my stepfather to her back in the early '60s. She would have rather died than lose that necklace. It not only has sentimental value, but the piece probably is worth at least $10,000— AND she was wearing it at the Toadlena raffle, which means she would have had to sell it in the last week, which seems unlikely. Then she turns up dead in a robbery?"

"Ten thousand dollars for a Navajo necklace?" Marshall said in disbelief. He had lived in Gallup most of his life, and knew squash blossom necklaces weren't worth that much. Moss could see the detective's skepticism and tried to answer in a way that would not bring any suspicion upon himself.

"Yes, I know most aren't that valuable, but this one was by a famous early silversmith named Slender Maker. It's a real museum piece, which is why it's so easy to identify. My aunt would never sell that piece. I just know it. Manycoats stole the necklace and probably killed her, that's what makes the most sense to me."

Moss's story seemed plausible, and the amount of money involved was more than enough motivation to murder someone. The only way to get a better sense of what was going on was to talk to Manycoats.

Detective Marshall dug deeper. "Is there any reason Manycoats might want to steal this necklace, besides its value?"

"Well, in fact, there might be one. Aunt Pingry was a teacher and my stepfather was a well-respected principal in the Indian school system in the 1960s. Manycoats is of the age that would have attended Indian boarding school. Maybe he had some old grudge and knew my relatives from there. Lots of Navajo have bad feelings about those schools. Maybe some of their complaints are justified; I don't know about that. What I do know is that my stepfather and aunt were good, honest people—and so am I."

"OK, we will check out all these leads and get back to you."

Marshall's cell phone buzzed. "Excuse me for one second," he said as he answered the call. "Uh, huh. Uh, huh. OK. Thanks, this changes things," Marshall replied to the voice on the other end of the line.

"We got a fingerprint hit, two actually—one set from Marvin Manycoats, who is apparently ex-military, and another set from a former jailbird, an Ernie Yazzie. Both men's prints were all over the place. We will find out what Yazzie's role in this might be, and if he and Manycoats were associates.

"You ever hear of Mr. Yazzie?"

"Nope, never have."

※ ※ ※ ※

Moss left the police station. "No more loose ends, time is of the essence," he thought as he floored the gas pedal, pushing the speed limit on his way home. For the first time, he was worried. He hadn't figured Ernie Yazzie into the equation, and the dent in Pingry's car that the cops had noticed meant they had samples of green paint that would put him at the crime scene if anyone in Gallup had recognized him on his Green Monster.

The more pressing question was when Yazzie went to Pingry's house and why? He was a friend of Marvin's, and they both had heirlooms stolen from them at the Indian boarding school, so it was hard to imagine that this was a coincidence. When Moss had asked if anyone else had called or come over, Pingry had said, "No."

"I was mad, and she was scared, so I'm sure she was telling the truth," Moss said to himself, as he desperately tried to work out the sequence of events in his mind.

"Ernie must have come after I killed her—or maybe when I killed her! Could he have seen me coming and going?"

Moss realized the scenario was a dangerous possibility. "He had to have seen Pingry dead. The only question is whether he also saw me."

This question had to be answered soon; Moss needed to find Ernie Yazzie and have a man-to-man chat with him. Satisfied he had a rough plan, Moss turned his attention back to Marvin, the designated fall guy.

"Marvin will be arrested for Pingry's death—he has to be, it's a slam-dunk case." Moss smiled, thinking about his performance at the morgue. Then he wondered if Ernie could have talked with Marvin about finding Pingry dead. Moss didn't think this was a possibility; there was absolutely no sign of concern in Marvin's demeanor. When they talked earlier this morning, the Navajo seemed upbeat.

"But what if he talks with Ernie today? Marvin will know he's been had. And where does Ruth fit into this picture? She knows Ernie somehow, and his place isn't far from where she's working...."

Concerned by this unexpected turn of events, Moss would begin the cleansing process as soon as he got back to Farmington. There were questions to be answered—and rats to be drowned.

CHAPTER 45

I TOLD YOU SO

When Rachel received Preston's text saying that Ruth was safe, she walked over to Mrs. Bennally's hogan to give her the good news. Mrs.

Bennally was grateful, as was Rachael, though her inner voice was not so sure her son was out of harm's way.

Preston was dealing with a man who had no scruples, and he was in the middle. She was glad this was her son's last workday. She would wait until 5 p.m. and then text him to find out when he planned to arrive. Rachel, who didn't own a wristwatch, set her phone's alarm to 5 p.m.

She jumped when the alarm sounded, her nerves on edge.

"How goes it? See you soon. (Heart emoji)" Rachael texted Preston—his preferred method of communication.

No answer. She waited 10 minutes and texted again, this time leaving out the heart and adding a question-mark emoji.

Another text followed shortly after. "You OK?" (emoji of praying hands.) Rachael repeated this text two more times, then tried calling. Still no answer.

Her next call was to Bloom, whom she had kept in the loop via texts.

"Bloom, as you can see, Preston's not answering my text or his phone. What do you think we should do? I'm worried!"

"Let's not freak out yet," Bloom replied. "This is not the first time Preston has failed to answer texts, and he never seems to answer your calls. He's probably preoccupied. Remember that time last Christmas when he didn't answer for almost a day?"

"Well, that was different. He was with a girl, not working for a man who hates you, has no morals, is in the process of breaking antiquity laws and who knows what else."

Bloom had no way to respond to this line of reasoning. She was right. He was worried, but didn't want to alarm Rachael.

"OK, I'll be home shortly. We'll figure this out, maybe head up to Farmington and knock on Moss's door."

"Thanks, Bloom. I'm probably overreacting, but you know I have a sixth sense for these kinds of things."

Bloom always trusted Rachael's gut instincts; she was rarely wrong. A call came into the post's phone as Bloom was turning off the lights.

"Charles Bloom, how can I help you...?"

"Mr. Bloom, this is Detective Dave Marshall of the Gallup Police Department."

Bloom's stomach turned; calls from cops were never good.

"I'm looking for a Marvin Manycoats. I was told that he likes to hang out at the post most days. Have you seen him today by any chance?"

Bloom's stomach relaxed as he realized the call wasn't about Preston.

"I saw him earlier today when I opened the store."

"Do you know where he might be now, or where he was yesterday?"

"I don't know his whereabouts yesterday. I didn't see him all day, or for that matter, for a couple of days. But he did come by this morning at around 9:30 a.m. He told me he was heading up to Billy Moss's store in Farmington. Is Marvin OK?" Bloom's concern came through in his voice.

"I'm not at liberty to say a whole lot, but what I can share is that there was what appears to be a homicide, a Mrs. Mary Pingry, at her home in Gallup, which appears to have occurred approximately forty-eight hours ago. Mr. Manycoats is a person of interest."

Bloom was now very concerned. "Pingry on Oak Avenue?"

"Yes, that is correct. Is there anything you can tell me with regards to Pingry or Manycoats?"

"Well, she recently purchased a small Two Grey Hills rug by Violet Roundhouse for $250 here at the Toadlena Trading Post the evening of our Halloween party on October 31. I haven't heard anything else from her."

"Anything you can tell me about Manycoats' activities in the last forty-eight hours?"

"Well, he told me he had swapped antique squash blossom necklaces with Mrs. Pingry. He had a very nice squash blossom around his neck, not the kind thing that I would expect Marvin to own."

"Why would you say that?"

"Well, it's antique and very valuable."

"By Slender Maker, by chance?" the detective asked.

"Yes, that's right. How did you know?"

"Can't say right now, but this helps us a lot. If you hear from Mr. Manycoats, please let us know. By the way, do you know an Ernie Yazzie?"

"No, I don't recognize that name."

"OK. If you hear anything about Mr. Yazzie or Mr. Manycoats, or if either man happens to come by the post, please let me know. Yazzie is the same age as Mr. Manycoats. I hope to get a recent photo of him shortly, but for now I'll email you his mug shot from 35 years ago, though I doubt it will be of much use. Should I use the post's email address?"

"Yes, that's fine. I check all the emails. What was Yazzie in jail for?"

"Drinking and assault. He's not the kind of guy you would want to mess with, so call 911 if you see him. I appreciate your help, Mr. Bloom. We will be in contact.

"Oh, one more thing... Do you know a Billy Moss from Farmington?"

Bloom's stomach cramped back up. "Yes, I do. Why do you ask?"

"Well, he was the one who called in the missing person report today. Mrs. Pingry was his aunt. What kind of a guy is he?"

"Not the kind I would keep as a friend. He seems like a man who has no problem skirting the law."

"Interesting... I'll call you tomorrow when I know more. Is it possible you could come down to Gallup so we can talk in more detail?"

"Sure, I'll be there at 10 a.m. if that works."

"Perfect. Thanks again, Mr. Bloom. I'll see you tomorrow."

As soon as Bloom hung up the phone he called Marvin's cell, leaving a message when there was no answer.

"Marvin, this is Charles Bloom. A detective named Marshall called asking about you. Pingry is dead, and I think they believe you are involved. Also, Preston is not answering his phone and Rachael is very concerned. Please call me when you get this message, no matter how late it is."

Bloom then ran out of the trading post and headed home to let Rachael know what had transpired. He was anxious. All paths were leading to Moss, and it didn't look good.

Rachael was pacing the floor when Bloom arrived home.

"No word from Preston, nothing."

Rachael's face contorted as Bloom delivered the bad news. The rundown of Detective Marshall's call was helpful to Rachael; she interrupted Bloom numerous times, trying to fish out an obscure missed detail that would somehow answer all her mounting questions.

"We have to do something, Bloom. Preston is in trouble. I can feel something is wrong. I knew we shouldn't have allowed my child to work for that man!"

"I understand you're worried, and so am I, but let's not go off the rails yet. Maybe try calling Preston again?"

Rachael whipped out her phone and shoved her call history in Bloom's face.

"Really, Charles Bloom. See those ten phone calls in a row? They have all gone directly to voice mail. Now let me ask you if you've called Marvin yet. I think maybe he could answer a lot of our questions."

"Yes, I called and left a detailed message. He knows what's going on now if he didn't before."

"We need to go to Marvin's hogan—and we need to go now!"

Bloom didn't know what the right next step was, but he knew that Rachael couldn't be stopped. They were headed to Marvin's home, dropping their kids off with Mrs. Bennally. They told the weaver there was some trouble and they hoped to be home soon, but it could be quite late.

Marvin's door was unlocked, something not unusual on the rez, and Rachael and Bloom entered the house carefully. Bloom had procured a four iron from his cobweb-covered golf bag just in case there was trouble. It was the only weapon he owned.

The hogan was typical of many older Navajo residences. There was a large 1987 Ford dealership calendar featuring wild running horses on the back wall. Directly below it was a neatly made military cot from the Korean war era, an oak clothing dresser next to the bed, a large pine writing table with a single drawer, and a plastic chair in the other corner of the building. No signs of trouble or Marvin. The two worn black notebooks Marvin had left pushed under the pillow were camouflaged by the dark gray wool army blanket.

"Now what?" Bloom asked.

"I don't know what I was hoping to find, maybe Marvin asleep on his bed or some obvious clue in plain sight. Check his desk. I know he likes to write. Maybe there is an answer there."

Bloom opened the drawer and pulled out a checklist written in Marvin's hand.

"Clue!" Bloom started reading the note out loud:

> 1) Talk to Matchstick Woman, see if she might understand. She's old, maybe she has no one to leave the piece to.

2) Break in and take it, like Soliday took it from me.

3) Hire a professional to take it.

4) Take care of Matchstick Woman in some other way.

"Do you think Matchstick Woman is Marvin's code name for Mrs. Pingry?" Bloom asked.

"Could be. We Navajo like to name people by the way they look. She was so skinny, it fits—and he refers to Matchstick Woman as 'she' and 'old.'"

"Rachael, I didn't tell you this before, but Marvin said Pingry liked the raffle squash blossom necklace more than the Slender Maker piece but that's not what Pingry had told me—just the opposite in fact."

"Really? What did she say?"

"Something about how our necklace wasn't nearly as good as hers, and that hers was very old and special. I just figured Marvin must have traded something else to sweeten the pot, but this 'take care of Matchstick Woman, get what belongs to you' talk sounds pretty damned ominous. If he's talking about Mrs. Pingry, I'm not sure he didn't steal it."

"What do you think he means by 'she might understand and get what belongs to you?'" Rachael said as she sat down on the bed. Seeing the edge of one of the notebooks peeking out from under the pillow, she pulled the books out and started flipping through the pages.

"Bloom look at these! They're diaries Marvin kept when he was a kid in Indian school. He must have left them here for a reason."

Both Bloom and Rachael begin scanning the notebooks and reading passages back and forth to each other, each more horrific than the last.

"Here, right here. Ernie Yazzie was with him at school. This has got to be the same guy the detective was asking about," Rachael said.

"It gets worse, Rachael. Marvin's father's squash blossom, a piece by Slender Maker, and Ernie Yazzie's blanket were apparently stolen by the headmaster, a man named Soliday. That's the name in the number two solution in the note we found! Matchstick Woman is Pingry and she was Marvin's and Ernie's teacher. This doesn't look good for either one of them."

"I don't know about Yazzie, but I don't believe Marvin could kill that old lady. If he had wanted to that, he could have followed her home the night of the party," Rachael reasoned.

"That's true. Marvin asked me about her address, but he could have just left when Pingry took off. His truck was parked right in front because he was helping me load in food, and he stayed late helping us clean up. He had the opportunity to follow her right then, but he didn't," Bloom agreed.

"You think maybe Ernie and Marvin killed Pingry for that necklace or maybe Yazzie's blanket was there?" Rachael's eyes filled with tears.

"I don't know, but it looks like there were plenty of motives to go around. It doesn't look good for either one of those men, but if I had to make a guess, even if Marvin was pushed by Yazzie to do something violent, I don't believe he is that type of man. And he's very intelligent, so why would he show me that necklace this morning so freely? He was proud of the piece, not trying to hide anything—unless he's a psychopath."

Bloom paused, wondering if Marvin could be that sick, then added, "Moss is involved. It's clear he's part of the equation—I just don't know how. The first step is finding Marvin, and I'm guessing he is with his Indian school buddy Ernie Yazzie. Let's call around and see if we can find out where Yazzie lives. Someone in the community will know."

"What about the notebooks, Bloom? Should we take them? They support what happened to them as kids. Do you think Marvin may have hidden them under the pillow for a reason?"

Bloom thought about her question, then said, "No, we shouldn't remove anything. It's evidence."

"Bloom, I'm taking that note Marvin wrote," Rachael announced in no uncertain terms. "I'll hand it over to the cops if Marvin's guilt becomes clear, but honey, you're not Navajo, so it's harder for you to understand. The Gallup cops won't look any further than the Indian in the room if they see this note. They won't care that Marvin and Ernie were abused as children and that their heirlooms were stolen. All they will focus on is Marvin's note, white woman dead, case closed."

"You're right that I'm not Navajo, my love, but I'm married to one and both my kids are Navajo. Take Marvin's note if you must. We may get into trouble later, but I'm always in your corner, no matter what the consequences. Let's find out where Ernie Yazzie lives." Bloom smiled, and Rachael was glad she had married this bilagáana.

"I know where to go. Thelma Brown knows everyone, and she lives fairly close by," Rachael suggested.

"Give her a call. It will save time."

"Really, Bloom, call Thelma? This is the same person who had to wait a couple of weeks to get her sister from her hogan because her truck broke down. Maybe we can just FaceTime Thelma on her iPhone X?"

Bloom smiled sheepishly, realizing he still had a lot to learn about life on the rez.

Rachael and Bloom didn't wait the standard courtesy time before knocking on Brown's east-facing front door. Thelma answered the door and Rachael unleashed a flood of Navajo questions. Bloom followed her into the house and waited.

Thelma limped over to the dining room table and sat next to her sister Darlene, who was staying with her until the winter storm had passed. She picked up a scrap of paper and a grandchild's crayon and drew a rough map. The three women talked for a couple of minutes, with both Grandmothers pointing to Rachael's wrists. She then thanked them for their help.

"Let's go. I know where Marvin lives. He's ten miles from the base of Beautiful Mountain, not far from those sheer white cliffs you and I liked to hike when we first started dating."

"What else did she say? They pointed at your wrists. Do they know about your injuries? Are they concerned?"

Rachael tried not to smile. "Well, not exactly. Thelma says that, like her sister Darlene, she's got two wrists and will be by to see you next week—and you're welcome for the information."

Bloom was once again outmatched by the Brown sisters.

CHAPTER 46

HAND ME THE GUN

The spotty cell phone coverage kicked in for a brief moment at the Yazzie house. A beep alerted Marvin that he had a message. He had forgotten about his phone while he and Ernie discussed their limited options. Marvin listened to a short message from a Detective Marshall of the Gallup Police Department asking him to call, followed by a long message from Bloom saying Marvin was a suspect in the Pingry murder, then one final message from Bloom advising that as soon as they got directions to Ernie Yazzie's house they would come directly there, figuring that's where they'd find him. Marvin played the messages for Ernie and waited for his reply—which was when Ruth popped back into Ernie's mind.

"Ruth!"

"What does 'Ruth' mean?" Marvin asked.

"Ruth Bennally. She is working for Moss not far from here. I was supposed to go back, but I forgot." Ernie looked out of his one window: the sky was dark and it was snowing lightly.

"What's this all about? Is she outside now? It's snowy and getting cold, and there is bad weather coming soon. And why is she working for Moss?"

Marvin was at a complete loss; the circle of life was taking an unexpected detour. Ernie quickly filled him in on the details as he knew them.

"If Moss is involved, and he's anything like his stepfather, I think Ruth could be in trouble. You need to go check on her now. Let me see if I can get ahold of Bloom."

Marvin looked at his phone: one bar, then no service. He walked outside to see if the cell coverage was any better. Still no service, and the storm wouldn't help reception this night. Marvin knew better than to ask if there was a landline in the hogan; Ernie had no running water and only solar electricity.

"Ernie, draw me a map of where Ruth is working in case you don't come back. You got any weapons?"

"Weapons? You mean guns?" Ernie asked.

"Yeah, guns preferably. You might need one, maybe me too."

Ernie smiled as he lifted his shirt, revealing a Colt .38 Special revolver, and then pulled a .30-06 Springfield rifle from beneath his bed.

Ernie removed the pistol from his waist and handed it to Marvin, handle first.

"It's loaded and ready for bear," he said as he showed his friend the safety lock and the six rounds in its cylinder.

"Not sure I want to go against a bear with this pea shooter," Marvin said, trying to lighten the mood.

"OK Marvin, I'm going. If you don't hear from me in about an hour, there has been a problem and you got two choices: hit the road and don't ever come back to the rez 'cause more than likely the bilagáana cops are going to string you up—or come find me."

The two old friends smiled at each other, taking one last look as if it were required, then Ernie sprinted out the door to his horse and was gone. Marvin could hear the hooves pounding away at full speed.

"It's hard to imagine going full-out like that at night," he thought. "That is one bad-ass Navajo. I hope he doesn't run into Soliday's stepson," Marvin said to the empty room.

The snow was starting to stick. The bad storm promised for tomorrow was coming in early. Rachael was driving her truck toward the Yazzie homestead; she knew how to handle the back roads on the rez, especially the wet ones. When her vehicle fishtailed rounding a slick corner, she took her foot off the accelerator, didn't break, then turned into the slide. Once the worst was behind her, she gently accelerated out of the skid, never missing a beat.

Charles' right hand was pure white as he gripped the front dash; he was glad she was behind the wheel and in charge.

"Over the next rise, that should be his house. Look for a small trailer tire; it marks the road, though it will be hard to see tonight." Rachael started to slow as they crested the hill, the snow coming down harder now.

"There!" Rachael said. Bloom didn't see the tire or the road.

"See those horse tracks? They're fresh," she said as she turned into the drive. There was just one faint lantern light on the entire mesa—Ernie's hogan. Both Rachael and Bloom were amazed at the vast complex of buildings: it looked like the second coming of Chaco Canyon. Rachael had noticed the edifice before, but only from a distance while hiking the white cliffs. Up close and in person, the structure was impressive.

"Look at this place! I've never seen anything like this before," Bloom said in amazement.

"Yeah, Grandmother Thelma said that Ernie was an 'odd duck.' I guess this is what she meant."

Rachael rolled her vehicle to a stop, leaving the engine going and the lights on. Three trucks, all at opposing angles, were parked in front.

"That's Marvin's truck," Bloom said, pointing to the '87 Ford.

As the two got out of Rachael's vehicle, Marvin walked out on the porch with a .38 Special in his left hand. Bloom saw the gun and stopped. Rachael pressed on.

"Hey, Marvin, why you got a gun in your hand?" she asked matter-of-factly.

"Bad night not to," he replied. "I got Bloom's message. It sounds like big trouble brewing and that I'm in the middle of a pot that's about to boil over."

"I'm afraid so. Come on, let's talk. My Preston is not answering his phone and I need some information."

Bloom, who had not moved, began to edge toward the hogan's traditional entrance. He was not a fan of guns; he had seen what they could do to the human body at close range.

The three sat down. Marvin laid the gun on the table and shared everything he knew with Rachael and Bloom, leaving nothing out.

"Marvin, I believe you, but what about Ernie? Are you sure he didn't kill that old woman? He had lots of reason to do it and, according to the detective, he has been in jail before for assault," Rachael said, watching Marvin's eyes for any hint of untruthfulness.

"Rachael, I have known that man since he was eleven years old. The assault charge was thirty-five years ago when he was drinking heavily. He's been in no trouble since then and he no longer boozes. Yes, he may be angry. He's a loner and even mean sometimes, but I believe him—he's no killer. He asked me the same thing, thinking that maybe I killed the old lady. That tells me he's not involved."

Rachael thought about Marvin's words, then said, "OK, I'm putting my life and my family's welfare on your shoulders."

"I know all about the heavy burdens of family, Rachael. I am willing to bear this as I have born the loss of Ernie's blanket. He is not a murderer of old women and neither am I—but I think Moss is."

Bloom considered calling Detective Marshall, but his phone had no bars. "No Service" was all it had to say—a common theme on the reservation. They couldn't wait for the law.

"How long ago did Ernie go to find Ruth?" Bloom asked.

"About fifty minutes ago," Marvin estimated, then showed them the map that Ernie had drawn. "Even on a horse, he should be back by now. I think something bad may have happened."

Rachael looked at the two men and took over. "Let's go. If Moss has involved Ruth with illegal Nasazi stuff and maybe that old woman's death, then my boy is in serious trouble too. All roads lead to Billy Moss—and that road is apparently not far from this hogan."

Rachael picked up Marvin's .38 revolver from the dining table, spun the cylinder to make sure the gun was loaded, and headed for the door, the two men in tow.

"I'll drive. Marvin, you get me to Ruth's spot and Bloom... Well, I love you, Bloom. Just make sure everything turns out OK."

"Don't worry I will. Why don't you hand me the gun...?" Bloom asked.

"Do you know how to use it?"

"No, not really."

"I do. I killed many coyotes in my sheep tending days with my grandfather's .22 pistol. I'll be fine. I'm an excellent shot. You watch for that horse. It's black, and I don't want to run Ernie and Ruth down."

The three drove off into the white darkness of the Navajolands, hunting a bad coyote spirit.

CHAPTER 47

TIME TO CLEAN UP THE LOOSE ENDS

The sun was parallel with the brooding dark horizon as Moss arrived back at his store. The weather was changing, and not for the better. Marvin Manycoats' rat trap had been set and looked promising. Tomorrow might bring some cops making a personal visit to Moss Pawn and Trading Post—not something Moss relished—so tonight he needed to take care of any and all loose ends.

Using the confiscated car keys, he drove Preston's car down to the out-of-the-way liquor store near his pawn shop, making sure not to leave any fingerprints on the vehicle, then he tossed the keys and Preston's phone down a nearby sewage drain.

"Another missing drunken Indian," Moss laughed to himself. He hiked back down the wash and entered his store through the back door.

Preston hadn't moved since Moss left him lying face up on the concrete floor. His arm and leg were still smarting something fierce from Moss's brutal blows. If he wanted to avoid a vicious death at the end of a wooden club, Preston would do as Moss ordered. The heavy door opened and the young silversmith braced for more punishing blows.

"Good boy, you listened," Moss sneered. "That's the first smart thing you've done all day. Now stand up, it's time to go."

Moss grabbed Preston roughly by the arm and pulled him to his feet. He cut off the duct tape wrapped around the boy's ankles so he could walk, and removed his athletic socks just in case he got any bright ideas of making a run for it. Not able to see or speak, Preston stumbled as Moss led him along, stubbing his big toe. He winced but kept moving forward, now hobbling. There was the sound of another door opening and Preston was outside, standing in fresh snow. His toes were pulling back like a snail's head, the big one on his right foot pulsating where his nail had been partially ripped off. He started shaking, waiting for Moss's next order.

"Preston, did you leave that ingot bracelet you made for me on the mesquite bench?"

Preston nodded his head, "Yes."

"Is it finished?" Again Preston shook his head, "Yes."

"You didn't sign it, did you?"

Preston had engraved his initials on the piece on an out-of-the way terminal end, but at this point he hoped Moss would have at least one bad thing happen to him—a kind of screw-you from the grave—and shook his head, "No."

"Good boy. OK, I'm going to pick you up. Don't struggle or I will knock the living shit out of you. Do you understand?"

Preston nodded. Moss picked the boy up and put him on the tailgate of his truck, which was parked by the back door. Preston's head was pushed down to a prone position, and his entire body was rolled into the back of the truck and tucked beneath the plastic bed top.

"Listen, we're going on a little ride. If you try to sit up, you're going to knock your head something powerful, and if you start kicking or yelling, I'm going to pull over somewhere nice and quiet and use my billy club on you until you can't speak or move no more. Got me, pard?"

Again Preston nodded his head in the affirmative, and Moss slammed the tailgate shut.

Moss went back into his store for supplies. With gloves on, he gathered some rope, placed a large knife in an open scabbard on the right side of his belt, and stuffed five tallboy beers into a green duffle bag. As he walked out the door, he grabbed his favorite CD.

"Might as well have some good tunes for the drive." He revved the engine, turned up the heat, and headed out to dispose of today's garbage.

The ride to the spot near Beautiful Mountain took an hour in good weather; with snow coming down it would take closer to an hour and twenty minutes. Moss was wondering if Ruth would be OK—not that he was worried. She was already toast in his mind, but he did have some questions he wanted to ask before he killed her.

Moss slowed down to a crawl, almost missing the snow-covered trail leading down toward the slot canyon where he had left Ruth. There were no real roads there, only cow trails and bushwhacking paths. It was more comfortable going there on his dirt bike so he could miss the big holes and drive between the ruts. The truck bounced up and down as Moss hurried along, wanting to be finished and back home before the roads became treacherous. He could hear Preston's head smashing against the hard plastic, and laughed at the thought that, with his hands tied to his sides, the boy was helpless to lessen the blows.

Finally, he saw Ruth's headlamp. She was still at work, diligently picking through the rocks.

"God, I hate to see this one go. What a find," he thought. "There are thousands of ant beds to pick though. It's a real loss, but that's the way it goes out on the rez." Moss chuckled to himself, hoping Ruth had managed to get one good last haul of beads.

He slowed the truck even more. There was just the faint sound of moaning coming from the back, so Moss turned up his Patsy Cline CD to drown Preston out. He didn't want Ruth to get scared before he found out what she knew.

"Ruth, my girl, you are one hard worker, aren't you? I can't believe you're still at it. It's awful cold. Your fingers must be half-frozen...."

"The gloves help," Ruth replied, "but they make it harder to pick up the tiny beads. I have to take them off and then put them back on. It's kind of a pain, but look, Billy—I done real good today, found a bunch," Ruth said, holding up a half-filled bowl of beads. "It did get hard to pick the last hour as the snow started to cover my pile, but I lit a branch and melted off the snow, see?"

The juniper branch was smoldering nearby, under a small lean-to Ruth had constructed.

"Ruth, how about you and me have a beer together? You've worked enough today, so let's talk about some things. What do you say?"

"Well, you know I got a problem with booze. I'm an alcoholic. I can't hold my liquor, and if I start drinking, I can't stop. Probably better I don't have that beer, but we can talk."

"Oh, come on, Ruth. One beer ain't going to hurt. You deserve it. Look how many beads you found."

"Well...."

Moss reached into the duffel bag he had brought with him, pulled out two forties and handed her one. "Come on, I'm the boss so you got to drink with me."

Ruth reluctantly opened the can, took a long, hard drag and smiled. It tasted good.

"See, that wasn't so bad. Nice, huh?"

"Yeah, I like beer, even when it's cold outside—that's my problem." Ruth guzzled the beer, and Moss handed her a second, barely touching his own. Once Ruth was feeling no pain, Moss started asking his questions.

"What did you and Preston talk about? He told me you guys got together this morning outside your window."

"He did, huh? He told me not to say anything about that to you. We talked about what I did with you, and how happy I was working."

"Did he understand these beads were Anasazi?"

"Yeah, he knew they were from the old ones. I told him. He didn't care, and I don't neither."

Moss was wondering if he could simply kill Preston and not worry about Ruth. She was harmless… then she unwittingly sealed her fate when she confirmed that she knew Ernie Yazzie.

"I love to sit out here. When Ernie visits me, the time flies like a hummingbird's wings in the air," she smiled.

"Does Ernie come out here and sit with you a lot?"

"Yeah, he does. He's a real great guy. I enjoy our talks, but I keep working. I promise I'm not messing around."

"I believe you Ruth. Does Ernie know you work for me?"

"Sure he does. We talk about all sorts of stuff."

It was time to dump the garbage. Moss pulled an automatic pistol out of his bag and walked back over to his truck. When he opened the tailgate and grabbed one of Preston's bare feet, the boy started to kick to get away. Moss held on tightly and slid the kid off the plastic liner like a slab of beef on a slip 'n slide. When he hit the ground with a hard THUD, Preston rolled back and forth groaning.

"Get up now, and no more kicking." Moss hit the boy on the side with the tip of his boot, grabbed his tied arms, and manhandled him to his bare feet.

Ruth, who had been enjoying her buzz, came back to the present.

"Hey, why you doing that to Preston, Mr. Moss?"

Moss walked over and hit the girl with all his strength, sending her body tumbling to the ground like a ragdoll, her beer can careening down the hard, rocky terrain. The sound of the furious slap echoed in the distant canyon walls.

Moss grabbed the sobbing girl by the throat, pulled her up to her feet and yelled in her face. "Shut up, Ruth, and listen to every word I say or I'll hit you again—harder this time and not with my hand."

Ruth, who had been hit by strong men in the past, did her best to mute the pain, her jaw now resembling a half-filled water balloon.

"OK, you two. Enough fun; it's time for a little walk. Ruth, take Preston's arm and guide him so he doesn't fall. We're going on a hike, and we wouldn't want him to get hurt, would we?"

The ground was white and slippery as the three started climbing up a steep embankment. With no arms available for balance, Preston fell hard twice. Ruth helped him to his feet. Moss was heading for the mesa top and its deep crevices, which lay just ahead. It was an area he knew well, having plundered old Navajo burial sites there in his never-ending quest for antique jewelry.

The bottomless cracks in the earth were soon to become a new burial site, but the latest occupants wouldn't be wearing their finest jewelry—and they would be alive, at least on the way down.

CHAPTER 48

SAVING RUTH AND PRESTON

Ernie had positioned himself above Ruth's last known whereabouts. His stallion was recovering from the hard ride, the animal's warm breath filling the surrounding air. Smoke from a burning juniper stick was faintly visible in the night sky. There was a full-sized Ram pickup truck down there, and country music playing in the background.

The hunter in Ernie Yazzie listened carefully. He could hear voices and the distinctive sound of a brutal slap on human skin, followed by a female cry of pain. He continued to listen. The bilagáana voice, maybe Moss's, started to trail off, heading due east away from Ernie's ears and toward the cliff faces of his ancestors.

There were two possible ways to proceed: one was to follow the man's voice, like he would track a wounded animal; the other was go back to the top of the mesa and circle around, anticipating where Moss was headed. Ambush was Ernie's preferred way to hunt prey; he would go around.

Ernie checked his horse's tether. The square knot was solid, so the animal couldn't break free—even if spooked by the retort of a gun ricocheting through the canyon walls. He headed up the hill with his rifle. The wet ground was slick, making the slope difficult to climb. Ernie was out of breath when he reached the top of the mesa. Then he heard a new sound, the whine of a vehicle's engine. He removed a large hunting knife from its scabbard and set his rifle under a covered stone ledge.

"Stealth might be needed to make this kill," he reasoned. The truck's lights were off as the wheels crept along the mesa's edge. "Big trouble," he thought as he watched the truck driving without headlights.

The vehicle rolled to a stop and three doors opened. Ernie was outgunned; he stood his ground, waiting to see what happened next. He heard two Navajo and one white voice; one of the truck's occupants was a woman. "Must be Marvin and his Toadlena friends," he thought. "I've been gone for awhile."

He slipped behind the intruders' truck and crouched behind the back bumper. The three started to walk in the direction from which Ernie had come.

"Shhee... sheee," Ernie whistled in a distinctively Navajo fashion. Marvin and Rachael recognized the call immediately and turned to face the sound. Bloom kept walking, oblivious to the danger.

"Ernie?" Marvin whispered, turning his good ear toward the sound to hear a response.

"Yeah, it's me. I'm right behind you." Ernie stepped out of the shadows.

Rachael tightened the grip on her revolver when she heard Ernie's voice. Bloom finally turned around and stopped, ten feet ahead of his companions. Ernie walked over to the uninvited guests, his large knife still positioned for action.

"You're here now, let me tell you what I know," Ernie said as he holstered his knife in the buckskin scabbard, and Rachael slightly loosened her grip on the gun's handle. "There are at least two, maybe three people heading east toward the cliff drop-offs. One is Ruth. A man with a white voice hit her, maybe Moss. I heard shuffling feet, so I think at least one more person is with Ruth and the bilagáana, but it's hard to tell for sure until I get closer. There is a truck down the hill with country music playing, making it hard to hear."

Marvin interrupted. "What artist was singing?"

"I don't know, some girl's voice, high old-style singing," Ernie answered.

"Patsy Cline, maybe?"

"I don't know, I was more concerned with Ruth than the station's song selection," Ernie replied, not understanding why it mattered.

"That's not a station, Ernie. That's a CD. Pasty Cline is Moss's favorite country artist and she was Soliday's too."

Ernie shuddered, realizing the implications.

This time Rachael interrupted: "Let's go. Moss has my Preston. I'm sure he killed Pingry, and now he's going to kill Ruth and Preston. Why else would he be out here brutalizing a poor girl?"

"No, I go alone, my way. I'm the hunter. You three stay here. I'll come back when I know more," Ernie countered.

Before Rachael could protest, Marvin spoke up. "Listen, brother, you and I are in this together—and we are going to either get out of it together or die together. You may be a great hunter of animals, but I'm a two-time decorated Marine who hunted men!"

Ernie realized Marvin was right. He had been well trained by the military—and Marvin understood that this particular circle could only be completed if they worked as a team.

"OK, Rachael. You and Bloom go down to that truck that's playing the music, take the keys and hide. If Moss comes back, stop him. He'll know something's wrong because the music will have stopped. Shoot him if he won't listen. A man that hits a woman that hard won't think nothing about killing you. Can you shoot him, Rachael?" Ernie asked.

"What do you think?" Her grip was once again firm on the handle as she pointed the pistol's barrel a hair past Ernie's right ear. A steely look and an outstretched, unflinching arm told of her unwavering determination.

Before Ernie could answer Rachael's question, she asked another: "Ernie, believe me, I can use this weapon on any man who threatens me or my family. Do you understand?" She was making sure that if Ernie had killed Pingry, he knew she would not be a pushover like the old lady.

"I do understand. I am with you. Mommy bear, you can take care of yourself. Bloom, stay behind that woman if you don't want to get hurt."

Bloom nodded his head in agreement, knowing the strength of his Diné wife's resolve when it came to her cubs.

Rachael and Bloom headed down to the truck. Ernie retrieved his rifle and the two Navajo brothers silently moved off to meet their destiny.

CHAPTER 49

RAINING TURQUOISE

"Ruth! Sit down right here next to me," Moss barked, pointing to a sandy area not far from the edge of the cliff with the end of his 9MM Luger pistol. Preston was now visibly shaking in the cold air, his bare feet blue as Moss pushed him to the hard ground next to Ruth, then brutally tore the duck-tape bonds off his mouth and eyes. Preston winced, then spit out the cloth in his mouth and breathed deeply, trying to comprehend his predicament.

"Moss, you have to stop. Nothing bad has happened here. I won't tell them anything," Preston said, his heart rate racing and his backside numb from being thrown on the rocky ground.

"Tell them what, Preston Yellowhorse? Who's 'them?'"

"The... uh... the authorities. I won't say a word about the guns I saw," Preston offered.

"How about the Anasazi beads poor old Ruth has been collecting—don't forget those."

Moss looked over at Ruth, who had gone into a trance picking up the pebbles around her and putting them in small piles.

"No, not that either. I won't say a word. I promise!" Preston begged.

Moss chuckled to himself knowing his silence wouldn't matter as he would never allow Preston to live past tonight.

"Tell me, Preston, why did you really come to spy on me? Was it for Bloom? Is he working for the ATF? Is he a fed?" Moss sounded serious.

"No, no. He's an art dealer filling in for Sal Lito. I told you I came to find Ruth to make sure she was safe. That's all."

"Hmm, hope that's true. Otherwise I'm going to kill your mom too. I was only going to have Bloom killed, but if I find out you lied, I will give your mom a slow, painful death. You understand me, boy?"

Preston's voice was quivering as he realized his time was running out. "I… I promise. I was just wanting to check on Ruth, nothing else. I'm sorry I opened your locked door. I'm just a dumb, nosey kid." Tears were running down Preston's high cheekbones.

To Moss's amazement, he heard another Navajo voice coming from a large, shadowy form. The apparition rose one hundred-fifty feet from the trio, shrouded by the now fast-falling snow. A massive human in moonlight, he appeared unarmed, but it was night and hard to see in any detail.

"What about me, Moss," the figure asked. "You man enough to kill a full-grown Navajo? I've seen what you do to old ladies, women and children, like your daddy did when he was alive, but I'm no kid. I'm Ernie Yazzie, a spirit born of my ancestors' pain—and your time is running out."

Moss was dumbfounded both by Yazzie's bravado and his own good fortune. Now he wouldn't have to track the man down as he had planned.

"Wow, you're one crazy Navajo, my friend. You better hope you are a shapeshifter in disguise, otherwise you're dead meat." Moss realized he had to kill this man on the spot; Yazzie had seen him leave Pingry's murder scene, and he knew Ruth was helping him rob Anasazi graves.

Moss stood up from his squatting position and started walking toward the silhouette, firing his pistol twice at the moving target. As the second shot's retort bounced off the surrounding cliffs, a charging bull appeared from his rear. Moss turned to fire, but it was too late. Marvin tackled the bilagáana harder then he planned. A huge adrenaline rush triggered by the sound of gunfire transported him back to Nam, and he was unable to control the force of his shoulder hit. Both men tumbled over the slippery cliff's edge, Moss's expensive Lugar tinkling as the metal hit the canyon walls below.

Marvin instinctively grabbed an ancient juniper tree limb, as he had done many times as a kid, his left hand making solid contact with the tree and his feet catching under an old pack rat's nest before both men plunged to a certain death. Moss, who wasn't as agile or familiar with climbing trees, found the only handhold he could muster and grabbed Marvin's squash blossom necklace.

"Pull me up, pull me up," Moss screamed. His left arm dangled uselessly at his side; Marvin's hard tackle had dislocated Moss's shoulder.

"Tell me, white devil, why I should help you. You murdered that old lady and maybe my friend...."

"I'm sorry, I'm sorry. It was self-defense. He was coming to kill me, you heard him, and I didn't mean to kill Pingry—it was an accident, all an accident. I can't hold on much longer, please!" Moss cried, his grip tenuous at best.

"And why is Preston barefoot and tied up on the cliff's edge?" Marvin asked in two separate, labored breaths. The weight of Moss's body was taking a toll on his neck.

"Mistake. Mistake. Pleeaassee." Moss begged for his life, but Marvin had one final question.

"Do you know anything about my friend's blanket—and don't lie to me, you white devil, or I will let you fall."

"No, I know nothing. I don't have any of my dad's papers. I lied. Pleeaassee pull me up. I'm sorry."

Marvin decided he was better than this evil white man whose stepfather had poisoned all he touched, so he would pull his useless ass to safety and let the law do the killing.

"OK, I'll help you, but don't try anything stupid. It's a long way down."

"I won't, I promise. Just pull me up!"

Marvin arched his body, pushing his back against the cliff wall. Using strong legs that were accustomed to walking ten miles a day, he simultaneously steadied his feet and grabbed at Moss's shirt, lifting him up from the bottomless crevice below.

As soon as Moss felt his feet back on terra firma, he let go of Marvin's necklace, grabbed a Bowie-style knife from his belt, and lunged at Marvin's throat with his one good arm.

Marvin was prepared for a struggle and propelled himself backward at the same time Moss made his fatal attack. The bilagáana's wild swing missed his target, causing Moss to lose his balance. His slick boots couldn't find any traction, and Moss started to rock backward, the knife making a clinking noise as it fell, following the same route as his gun had earlier.

Moss's only functional arm thrashed in the snowy night air, looking for any handhold to help right his precarious balance. Marvin's long necklace once again provided a safety hold for Moss, though this time the necklace had been irrevocably damaged. The knife had nicked the antique sinew and the string popped like a firecracker as soon as Moss's full weight took was on it. Beads flew skyward, and Marvin ricocheted against the cliff in a shower of snow and turquoise.

Moss also fell, but in the opposite—and wrong—direction. He careened down a black hole, breaking his neck on the first rock, his right hand still grasping the remains of Marvin's father's squash blossom necklace. A deep, dull thud signaled Moss's demise.

Ernie, who had gotten to the ledge in time to hear Moss's confession, grabbed his old friend's collar and held him tightly against the rock wall with a giant, calloused hand used to hauling mighty stones.

"OK, we're even now," Marvin said weakly, his lips trembling. Only the sound of the two men's hearts pounding was audible in the cold, snowy air.

"Ernie, I'm glad you're not dead. I like your funny face, and I don't want to hear your voice haunting me, asking why I was so slow to hit that bilagáana."

Marvin smiled up at his best friend, hoping both would now be on the road to recovery.

"I like your smiling face too, Marvin. I always have."

"Ernie, I'm sorry about your blanket, but maybe now our bad dreams will stay in our past, and we can finally be free of our childhood chains."

"Marvin, my mind is clear. I don't need my grandmother's chief's blanket no more. It has found its own course in life. I already have a good trade blanket back at the hogan, and it will warm us up as good as any old Navajo weaving. That's all the blanket I'll ever need."

"You're right Ernie. All anyone needs in life is a best friend, a good warm blanket, and a carton of Blue Bunny ice cream in the fridge."

Tears ran down both men's faces as they realized their circle was finally complete.

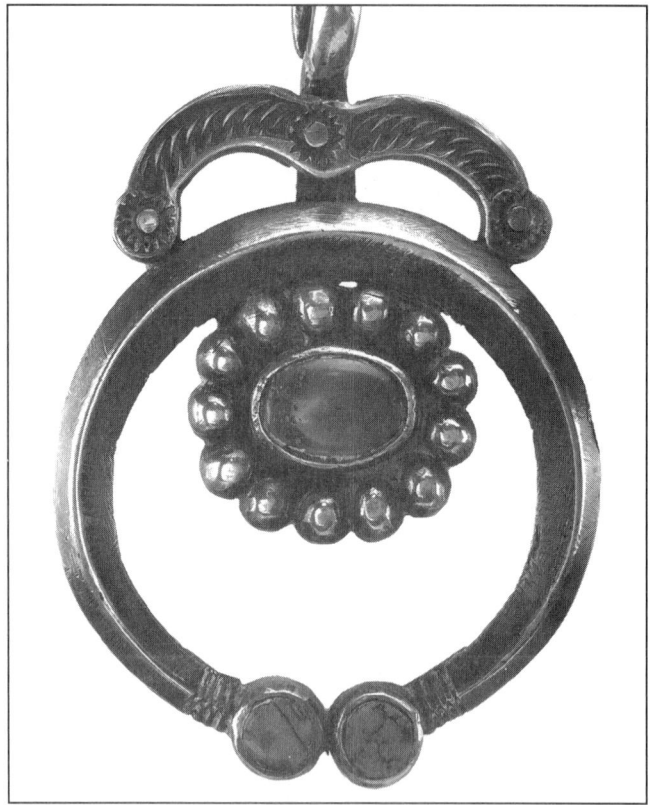

CHAPTER 50

AFTERMATH

Thanksgiving was the next week, and there was much to be thankful for at the Toadlena Trading Post. Rachael's hózhó curing ceremony was scheduled for the first week in December. Preston would no longer be assisting in the ritual, as he, along with Ruth Bennally, Marvin Manycoats and Ernie Yazzie would also be participants. An additional medicine man has been hired to help the elderly Hastiin Johnson treat five patients instead of one.

Rachael's arms were finally starting to heal, and she was once again spinning wool. She hoped to have a new rug on the loom by the first of the year. Sal Lito was expected home in three weeks. Bloom had decided he would ask the old man if he could stay on to help run the post at least through the spring. Rachael was thrilled not to be moving anytime soon, and Willy could finish the year in the Navajo school system.

As it turned out, Moss Pawn and Trading Post was less a pawn shop than a fence for illegal weapons. Jane had been arrested; she turned state's evidence to help close the case and turn over the names of those who had bought guns from Moss. The FBI confiscated the contents of the Moss's precious Museum of the Ancients, which they would hold for an undetermined period; the artifacts were deemed illegally collected until proven otherwise.

It took nearly a full day to recover Moss's body. It had wedged into a crack of the ancient Navajo burial grounds, and when the broken cadaver was finally pulled up, an old Navajo naja fell out on the hard sandstone floor. The Slender Maker naja had been tightly wedged in Moss's death grip through the ride up the canyon walls. A Navajo tribal officer quietly returned the silver crescent to its rightful owner, Marvin Manycoats, no questions asked.

Marvin spent two days looking for the Number 8 beads, the only pieces of the necklace not lost down the bottomless crevice. Ernie and Ruth offered to help, and Ruth's natural gift for pattern recognition allowed her to locate more than two dozen turquoise beads.

The police found Moss's Green Monster, whose paint matched the samples on Pingry's Volvo's bumper. A note written by Marvin and signed by Pingry spelling out their trade had been recovered by the

Gallup police from under the woman's couch pillows during their homicide investigation. This critical piece of evidence, along with the appraisal certificate for the raffle squash blossom that was found in her mailbox, supported Manycoats' story.

After reviewing his 1961 school notebooks, it was determined that the Slender Maker necklace had indeed been stolen from Marvin Manycoats during his boarding school stay. The police nullified the trade and Marvin retained ownership rights to both necklaces: case closed.

Marvin had one final deal to make. He took his Number 8 beads, the Slender Maker naja and asked Preston to fill in the rest.

"Make me a new necklace of your own design, and I'll trade you my squash blossom raffle necklace as payment."

Preston, who was thrilled to get a $2,500 squash blossom, eagerly agreed to make Marvin a new piece. A marriage of old Navajo design, memories of courage, and modern Diné aesthetics would become the latest Manycoats heirloom. Marvin was sure his late father, Ned Manycoats Sr., would approve of keeping Navajo silversmithing skills alive for another generation. The new necklace would follow the family tradition of creating a personal piece that could be passed on and cherished.

Marvin secretly told Bloom and Rachael he was going to leave Preston the new necklace when he died. And when he crossed the great divide from this world to the next, he asked Bloom to remove the piece from around his neck and retrieve a note in the top drawer of his clothes bureau that gave the jewelry to Preston. There would be no doubt about who owned the heirloom the next go-round. Marvin understood the importance of a good paper trail.

Ruth Bennally moved in next to Ernie's hogan, the multi-room structure he had tirelessly worked on for many years now serving a purpose. She was going to help him gather stones for his next project, a hall to connect the family hogan to her side of the property. Ruth's mother had never been happier for her daughter. To celebrate, she had a new weaving on her loom, a full-sized Revival-style Third Phase Chief's Blanket, one that would fit Ernie's massive shoulders—a thank-you gift of sorts, or maybe even a wedding present to a future son-in-law.

On a warmer than average December day, not long after Rachael Yellowhorse's expanded hózhó ceremony had been completed, the curator of the Navajo Nation Museum in Window Rock received a special gift. It came in a nondescript cardboard box with no return address, accompanied by a note that read, "Please accept this gift from the estate of Mary Pingry, Gallup, NM, for your museum's permanent collection."

Inside the package was a small, folded Toadlena/Two Grey Hills rug with a tag that said "Violet Roundhouse, $250." Underneath the chocolate-colored textile were two ragged journals with yellowed paper and entries dated 1961. The labels on the book covers read: "Two Trees Journals from My Indian School Days."

    The End

GLOSSARY

Anasazi/Old Ones: Ancestral Puebloans who occupied the Four Corners region of the United States; commonly defined as "ancient people," the Navajo word translates as "enemy ancestors"

Beautiful Mountain: Part of the Chuska Mountain range, about 26 miles southwest of Shiprock in the New Mexico section of the Four Corners region

Bench silversmith: An artisan who makes and repairs jewelry at least partly by hand; as used in this book, a jeweler, often paid minimum wage, who works for a trading post creating jewelry that is then sold under the post's brand

Beso: This is the Navajo slang term for *dinero* to mean money

Bilagáana/bilágaanas: White man/men or white woman/women

Bisti Badlands (Di-Na-Zin Wilderness Area): A desolate desert wilderness area located between Farmington and Crownpoint, New Mexico; once the site of a coastal swamp of an inland sea, it's now known for its unusual rock and sandstone formations

Bow drill: A hand tool used by silversmiths until the early part of the twentieth century to bore small holes in precious metals and stones

Box and bow squash blossom necklace: A lighter weight squash blossom necklace with the primary "blossom" in the shape of a bowtie with a little box, usually set with turquoise, in its the center; developed by Navajo silversmiths between 1930 and 1950 for the Southwest tourist trade

Capisce: To understand, in Italian; often used in a threatening way

Cerrillos turquoise: Turquoise from historic mines south of Santa Fe; an important source of stones for Ancient Puebloans

Chaco/Chacoan: Chaco Canyon was a major center of Ancient Puebloan (or Chacoan) culture between 850 and 1250 CE, when the site was abandoned. Now a National Historic Park located in northwestern New Mexico, it contains the largest collection of ancient pueblos in the American Southwest

Chiefs' blankets: Navajo weavings, longer than wide in construction, woven between 1840 and 1900 and divided into three phases, or design styles, all highly collectible; the third phase as cited in this book dates from 1860 to 1870

Chindi: The ghost left behind when a person dies; the Navajo believe chindi should be avoided because they are often "unbalanced," or malevolent, and can negatively affect the living

Chuska Mountains: A heavily forested mountain range towering almost 10,000 feet above the San Juan Basin, the Chuskas lie within the Navajo Nation near Gallup and Toadlena; Beautiful Mountain is a satellite of the range

Code Talkers: A top secret World War II program that created an unbreakable code based on the Navajo language to send and receive key information in the Pacific theater; Code Talkers were not publically acknowledged or allowed to speak of their service until the program was declassified in 1968

Coyote/coyote spirit: A major figure in Navajo cosmology, the coyote is a Trickster, sometimes loved and sometimes feared

Diné: Translating as "The People," it is the name the Navajo use to refer to themselves and their language

Emoji: The *Oxford Dictionaries* Word of the Year in 2015, these ideograms can be attached to text messages, emails, and websites

Farmington: The largest city in the Four Corners area; bordered by the Navajo Reservation on its west and southwest edges, Farmington is both a commercial hub and the traditional home of a number of Native American tribes

Four Corners: A remote region of the Southwest where four states—Arizona, Colorado, New Mexico, and Utah—intersect at one point

Fred Harvey bracelet: Mass-produced lightweight silver jewelry made specifically for sale to tourists at various Santa Fe Railroad train stops, Harvey House and "Indian Detour" locations

Gallup: A small town in McKinley County, New Mexico, on the edge of the Navajo Nation; according to the 2000 U.S. Census, more than 30 percent of the population is American Indian

Hastiin: A title of respect for men, it's the Navajo equivalent of "Mr."

Heishi: Small, thin, disc- or tube-shaped beads made from shells, turquoise or other stones

Hogan: A traditional eight-sided Navajo dwelling with a center hole to allow smoke from the fire at the center of the floor to escape and a doorway that faces east so the family can greet and be blessed by the morning sun

Hopi kachina: Figures representing messengers between humans and the gods, kachinas (a.k.a. katsinas) are usually carved from the roots of cottonwood trees

Hóhzó: One of the most important concepts in the Navajo belief system, hózhó refers to the beauty, order, and balance that are at the core of a healthy and happy life

Ingot: A poured, rectangular bar or block of metal (in this case silver) that can be pounded down to make jewelry; Navajo silversmiths often used Mexican silver dollars as their source of ingots; wrinkles or minute cracks on the surface and tool marks on the edges of pieces distinguish hand-hammered silver from machine-rolled sheets

Naja: An inverted crescent-shaped pendant, the naja was a Moorish good luck charm adopted up by the Spanish, who then passed it on to Navajo silversmiths; the naja hangs at the bottom of the squash blossom necklace

Nasazi: What the Navajo call the Anasazi, or Ancient Puebloans, who lived in the Four Corners region of the Southwest

Noodle: Flat-shaped, carded virgin wool ready for spinning

Number 8 turquoise: Turquoise with a distinctive spider-web matrix mined in Eureka County, Nevada, from 1929 to the mid-1970s, it is highly valued by Navajo silversmiths and collectors of historic and contemporary Native American jewelry

Pawn jewelry: Personal or family Native American pieces exchanged for cash, which could be (but often were not) redeemed by the original owner; old pawn is highly collectible

Prickly pear cactus: Also known as Opuntia, the prickly pear's pads are covered with difficult-to-remove, needle-sharp spines

Shapeshifter: In Navajo culture, a witch who has the ability to turn him- or herself into an animal is known as a shapeshifter or skinwalker

Sings: Complex healing ceremonies that include sand painting and chanting led by a Navajo medicine man; the sing most often used to re-establish hózhó is the Blessingway

Shiprock: Called Tsé Bit'a'í—winged rock or rock with wings—by the Navajo, the volcanic remnant is extremely important to the tribe's history, mythology and religion; its Anglo name refers to its resemblance to a nineteenth-century clipper ship

Slender Maker of Silver: A highly regarded Navajo silversmith active in the mid-nineteenth century, Slender Maker lived near Toadlena on the Navajo Nation

Spider Woman: In Navajo legend, Spider Woman wove the web that helped create the universe; she also taught Navajo women how to weave the tribe's distinctive textiles, guiding and inspiring them with her song

Squash beads (chil bitan): In the Navajo language, chil bitan means "bead that spreads out," a good description of the distinctive shape of the flower-like squash bead

Squash blossom necklace: A large, heavy silver necklace that intersperses tri-petal blossom beads (usually a total of twelve) with round spacer beads and a central pendant known as a naja

Toadlena Trading Post: Founded in 1909, the Toadlena post is the historic home of the Two Grey Hills style of Navajo weaving; closed by its last owner in 1996, rug trader Mark Winter negotiated a lease with the tribe and reopened the carefully renovated post in 1997; it continues to provide goods and services to local families and Winter purchases their rugs, and sells them along with jewelry and other handcrafts to visitors

Tsénaajin and Tsénaajin Yázhí: The Two Grey Hills

Yá' át ééh: The traditional Navajo greeting, it translates literally as "It is good."

Yei winds: From the word Yeibicheii (The Holy People), Yei are spirits believed to control natural elements such as wind, rain and snow

Photography courtesy Mark Sublette, unless otherwise noted

Page 1: *Came to Late*, Near Toadlena, New Mexico
Page 6: *Open Range*, Near Sheep Springs, New Mexico
Page 15: Top - *Chiracahua Apaches Upon Arrival at Carlisle Indian School from Fort Marion, Florida*, John Nicholas Choate (c. 1850-1902), Pennsylvania, November 4, 1886
Bottom - *Chiracahua Apaches 4 Months After Arriving at Carlisle Indian School*, John Nicholas Choate (c. 1850-1902), Pennsylvania, March 1887
Page 20: Navajo Late Classic Third Phase Chief's Blanket with Cochineal and Indigo Dyes, circa 1870s, 57" x 70.5"
Page 26: Canyon Road Sign, Santa Fe, New Mexico
Page 31: *Four in October*, Canyon de Chelly, Arizona
Page 38: *Along 491 Near Toadlena*, New Mexico
Page 45: *Shelter Near Beautiful Mountain*, New Mexico
Page 52: *Hogan Smoke Hole*, Navajo Reservation
Page 57: *Desert Rat Hiding*, Toadlena, New Mexico
Page 61: *Rusted Reservation Can*, Navajo Reservation
Page 64: *Rattlesnake*, Tucson, Arizona
Page 67: Benham Indian Trading Company Bill of Sale, 1907
Page 75: *Two Trees, Cottonwoods, October*, Canyon de Chelly, Arizona
Page 81: *Tabletop Jukebox*, Dennis Ziemienski, oil on canvas board, 11" x 14"
Page 87: Toadlena Trading Post Entrance Sign, New Mexico
Page 92: *The Sweet Tooth*, Historic Toadlena Trading Post, New Mexico
Page 97: Top - Navajo Fred Harvey Turquoise and Silver Bracelet with Butterfly, Snake, and Saguaro Designs, circa 1930s
Bottom - Navajo Fred Harvey Turquoise and Silver Bracelet with Thunderbird and Arrow Designs, circa 1940s
Page 105: Navajo Turquoise Chip Inlay Peyote Bird Decorated Skoal Can with Leather and Beadwork circa 1970s, 1" x 2.75"
Page 111: Navajo Blue Gem Turquoise and Silver Squash Blossom Necklace, circa 1930s, naja 1.875" x 2"

Page 116: Trading Post, Historic Toadlena Trading Post, New Mexico
Page 123: Navajo Ingot Silver and Turquoise Squash Blossom Necklace, circa 1890s
Page 130: *View from the Porch*, Toadlena, New Mexico
Page 136: *White Cross*, Western United States of America
Page 142: Chaco Architecture, Chaco, New Mexico
Page 148: Historic Hogan, Canyon de Chelly, Arizona
Page 152: *Farmington Accomodations and Dining*, New Mexico
Page 156: *Near Sheep Springs*, New Mexico
Page 162: White Hogan Shop Hallmark
Page 167: Trading Post 1956 Pawn Ticket
Page 173: Navajo Silversmith Toolbox, circa 1900s
Page 179: *Ant Hill on the Rez*, Canyon de Chelly, Arizona
Page 186: *Hero of the Plateau*, Near Toadlena, New Mexico
Page 194: Prehistoric Beads, 1200 CE
Page 204: Navajo Second Phase Chief's Blanket with Indigo and Cochineal Dyes and Raveled Bayeta, circa 1950-60s, 50.5" x 59"
Page 208: *March of Time*, Josh Elliott, oil on panel, 14" x 16"
Page 216: Navajo Bow Drill, circa 1900s
Page 221: *Red Truck*, Historic Toadlena Trading Post, New Mexico
Page 229: *Near Beautiful Mountain*, New Mexico
Page 233: *Juanita, Favorite of the Five Wives of Manulito, Great War Chief of Navajos*, Charles Milt Bell (1848-1893), Photograph, circa 1870s, 7.5" x 5.5"
Page 237: *Shiprock at Eclipse*, New Mexico
Page 240: *Not Dead Yet, Rez Horse*, West of Shiprock, New Mexico
Page 247: *Ancient Grounds*, Canyon de Chelly, Arizona
Page 252: Navajo Turquoise and Silver Squash Blossom Necklace circa 1920s, naja 3" x 2.5"
Page 260: Screenshot of Racheal Yellowhorse's Text Message
Page 270: *Coyote Stalking*, Canyon del Muerto
Page 275: *Nasazi View*, Near Toadlena, New Mexico
Page 281: *Last Glimpse*, Chuska Mountains, New Mexico
Page 285: *Distant Memories*, Tsénaajin, near Toadlena, New Mexico

Page 290: Top - Toadlena Trading Post Tag
Bottom - Navajo Turquoise and Silver Naja, circa 1900s, 2.625″ x 2.25″

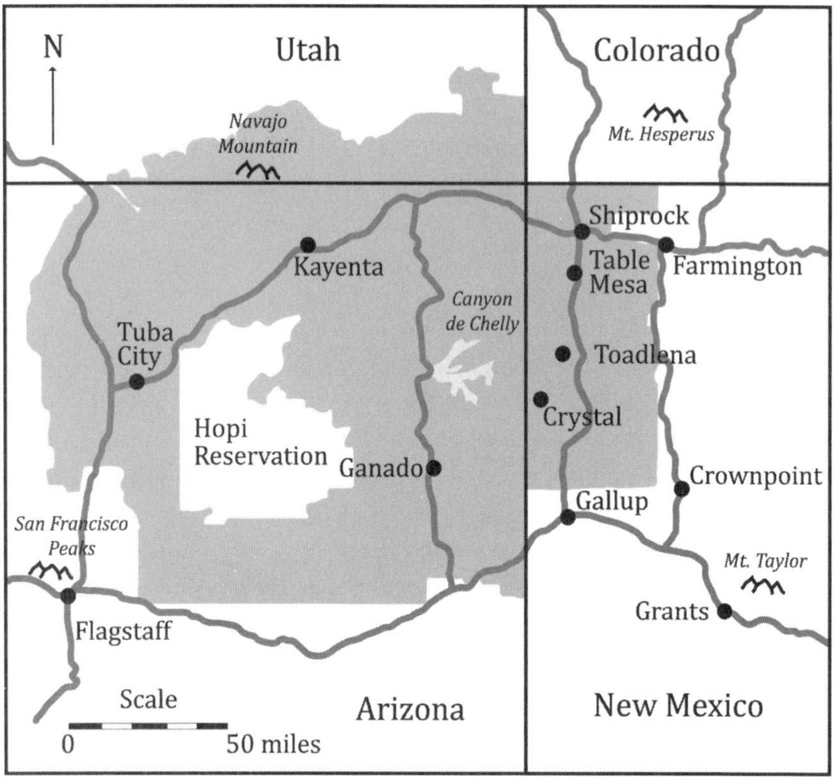
N
Utah
Colorado
Navajo Mountain
Mt. Hesperus
Shiprock
Kayenta
Table Mesa
Farmington
Canyon de Chelly
Tuba City
Toadlena
Crystal
Hopi Reservation
Ganado
Crownpoint
Gallup
San Francisco Peaks
Mt. Taylor
Grants
Flagstaff
Scale
0
50 miles
Arizona
New Mexico